Homing

Also Available in Large Print by
Elswyth Thane:

Dawn's Early Light
Yankee Stranger
Ever After
The Light Heart
Kissing Kin
This Was Tomorrow

Homing

Elswyth Thane

G.K.HALL&CO.

Boston, Massachusetts

1981

Library of Congress Cataloging in Publication Data

Thane, Elswyth, 1900-
  Homing.

  Large print ed.
  1. Large type books. I. Title.
[PS3539.H143H6 1981]   813'.52   80-25636
ISBN 0-8161-3164-3

Published in Large Print by arrangement with Elsevier/Nelson Books

Set in Compugraphic 18 pt English Times by Marilyn Ann Richards and Cheryl Yodlin

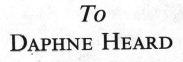

To
DAPHNE HEARD

Acknowledgments

I am again grateful to many people in England who have gone to a great deal of trouble to answer questions regarding details of the war years and to send me notes and publications which were not available here; in particular, Derrick de Marney, Daphne Heard, Mary Clarke, Christine de Stadler, and Lt.-Colonel W. E. G. Ord-Statter. Alice Grant Rosman, whose enchanting book, *Nine Lives,* gives many a clue on the Animal ARP, put me in touch with M. O. Larwood of the National Register of Animals Service, who was most helpful, as was the Royal Society for the Prevention of Cruelty to Animals, and Mr. Carpmael of the Blue Cross, concerning an almost forgotten aspect of the blitz. The British Information Services rendered their usual prompt assistance.

Miss Susan Armstrong of Colonial Williamsburg supplied maps and information. The chronological sequence and news details were drawn from my own extensive files of the British weekly periodicals and newspapers, for the war years.

E. T.

Contents

The Days AND

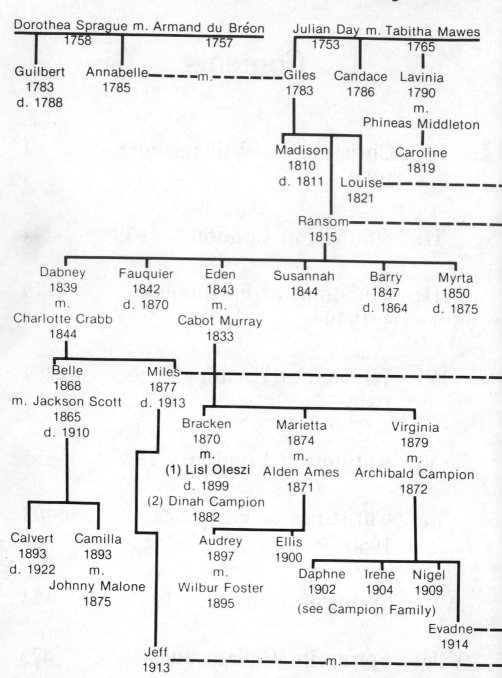

Dorothea Sprague m. Armand du Bréon
1758   1757

Julian Day m. Tabitha Mawes
1753   1765

Guilbert
1783
d. 1788

Annabelle ------ m. ------ Giles
1785   1783

Candace
1786

Lavinia
1790
m.
Phineas Middleton

Madison
1810
d. 1811

Louise
1821

Caroline
1819

Ransom
1815

Dabney
1839
m.
Charlotte Crabb
1844

Fauquier
1842
d. 1870

Eden
1843
m.
Cabot Murray
1833

Susannah
1844

Barry
1847
d. 1864

Myrta
1850
d. 1875

Belle
1868
m. Jackson Scott
1865
d. 1910

Miles
1877
d. 1913

Bracken
1870
m.
(1) Lisl Oleszi
d. 1899
(2) Dinah Campion
1882

Marietta
1874
m.
Alden Ames
1871

Virginia
1879
m.
Archibald Campion
1872

Calvert
1893
d. 1922

Camilla
1893
m.
Johnny Malone
1875

Audrey
1897
m.
Wilbur Foster
1895

Ellis
1900

Daphne
1902

Irene
1904

Nigel
1909

(see Campion Family)

Evadne
1914

Jeff
1913 ------ m. ------

The Spragues

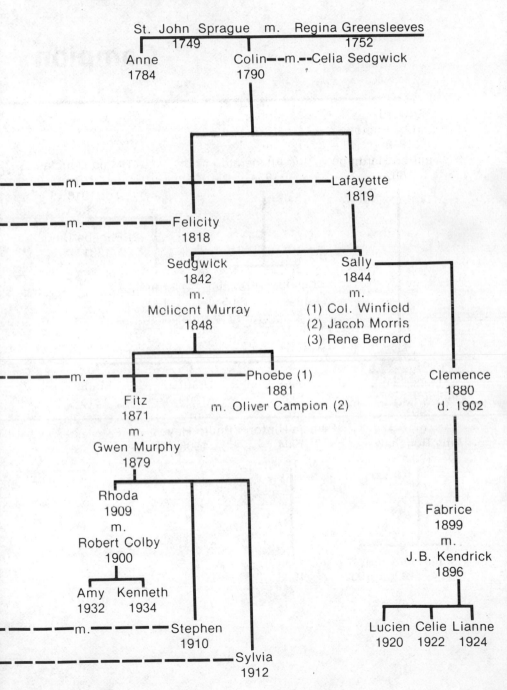

St. John Sprague m. Regina Greensleeves
1749   1752

Anne   Colin––m.––Celia Sedgwick
1784   1790

m.   Lafayette
                                            1819

m.–––––––Felicity
         1818

         Sedgwick   Sally
         1842   1844
         m.   m.
         Melicent Murray   (1) Col. Winfield
         1848   (2) Jacob Morris
                             (3) Rene Bernard

m.––––––––––––––––Phoebe (1)   Clemence
                  1881   1880
    Fitz   m. Oliver Campion (2)   d. 1902
    1871
    m.
    Gwen Murphy
    1879

    Rhoda
    1909
    m.
    Robert Colby   Fabrice
    1900   1899
                                          m.
                                          J.B. Kendrick
                                          1896
    Amy   Kenneth
    1932 1934

m.––––––––––Stephen   Lucien Celie Lianne
            1910   1920   1922 1924
                    Sylvia
                    1912

Campion

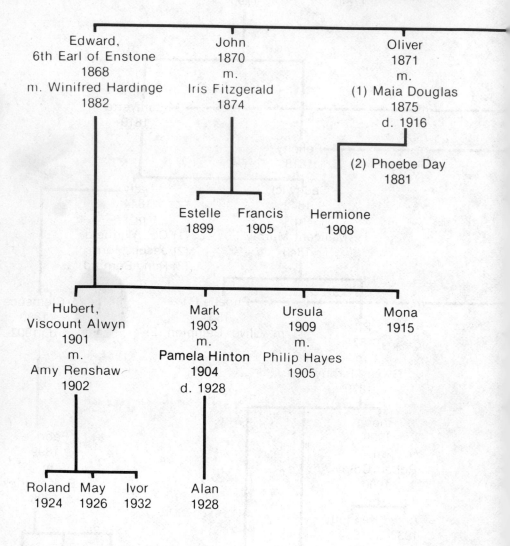

Edward,
6th Earl of Enstone
1868
m. Winifred Hardinge
1882

John
1870
m.
Iris Fitzgerald
1874

Oliver
1871
m.
(1) Maia Douglas
1875
d. 1916

(2) Phoebe Day
1881

Estelle
1899

Francis
1905

Hermione
1908

Hubert,
Viscount Alwyn
1901
m.
Amy Renshaw
1902

Mark
1903
m.
Pamela Hinton
1904
d. 1928

Ursula
1909
m.
Philip Hayes
1905

Mona
1915

Roland
1924

May
1926

Ivor
1932

Alan
1928

Family

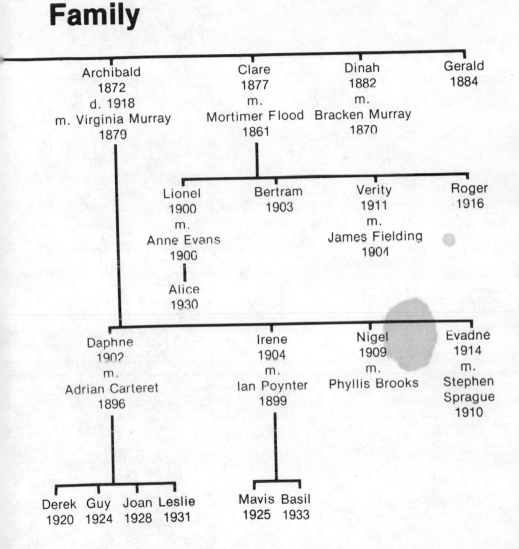

Archibald
1872
d. 1918
m. Virginia Murray
1879

Clare
1877
m.
Mortimer Flood
1861

Dinah
1882
m.
Bracken Murray
1870

Gerald
1884

Lionel
1900
m.
Anne Evans
1900

Bertram
1903

Verity
1911
m.
James Fielding
1904

Roger
1916

Alice
1930

Daphne
1902
m.
Adrian Carteret
1896

Irene
1904
m.
Ian Poynter
1899

Nigel
1909
m.
Phyllis Brooks

Evadne
1914
m.
Stephen
Sprague
1910

Derek   Guy   Joan   Leslie
1920   1924   1928   1931

Mavis Basil
1925   1933

I.

Christmas at Williamsburg.

1938

1

"You scared?" Stephen suggested, glancing at her speechlessness and then attending again to the road ahead of the car.

Evadne smiled, and leaned a little towards him — an instinctive nestling movement which acknowledged her need of reassurance.

"I wouldn't have been a good pioneer woman," she murmured. "Every shadow would have been an Indian, every twig would have sounded like a rifle shot. I would have woken up screaming with nightmares about being scalped. Just think if those trees came right in on a narrow trail — just think if we were in a covered wagon with arrows zinging past our ears!"

"Honey, you've got it all wrong. No covered wagons in Virginia — that was Death Valley. I thought you'd like this road — there's a sort of Feel to it, I always think."

"You mean there's another road?"

"Yes, the main highway's over there. We always take this one, along the River."

"Because of the Feel."

"Mm-hm."

It was the back way to Williamsburg, running behind the big house which faced the East bank of the James. As the day drew in, the trees either side the road stood tall and aloof, cutting off the setting sun, too close together to allow more than a suspicion of the River on the right. Little dusty lanes led off at angles, with obscure, tipsy signs. Almost uninhabited crossroads occurred at long intervals. You met nothing coming the other way. Very different from Highway 60.

But she had surprised him again, because it was not the kind of scare he had had in mind. They had been married about three months ago in London, and he was bringing her home for a Southern

2

Christmas with his family. And now his English bride's shyness of the first meeting with his parents was overlaid by her reaction to a back road at dusk in Virginia — an intuitive awareness of a wilderness which no longer existed.

He touched a button on the dashboard and their lights came on, barely visible yet in the waning daylight.

"That better? You want a drink, maybe. That'll pull civilization towards you."

"I suppose they came this way on horseback," she brooded. "With nothing but a sword."

Again Stephen glanced at her over the wheel. Last September she was taking her First Aid and Air Warden training in London for a Hitler war, while his own stomach fluttered fussily at what she must encounter during the course. Last September he had worked beside her in a dimly lit parish school while she fitted gas-masks on tense, well-behaved children and anxious, well-behaved old ladies, and her tact and composure had never wavered. He had listened and cued her while she recited to him the varieties of poison-gas, their effects, and their detection — and her voice was as steady as though it read a bus schedule. The war hadn't happened after all. Not yet. But now she jibbed at a shadowy road beside the River James. Women.

"They came this way for picnics," he said cheerfully, and slowed the car as it emerged into a clearing with a grassy lane running off to the right. "That's the road to Jamestown. There's a museum there now, and a stone wall to keep the River from eating up the site of the town entirely. The old brick church is there still, what's left of it, and the tombs —"

"Picnics at Jamestown," she said thoughtfully, while the car slid on towards Williamsburg. "Amongst the tombs. I'm so ignorant. Who's buried there? What's Jamestown?"

"My dear girl!" said Stephen, registering marked horror. "Never let them hear you say *that!* How would you feel if I said, 'Dover? Never heard of it!' "

"You'll have to coach me," she said comfortably.

"I should think so. Grandfather

4

Julian won't rest."

"Oh, I do know something about him, vaguely. He was a Day, like Jeff, and his portrait hangs over the mantelpiece in Jeff's house here in Williamsburg."

"It's in the front bedroom upstairs, as a matter of fact."

"He came out from England while it was still colonies here, didn't he? Where do we come in — the Spragues, I mean."

"The Spragues were here when he arrived," said Stephen with some pride.

"The First Families."

"Absolutely. Grandfather Julian Day and Grandfather St. John Sprague both fought in the Revolution — which you may have heard about too, vaguely," said Stephen.

"Now I suppose we've come to Yorktown," said English Evadne. "Go on. The British got beaten. For once."

"Well, that depends how you look at it," Stephen conceded cautiously. "The colonists were mostly British too. And half the British Army was German troops."

"Oh. And the French, who turned up somewhere?"

"Yes, the French were in at the kill, on our side. But they weren't at Valley Forge. Did you ever hear of Valley Forge?"

"Where's that?" Evadne asked, and laughed, and nestled closer. "It was something about George Washington," she decided shamelessly. "I'll read up on it, truly I will. It's really a new world for me, don't forget. I never had any idea I'd come here."

"Well, I warned you," he reminded her, in view of his two years' resolute courtship.

He drove on, reflecting happily on the baffling, delightful creature he had married. A year ago she would have stammered and apologized for her ignorance of Jamestown and Valley Forge, in the maddening state of humble anxiety to please everyone in which she had then existed. A year ago she would have been in a pitiable twitter of nerves for fear his people might not like her as his wife. But now Evadne had changed. Almost overnight she had changed from a defensive, apprehensive, intense young woman who always tried much too hard, into this incandescent, philosophical bride who never seemed to worry much about anything any more. It was a miracle. And it was *his* miracle. He, Stephen, had taught her to laugh at herself — and at him — after demonstrating to her with colossal patience and wisdom that nothing would induce him to think otherwise than idolatrously of her. And now here she was, on the way to Williamsburg with him, home for Christmas.

It came of so much love, he thought, the wheel under his hands, his eyes on the road. Nothing evil or unhappy could endure against love like his for Evadne. Since that first time he saw her in the lobby at the Savoy in London, not knowing who she was, not having the faintest idea that they were bound for the same party and were linked by distant cousinship. A hell of a thing, he had thought more than once since then, if she hadn't got out of the lift at the same floor he meant to, and preceded him to the same door — she thought by then he was following her, and slew him with a glance — and then, when he made himself known, "Welcome to London, Stephen," she said, with her radiant smile, and he had kissed her, because after all they were kissing kin. . . .

"What are you thinking?" she asked, noticing his silence.

"Why?"

"You've got the most *idiot* grin on!"

It broadened.

"I was thinking about the Savoy — that first night we met."

"Bracken's party. How long ago it seems now!"

"You came marching into the lobby and pressed the bell for the lift, remember? I had already rung for the lift, or I wouldn't have been standing there, would I? But you bustle up, smelling of flowers, and press the bell. And I thought, *Women.* And then I took another look and it was all over with me, *boom!* I haven't been able to see straight ever since."

"I didn't know what to make of you that night." They had been over it before, but it never palled. Discovery. Always a fresh marvel of discovery, with him so sure from the beginning, and herself so unaware, so obtuse, and so misguided. "You went so fast," she mused, as she had done before. "But how you could fall in love with anybody so *hopeless* as I was then —"

"You were hopeless," he agreed. "And lost — and off on the wrong foot. But you didn't know. That was the hard part. You didn't know *from nothing*. I just go on thanking God it was me that came along in time!"

"I gave you a bad run, didn't I, Stephen?"

"Talk about wake up screaming!" He held out his right hand from the wheel, palm up, and she laid her left in it, warmly. "It will be years before I can be sure, in the dark, that you'll be there if I put out my hand —"

"It's all right, Stephen." Her tone was motherly. "You're in for it now. You'll never be rid of me now."

"For better, for worse."

"Till death do us part," said Evadne, and their fingers tightened with a swift, unspoken memory of last September's portent, and the gas-masks and the shelter

9

trenches scarring the green turf of London's parks.

2

In the Sprague parlor at Williamsburg, the new song trickled lightly from Fitz's fingers on the keyboard. Its lyric was lost in the muted whistle which carried the air, but it was a song about love at first sight — love for a stranger. Fitz had written it as a Christmas present for his son Stephen's English bride, and around it, eventually, the next Sprague musical comedy would be written. They were a team now — father and son — music and lyrics by Fitz, dancing and singing (he called it singing) by Stephen.

The girl had finally stopped her nonsense and married him, when they had all begun to think she never would. Until recently there had been very little to recommend English Evadne to Stephen's parents, but now they would see what they would see. Stephen's mother, who had herself once come to Williamsburg a stranger-bride, was sure Stephen knew what he was about. And Fitz, remembering his own sensations when he had faced his redoubtable father that day, was determined to welcome Stephen's choice as generously as the family received the unknown girl he himself had brought home almost forty years ago.

"I hope she won't be nervous," Gwen said from where she sat knitting by the fire, following his thoughts as she often seemed to do, even in their silence. "I was terrified, the day I came. Of course it's not quite the same."

Their eyes met, amused and rueful, across the room. Instead of replying, he changed the music smoothly, so that the new song ran into the old one, one of his oldest, and Gwen began to sing it softly, watching him from where she sat.

"Ef de sun set red on a weary
day,
De skies will clear ef de mornin's
grey,
An' dat's what I hope foh
me —

Ma shadow gettin' longer crost
        de grass,
Cool ob de ebenin' done come at
        las',
De sun goin down on me. . . ."

"It's *still* a good song," he admitted judicially, and, "It takes you back," said Gwen, resuming her knitting with a sigh.

Back to the time when he was a cub reporter on Cabot Murray's newspaper in New York, and she was a frightened girl singing in a third-rate music-hall — you couldn't blame the family for not knowing quite what to expect when he married her. They soon found out about that, though. Gwen had no tall ideas about a career on the stage, even after his musical comedies caught on and became almost annual fixtures on Broadway. Gwen only wanted to stay at home and raise babies, while the shows went on without her.

Baby Stephen grew up stage-struck and starred in the shows, with his sister Sylvia as his dancing partner. During the London engagement of the last show but one he had fallen in love with Evadne the

Problem Child. But it wasn't quite the same, no. The singing waif from the wrong side of the tracks which was the young Gwen, craving love and security — and this well brought up, protected Evadne, laboring under a Joan of Arc complex which had found more than one embarrassing outlet. She had kept Stephen dangling till everyone on both sides of the Atlantic wanted to shoot her, and then quite suddenly she had learned her lesson and began to eat out of his hand. Got it all out of her system, the family said in England, with visible relief. Grew up. Saw the light. Stopped being a crusader in lost causes. Fell in love. And about time too. Nevertheless in Williamsburg there was still the shadow of a doubt, and some suspense, for while Evadne's mother was Fitz's first cousin, Virginia had married abroad and her children were strangers to their American kin.

Stephen had got her at last, though. And because something had gone wrong with his left foot which hampered his dancing, he had closed the show in London and was bringing her home for

Christmas. The song was ready for them, and for the new show. Even if Hitler started a war in Europe, Fitz was hoping they could still open a new show in New York. The shows always opened in New York and went to England after the American run.

"There was a war coming up then too — when I came here the first time," said Gwen, abreast of his unspoken thoughts from across the room.

"Little bitty Richard Harding Davis kind of war," he agreed, still playing. "It wouldn't count nowadays."

"You and Bracken almost died of it."

"Almost. They do it better now. We were a bunch of amateurs."

Cuba, it was that time. He and his Cousin Bracken Murray had gone out as field correspondents for the newspaper — but that didn't mean they didn't get shot at, and Fitz had so far forgotten himself as to acquire a rifle and shoot back, though that was against the rules for correspondents.

Bracken was running the paper himself now, since his father's death. But for Fitz the youthful fling at journalism was only an interlude in his music. He had come back from Cuba full of malaria and tunes, to his piano and Gwen, and had settled down in the big white house in Williamsburg where his father and grandfathers had lived, just across the little town from the big white house where the Day cousins had always lived. Bracken's father, who was a Yankee, had married Eden Day. Fitz's own grandfather had married a Day, his sister Phoebe's first husband was a Day, and his daughter Sylvia had married a Day. The lines of courtship were entwined and entangled for generations.

"There aren't so many of us around here any more," said Gwen, with her effortless clairvoyance. "When you brought me home to meet the family there must have been — well, it felt like *dozens!* Now there's just us. It will seem kind of quiet to her, maybe. The children of the family are mostly in England now, on Virginia's side."

"Phoebe didn't do her share," he remarked, still playing. "She only had

15

Jeff. Maybe now Sylvia and Jeff — or Stephen and Evadne — or maybe if there's going to be another war it's just as well —''

"I'm glad we didn't think of that," said Gwen softly. "I'm glad we had ours."

Fitz rose from the piano and came round the end of the sofa and laid his hands on her shoulders from behind.

"Lucky you and me," he said. "I wonder if it will ever be so good again."

Her hands came up to his on her shoulders.

"Oh, Fitz, you don't really think —''

"I'm afraid I do."

"Another war?" she cried, echoing the ages. "When?"

"Any time now. Whenever Hitler's ready. He's callin' the tune this time."

"Will we be in it too? Will Stevie have to fight?"

"We're always in it sooner or later. It'll be a young man's war this time — flying and all. Stevie's pushing thirty. But it won't matter what you're doing or what age you are, any more. Bombs dropped from a mile high don't ask questions."

Gwen shivered under his hands.

"Like Spain? Even the children?"

"They're going to evacuate the children from the towns, you know. Break up families. Imagine having to decide. Send your child away to strangers — or keep it by you and see it blown to bits."

"But not here, Fitz! In France and England, maybe — but not over here! If a war starts we must keep Stephen and Evadne here, especially if there are children."

He sighed, and sat down on the end of the sofa.

"They might not think that was right. It's for them to decide, remember — it's their lives they have to live."

"Listen," said Gwen. "Wasn't that a car stopping?"

3

Evadne had observed with appreciation the red brick and white clapboard of the little town, the green lawns and low hedges and picket fences. Lights were coming on at the College end of the street where the shops were. Beyond, the old mulberry trees made an arch of darkness all the way to the unseen Capitol at the other end.

Stephen turned the car off the main street and stopped in front of a white fence and a broad white house with lights behind the windows. When he opened the car door on her side she stepped down a little stiffly after the long ride, and stood still in the road looking round her gravely. It was a village, after all — like an English village, old and intimate and welcoming. . . .

"I'll come back for the bags," he said, and put his arm around her waist and moved her towards the house.

They entered the lighted hall, they kissed all round, they said all the usual things. Stephen carried the luggage in, and she went with him up the broad stairs to his old room. There he turned and held out his arms.

"Now I know it's true," he said, and she went to him.

Soon the rattle of ice in a cocktail-shaker came up from below, and they descended hastily to find Fitz at the foot of the stairs sounding the shaker like a bell to summon them. Behind him stood a stout colored woman, her beaming face upturned to the two on the stairs, and Evadne saw Stephen fling his arms around her and kiss the black cheek which shone wet with tears.

"This is Hagar," he said then. "She looks after us all."

Evadne held out her hand with her radiant smile, and Hagar took it in both hers and raised it against her bosom. And Gwen, in the drawing-room doorway, and Fitz with the cocktail-shaker, and Stephen at the bottom of the stairs, all stood enchanted, gazing at Evadne, with her short chestnut curls and her red-brown eyes and crimson mouth — there was a real look of her mother about her, Fitz thought, the same effortless vitality, the mischief, the *minxishness* of Virginia, but with something softer and less sure, something un-American and terribly appealing, which Virginia in her self-possessed girlhood had never had. Virginia at eighteen or so, when Fitz had seen her last, always knew the time of day. It was conceivable that Evadne could be lost and helpless and in need of rescue. A fatal quality in a woman, as Fitz very well knew, for Gwen had had it too.

"Welcome home, li'l dolly," Hagar was saying in her soft, husky voice. "Many's de time I hear my ol' granny tell 'bout de night Miss Gwen came home to dis yere house. 'Bout time we had nudder bride, seems like, Mas' Stevie —" Her high, sweet, colored laughter rang like music. "He was so all-fired *slow,*" she confided to Evadne, "I almost done gib up hope on him, but I kin see now he had a right to wait. Now he caught up on Mas' Jeff at las' —"

"Hagar only stays with us when Jeff isn't using his house here," Stephen explained. "And she'll desert fast enough when he and Sylvia show up again."

"Dey comin' soon, mebbe?" Hagar inquired with transparent hope.

"Not very soon, I'm afraid. You'll have to make do with us for a while. They sent you their love."

"Mas' Stevie — dis yere war — is Mas'

Jeff goin' to git mixed up in it?''

"It hasn't happened yet," Stephen reminded her. "No harm in hoping."

Fitz had poured the cocktails and now approached with them on the tray.

"Yassuh, yassuh, I fetch de can-*apes,*" said Hagar, and was off to the kitchen in a rustle of white apron and starched petticoats.

"She's wonderful," said Evadne, gazing after her. "Like *Gone With the Wind*. Was she your Mammy, Stephen?"

"Her sister was Jeff's Mammy, and she really belongs to the Day house. Mine was very old and died a long time ago. In a family like ours the maids are more or less interchangeable according to who's sick, or having a baby, or nursing a relative." Stephen raised his glass. "Well, Pop — Mother, darling — Home Sweet Home!"

They sipped.

"To Stevie's bride," said Fitz gallantly then, smiling over his glass at Evadne. "God bless her!"

Later, in the dining-room as the pumpkin-pie came in, Evadne looked slowly round the table in the candlelight at the three waiting faces, watchful and kind and full of affectionate interest in what was on her mind to say — Fitz with his long, bony head and sensitive mouth, his grey hair still thick in a curving crest, Gwen slender and doe-eyed and, like all the Sprague women, cherished and serene — and Stephen, intrinsically gay, magnetic, charming, untheatrical even though acting was his job, and *hers*.

"Isn't this lovely?" she said, very low, and stretched out a hand to Fitz on one side and Gwen on the other. "No refuge-rooms, no gas-lectures, no bandage-classes, no need to think about blackout paint and buckets of sand and what to do about the children — it doesn't seem possible," said Evadne with a catch in her breath, "that all of a sudden nobody's *worrying!*"

Fitz and Gwen exchanged compassionate glances.

"Well, I wouldn't go as far as that," Fitz said reluctantly.

"No, of course Hitler's still there," Evadne conceded at once. "But he's a lot farther away from Williamsburg, isn't he!

I don't think anybody here in America can quite realize the difference that makes. I mean, it's so easy to say what Chamberlain should have done at Munich last October —"

She broke off in embarrassment. On the boat coming over she had had to listen more than once to outspoken comment on the Munich agreement, usually by homeward bound Americans. To anyone who understood the problems of civil defence which England had faced that autumn of 1938, ridicule or scorn of the reprieve seemed quite as unrealistic as short-sighted rejoicing. Even those who had supported Chamberlain two months ago were now unwillingly aware that it did not mean peace even for his time, and he was seventy. Air Raid Precautions proceeded doggedly even in the villages, with mock drills and public shelter plans. There was no attempt to minimize the likelihood of another European crisis in the spring. Rumania, they thought, would be next. Or Poland. And what would Italy do? And where did Russia really stand? So much for appeasement.

"Now, now," said Stephen gently, into the silence she had left. "Merry Christmas."

"I know. I *will* be merry." Evadne drew a breath and gave them her smile. "Surely we can snatch one more Christmas before it happens."

"And we'll trim a tree," said Gwen.

"Oh, definitely a tree!" cried Evadne. "We always have a tree at Farthingale, and my father used to read out the labels on the presents one by one. Christmas is always a hard time for Mummy — she was quite young when he died, but she never married again —" Evadne looked round the table, feeling suddenly rather far from home. "Am I talking too much? It seems queer that nobody here ever *knew* my father —"

"I knew your mother," said Fitz. "Long before you did!"

"Of course you did." Evadne beamed at him mistily. "You're some sort of cousin to Mummy, because after all, Stevie and I are vaguely related, aren't we. When did you see Mummy last?"

"Just before she went back to England

to marry your father. The same time Bracken married your Aunt Dinah. Brother and sister married brother and sister. It's happened that way before in our family. We never thought they'd forget to come home, though, once in a while."

"That happens too," said Gwen ruefully.

"Great-aunt Sally began it," Fitz recalled. "She married elderly millionaires, one after another, while she was young, and then lived and died in elegant Edwardian sin at Cannes. And then there was Cousin Camilla, who inherited Cannes — and all the elegance and maybe some of the sin — till she married Bracken's European representative and is now in Berlin, which I wouldn't wish on a dawg. And there's Bracken, married to a ladyship and spending half his time in London. And my own sister Phoebe, took a British Army officer for her second husband and settled down in London. And your mother, staying on at Farthingale after your father died —"

"And now Sylvia and Jeff," added Gwen. "With a perfectly good house here in Williamsburg, they seem to feel that London is their home —"

"Well, blame the newspaper business for one thing," Stephen reminded them. "It's worse even than acting — you can't settle down in it, Jeff can no more turn his back on the biggest story of the century than I could turn down a good show."

"This is fascinating," Evadne said, listening with her chin in her hand. "There's so much I don't know about people I'm related to. Somehow before Stephen came to England I never thought much about the American side of our family,. There was always Phoebe of course, and there was Phoebe's Jeff — but because she married Uncle Oliver at the end of the war everybody's forgotten she had another husband, it's almost as though Jeff was Oliver's son, or Bracken's. Who *was* Jeff's father?"

"Miles Day," said Fitz. "Cousin Miles. As near to a stick-in-the-mud as the family ever produced."

"Oh, poor Miles," said Gwen with a sigh. "He was second choice with Phoebe, and I'm afraid he knew it. Anyway, it didn't last long. He died quite suddenly before Jeff was born. So when Oliver's wife died too during the war it — it all came out right for Phoebe after all.''

"It's like opening a new book I can't wait to read," said Evadne. "How Mab would love to be here tonight! She knows lots more about the family than I do. That's my sister Irene's daughter," she explained to Gwen, unaware how simple the family intricacies were to the older generation. "She's only about twelve, but she's always had a Thing about America. She knows exactly who married which, on both sides of the Atlantic, all down the line from Grandfather Julian on. She got Mummy to make a sort of map of the generations, and she has it pinned up on the schoolroom wall. I wish now I'd taken more interest."

"Mab is one-quarter American, through your mother," Gwen reminded her, and Evadne began to count it up on a taper finger, while they watched her with delight.

"Let's see, now, Mummy was American

and married an Englishman. That makes me half American, so I backslide and marry one myself." She grinned at Stephen. "But Irene married another Englishman, so Mab is only one-quarter, but there is some sort of throw-back so that she and Mummy are more like mother and daughter than she and Irene. *I* think Irene is quite heartless," she told Gwen. "She's still dotty about Ian and won't lose sight of him even for a weekend if she can help it, and now that they've got a son, which is what they wanted in the first place, honestly, *anybody* can have poor Mab, so far as they're concerned! She's at Farthingale most of the time, and they leave everything to Mummy about clothes and governesses and even holidays."

"Mab likes it that way," said Stephen.

"Well, who wouldn't, Mummy's much more fun than Irene any day," said Evadne, dismissing her elder sister. "After Munich last October, when we were all at Farthingale recuperating, somebody said something about sending Mab out to Williamsburg if there was a war next year, and she said she couldn't leave Mummy.

Not a word about Irene! That just shows you," said Evadne.

"We've always hoped that Virginia would come back some day, even for a visit," Gwen mused. "I wonder now if she wouldn't bring the children here, if there's a war."

"Especially not if there's a war," Evadne said without hesitation. "We've all got our jobs there when it starts." Quick to sense an undercurrent, she looked from Stephen to his father. "But the theaters won't close here, if war is declared in England," she said contritely. "I forgot about that."

"Well, if the worst comes," Fitz drawled easily, "I reckon the new show will have to wait till Stevie wins the war for you."

"I want to get a mobile canteen going as my contribution," Stephen admitted. "I'd look fine doing a show in New York, with Evadne back at the post in London. Besides, it isn't ready yet, we've got a lot of work to do on it first. But you see how they are in England, Pop, they won't run out on the war. Farthingale will be full of evacuees, and Virginia will want to stay and see that they don't wreck the place."

"It's the house where she and Daddy lived together, and the four of us were born," Evadne explained. "She loves it as though it was another child, I think."

"Houses are like people, they hold you fast the same way," Fitz acknowledged. "We've come up against that, with the Restoration work here at Williamsburg. People whose families have lived here for generations, like ours — they react in a funny way. Some of them hate it from the ground up, what's been done to the town. Others are glad to know that the Rockefeller money is there to maintain the place as it should be when the old families die out or are forced to sell. Me, I'm glad. I can remember when ugly telephone poles went right down the middle of the street, and cows were grazing on the Palace Green."

"Even I can remember that," said Stephen. "I think it's worth it, myself. Tomorrow I'm going to buy Evadne a block of tickets and take her straight round the guided tour. After that she can go back and potter to suit herself.''

''I look forward to seeing Jeff's house,''
Evadne said.

''You won't need a ticket for that,''
Fitz grinned. ''Hagar keeps it always as
though they might be arriving any minute.
There are even flowers in the rooms.''

''To Hagar it's not an empty house,''
Gwen said gently. ''She feels that they are
all still living there, even if all we can see
now is their portraits.''

''I've heard about Grandfather Julian's
portrait.''

''It looks just like Jeff,'' said Stephen.
''Or perhaps I should say Jeff looks like
the portrait.''

''Stevie,'' Gwen began, out of what had
laid heavy on her mind all evening. ''What
about Sylvia — if there's a war?''

Stephen caught his father's eyes and
looked away, avoiding Gwen's as well. It
was bound to come — this question about
his sister Sylvia, who was Jeff's wife.

''Sylvia married a foreign correspondent,
even if he is Jeff Day of Williamsburg,
Virginia,'' he said slowly, unwillingly. ''If
Jeff decides to stay in London and see the

war, Sylvia won't come away without him. You wouldn't want her to, would you?"

"No," said Gwen obediently, and sat silent among them, thinking of Sylvia, her youngest, and the house a few streets away where she might be living with Jeff, where they might have settled down by now, where there might have been a baby or two, by now. . . .

There is always something about the youngest — especially when it is a girl — and Gwen drew a small sigh. Sylvia living in London with her husband — Stephen returning to it soon with his English wife — well, it was for them to decide, it was their lives they had to live. But in what a world, thought Gwen. And what did they really think, behind their frightening composure, their young, heart-breaking gaiety? How did they face up to their world, she wondered, hearing Evadne's ready laughter, watching Stephen, relaxed and easy, sitting with his bride's hand held unself-consciously in his.

The next day Stephen began conducting Evadne through the formal Restoration tour for the sake of her education. They listened gravely to the soft-voiced hostesses in their eighteenth-century gowns at the Palace and the Capitol, lingered to admire the immaculate charm of the Wythe House, and did not succumb to giggles at the stocks and the Gaol. They sauntered hand in hand down the wide central street, which runs seven-eighths of a mile between Capitol and College, straight as a Roman road under the arching mulberry trees.

Unhurried, bemused by the off-season leisure of the atmosphere, they made the turning to the Day house, which had now come by inheritance to Jeff, the last of that name, posthumous child of sober-minded Miles by Fitz's sister Phoebe. The last before Jeff to live there was Aunt Sue, who could remember Grandmother Tibby, who could remember Yorktown and George Washington. It was still Aunt Sue's house when Jeff came there as a child in the Twenties to recuperate from rheumatic fever. He was in Europe with Bracken when she died a few years later and left it to him. And as she had doubtless foreseen, inheriting the house had brought him back to Williamsburg and his childhood love for Sylvia.

Stephen unlocked the white door and they went into the big square hall with the stairs soaring up. There were vases of flowers, as Fitz had prophesied, and a small wood fire glowed behind a screen in the parlor grate. Evadne entered the parlor ahead of Stephen and stopped short, facing the mantelpiece.

"It's Mab!" she said.

"What?" said Stephen stupidly, glancing round as though some one else might be there.

"That picture! It's Mab! Didn't you *know?"*

His eyes followed her pointing finger to the portrait of Tibby which had always hung in that room above the mantelpiece. When it was painted, by a pupil of Gilbert Stuart, Tibby was in her forties and the mother of three, and Dolly Madison in the White House was setting the style for buxom beauty. Tibby looked frail and childish in the high-waisted white satin gown which left her small arms bare above the elbow and was cut low over her small bust. As Stephen and Evadne stood rooted on the hearthrug the greenish eyes, black-fringed, of the portrait returned their gaze, alert and listening, like a third person in the room.

"It's Grandmother Tibby," said Stephen at last, awed. "Julian's wife."

"It's our Mab in fancy dress!" said Evadne. "Can't you *see?*"

"I can now." Stephen was looking unusually grave. "Come upstairs," he said, and led the way. In the master's bedroom at the top of the stairs, where generations of Days had been born and had died in the four-poster, he fronted her up to another portrait and said tersely, "Who's that?"

"J-Jeff."

"Mm-hm. It is also Julian. We all knew about the resemblance between them. You're the first to spot the other one."

"Jeff and Julian. Mab and Tibby. It's — quite scarey," said Evadne. And after a moment — "Do you think Jeff has noticed? About Mab, I mean."

"He must have. He knows this house by heart."

"And — Sylvia?"

"I wonder."

They stood a moment more in contemplation of Julian, who was Jeff — the long chin and large, humorous mouth, the reflective grey eyes, the thick, brushed-looking dark hair with no wave in it. Then with one accord they returned to the drawing-room like sleepwalkers and stood in front of Tibby, looking up. She had not changed while their backs were turned. Except that now she seemed to be waiting.

"We're *not* seeing things," said Evadne. "Stevie, I feel very queer. What would Mummy say?" She glanced round the bright, warm room. "Stevie, I feel — *haunted.*"

"Now, now. Mustn't panic." But he lit a cigarette without smiling.

"It's when you think how Mab has always had such a Thing about America," Evadne went on, dropping into a corner of the sofa. "That's what makes it so odd. Learning the family tree the way she has — making those scrap-books of everything she can collect about Williamsburg — as though she *remembered,* you might say." Evadne looked up at him with large, incredulous eyes. "Jeff — and Mab," she whispered.

"She's only a kid. Besides, Jeff and Sylvia have been in love all their lives, more or less."

"But it's not Sylvia who looked like Julian's wife," said Evadne. "It's not Sylvia who repeats the pattern, like reincarnation — or do I mean atavism?"

"No," said Stephen slowly, and glanced up as though the portrait of Tibby could hear. "I hope you don't mean anything like that. Because it is Sylvia who has married him."

They looked at each other a long moment and Evadne stood up.

"Isn't it lunch time?" she asked matter-of-factly, and he glanced at his watch and said it was, almost, and they locked the white door behind them and walked back to Fitz's house without mentioning the portraits again.

By mutual consent they said nothing at luncheon about Evadne's discovery.

It was Evadne's misfortune to have her birthday only a fortnight before Christmas, and a letter from Virginia arrived for her in time to be opened on Christmas Eve. She read it in Fitz's drawing-room, with the rest of them sitting round occupied with their own letters and newspapers — and every now and then she would share with them a few lines of Virginia's report on the state of affairs in England since she and Stephen had sailed.

My darling, my youngest — [Virginia wrote]

Twenty-four years ago tonight you were being born here at Farthingale. The Kaiser's war was then nearly five months old. People had already got killed right and left in France — people we knew, people we'd danced with only a few weeks before. The ballrooms where we had danced were suddenly full of long trestle tables where we sat rolling bandages for the Red Cross, and some of the biggest houses were already being turned into hospitals, because in 1914 London was just as safe as anywhere else in England.

Your father was already in uniform, and didn't get home to see you till Christmas Day. I remember watching him bend over your cradle, looking tired and pleased and not quite the way I was used to him — the war marked them very quickly. Three Christmases later he was dead. I wish you could have known him better.

It is a strange twilight sort of Holidays this year. We are secretly thankful to be still whole, still able to do as we please, when so much of the world has lost that privilege — and I think secretly ashamed. So far all our civil defence service is voluntary as it was last time, but that can't last. I go round for the WVS, asking for this and that, and nobody refuses, but nothing is *enough,* and it's not sufficiently organized, hateful word. We have courses in everything — First Aid, Home Nursing, Communal

Cooking, Maternity Care, Gas Contamination — everybody is behaving very well, they offer to sew and mend for the evacuees if and when, to cook for invalids, to provide transportation. Of course we all know evacuation would have been the most frightful muddle if we had got it last autumn, and a good many of the same problems still plague us — such as what to do about the cows in the fields?

People are still arguing hotly about Munich, as though it mattered now. We must just get on with things, it *happened,* whether for better or worse, and we're stuck with it. There is a persistent rumor that an underground revolt in Germany might have got going if we had held out. But who really *knows?* And now, whenever war does come, if we have made good use of the time so dearly bought, we shall be readier.

What a dull letter. One gets in a mental rut these days, it's very narrowing. Basil has caught mumps, from God knows where, Irene is frantic, and Mab and the governess have been staying with me. Irene is a chump. You all had mumps in your day and nobody died. She'll make the most awful mollycoddle of him if she goes on like this.

Dull or not, this letter means to say we miss you, my darling, and hope and pray that you are well and happy and not a bit homesick. Give them all my love.

MUMMY

Then Evadne came to the postscript, without which Virginia could never send off a letter. She read it once over lightly, and again with a frown. And then she looked round rather helplessly for Stephen.

"There's a bit more at the end," she said, and responsive to her slightest inflection he rose and came towards her.

P.S. [Evadne read to them aloud] Mab has a very special request. She wants me to ask you to walk down to the Capitol and turn left. She wants to know exactly what you come to if you keep left along what the map calls Waller Street.

"The railway bridge," said Stephen promptly, and —

"That's funny," said Fitz at the same moment.

"What's funny?" Stephen inquired.

"Go far enough past the railway bridge along the Capitol Landing Road," said Fitz, "and you come approximately to the place where the Mawes cabin stood."

"Mawes?" It meant nothing to Evadne.

"Tibby Mawes, before she married Julian," Fitz reminded her patiently. "Where she lived as a child. Where she was living when he came to Williamsburg before the Revolution began."

"Oh, *no!*" cried Evadne, aghast. "Stephen, we'd better tell them!"

"'Tell us what?" Gwen looked up quickly at her tone.

"Well, the fact is," Stephen began unwillingly, busy with a cigarette, "Evadne noticed something, over at Jeff's house the other day." He glanced from his father to his mother, and went back to the cigarette.

"We all know that Jeff is the image of Julian's portrait. But what Evadne saw at once — and what Jeff must have realized before now — is that Mab looks exactly like Tibby."

There was a silence.

"I suppose there's no sense in getting spooky about it," Stephen continued then. "But the sort of — nostalgic feeling Mab has always shown about everything connected with Williamsburg does make you think, even without this. Do you *know* where the cabin was?"

"It was near the Landing," said Fitz. "You took the road which ran left of the Capitol."

"But it's not marked," Stephen insisted. "That is — there's no record. The Restoration people never heard of it."

"Of course not."

"Then how did she know?" said Stephen. "Or rather — why does she ask?"

The clock ticked perhaps ten times.

"What would happen if Mab ever came to Williamsburg?" Fitz wondered.

"Perhaps it would be better if she never did," said Gwen.

II.
Summer in London.
1939

1

The following August found Mab watching the approach of her thirteenth birthday with an impatience which the annual celebration had never roused before. The whole family as it were had their fingers crossed.

The Bank Holiday had gone by uneventfully except for the eerie feeling entertained by people like Virginia, who could remember 1914 — and everybody drew a cautious breath and looked over their shoulder because it was during a wave of irresponsible optimism in England only last March that Hitler had suddenly marched into Prague. That did it, as even the children in England could see.

That was the end of even Chamberlain's obstinate confidence that Hitler could be handled. England was angry right down to the ground, right to the last citizen. " 'E's broke 'is word," they said in the pubs and the buses, as though it were the first time — but this time his word had been given personally to their Prime Minister at Munich. There was even talk of a change of Government if Mr. Chamberlain didn't *do* something now. Mr. Chamberlain was furious too, if only in his schoolmasterish way, and before the end of March he had given Poland a guarantee that if Hitler moved on Danzig Britain would go to war.

Wise beyond her years in world affairs because of living in a family which allowed its young to mingle in adult society rather more than was customary in England then, Mab understood fairly well what they were all up against now. She had a father in the Home Office, her Great-uncle Bracken owned the American newspaper for which Jeff was a foreign correspondent, her Great-uncle Oliver had been for years at the War Office, and there were assorted cousins with Army and Navy connections.

Even if she had been less intelligently interested than she was, a good deal of it must have rubbed off on her. But it was because of Jeff that she followed the zigzagging international fever chart with such anxiety. Now that Jeff was broadcasting to America as well as writing dispatches for Bracken's newspaper, his job was likely to take him wherever things looked hottest. He had been in Vienna for the *Anschluss,* and in Prague during Munich, and Mab had begun to dread that next it would have to be Danzig, because everybody said the real shooting would start at Danzig.

"Correspondents are just like soldiers, they have to go where the trouble is," said Sylvia, when Mab asked her privately what she thought about Poland. Even though she was Jeff's wife, or perhaps because she was, Sylvia was firm about his obligations, and about theirs, which meant they were not to interfere in his assignments. "Bracken in his day went to the war in Cuba because his father had got too old to take the field work. Now

Bracken has turned sixty, though that doesn't seem possible, and it's Jeff's turn to go abroad for the paper, because Bracken has no son. It's Jeff's job," said Sylvia. "It's what he's been trained all his life to do, as Bracken's heir. We wouldn't have him let Bracken down now, would we, just because there might be some shooting —"

But Mab knew that Sylvia was talking for her own benefit as much as to convince her listener. Inseparable especially when Jeff was away, they made a picturesque pair — Sylvia's long-legged, honey-blonde beauty, and the thin, green-eyed child with straight dark hair held by an Alice comb.

"If we always wish him back hard enough," Sylvia said, with her chin up, "he's bound to come. We can only lose him if we let go and get frightened."

They had had him safe at Farthingale at Easter time this year when Mussolini shot his way into Albania in two days — the man from Bracken's Rome bureau covered that. But Easter was ruined because they all thought — *Now?* Then there was another perilous lull, during which people went on getting married in white satin, having babies, going to the races, even going abroad for holidays — everybody trying to behave just as usual, getting born, living, dying, and done with it, Virginia said — right through Whitsun without another crisis, until now even the dread anniversary of the Kaiser's war slipped by with nothing more alarming than a notice in the papers of a blackout rehearsal to be held in England on the night of August ninth, alongside another list of those household supplies which should be in everybody's emergency cupboard.

Mab was staying with Virginia at Farthingale during August, while her parents went off on their usual summer honeymoon abroad, leaving their idolized small son at home with his nurse. Virginia was always delighted to have Mab to stay, and was equally pleased to be spared the presence of little Basil, a spoilt, precocious child inclined to whine.

Mab and Virginia checked through the emergency list again — pretty dull stuff for the most part — corned beef, matches, lentils, dried onions, cocoa, sugar, tea, American canned beans (for Jeff), tinned dog biscuit for Mab's black cocker spaniel from whom she was never parted even overnight and whose name was Noel — not, as it was often necessary to explain, after Mr. Coward, but because he was a Christmas present. The newspaper reminded you that there would be a scarcity of table scraps and meat trimmings for dogs when you started eating out of tins. Sylvia had added birdseed to her list, in airtight containers, for the canary Midge who accompanied her everywhere, even on week-ends, in a specially made travelling-cage.

Virginia had promised that unless Something Happened they would send Miss Sim the governess home for a holiday in Scotland while they popped up to London for the birthday and bought a lot of clothes and generally let themselves go. Bracken had promised that if Nothing Went Wrong he would take them to dinner at the Hungaria and to the nine-something show of *Good-Bye, Mr. Chips.*

And Jeff had promised that if everything was still All Right they would go to the Wednesday matinee of whatever Mab chose to see. A little to their surprise she had chosen, instead of the Drury Lane show which had music and dancing and Ivor Novello, to see *The Importance of Being Earnest* at the Globe. No one suspected that the answer lay in the chance remark of Virginia's after attending the opening night — it took you back, said Virginia, to a time before Hitler, when the world was young and gay and a lot easier to live in. So the tickets back to Oscar Wilde's world were already bought and in Jeff's pocket.

Another of those random rumors ran round about some new crisis expected on August fifteenth — but nothing burst, and Jeff and Sylvia drove down for the week-end to take them back to Town. Bracken had a house in Upper Brook Street where the family came and went as to a sort of private hotel, and his wife Dinah was always there to pour out their tea, and a small devoted staff was ready to scare up a hot meal at any hour.

Staying at Bracken's was in itself always a treat for Mab because there was no nursery or schoolroom or governess routine there, and one was never treated like a child. Sometimes, if things were very busy and people were there from abroad, one even got to share a twin-bed room with Virginia or one of the girls, and there was grown-up bedtime chat and morning tea together.

It had been a wretched rainy summer so far, which was hard on the new conscript troops training under canvas — Jeff had done a story about that for the paper, though everybody knew it wasn't really as funny as they made it sound. But for Mab's birthday the sun came out and the drive up to London was delightful. Jeff was a trifle preoccupied with the news of a Russian-German trade agreement which had been completed last Saturday.

"The Germans are getting themselves out on a limb again," he brooded as they travelled through the rolling Cotswold countryside. "The first thing we know they'll have talked up another storm."

"There can't be much of anything

coming up this week — Chamberlain has gone fishing,'' Sylvia reminded him comfortably.

"He went fishing last year," said Jeff. "Just before he went to Munich."

"Now, Jeff," said Sylvia, because of the birthday.

"Sorry," said Jeff. "I was only talking out loud."

They reached London in time for late lunch, accompanied of course by the spaniel Noel, who wore a blue bow on his collar for the occasion. They found Dinah alone and rather tight around the mouth. Bracken had telephoned from the Fleet Street office to say that he couldn't make it home for luncheon. Mr. Chamberlain was back in London, said Dinah. Unexpectedly. There was to be a Cabinet meeting tomorrow.

Mab felt them looking at each other above her head. Jeff drifted away toward the telephone, while Dinah and Virginia escorted Mab to the dining-room where a heap of gaily wrapped presents marked her place at the table.

"Don't let's wait for Jeff, he may be

hours on that telephone," said Dinah. "The one with the green ribbon is from Bracken. I'd advise you to open it first."

The family had always made a specialty of presents, ever since the days when Bracken's father had sent his lavish Christmas and birthday gifts through the Yankee blockade to Eden Day at Williamsburg even while the Yankee army was sitting in the town. Soon Mab was surrounded by loose tissue paper and ribbons, enchanted to find that Stephen and Evadne had sent a parcel, with American stamps, all the way across the ocean.

She was a lovely child to give to, knowing by instinct how to express her thanks, as well as having been brought up on Virginia's parable of the Stingy Receiver, which she had drummed into the heads of all the young in the family: There was once a very old lady (Virginia would begin) who was bedridden but quite lively in her mind and heart, and enormously wealthy. She had no immediate family, so when the unknown daughter of a faraway niece was about to be married, the old lady made herself a divine game by taking over the trousseau as her wedding gift to the bride. Everything was brought to her bedside, said Virginia, until sometimes the coverlet and the furniture all around the room were strewn with fabulous garments, from the ivory brocade of the wedding-gown itself to dozens of pastel-tinted, cobwebby under-things — shoes, hats, furs, gloves, even the luggage to put it all in. Each smallest item was inspected and chosen by the rich old lady in bed, regardless of expense, her eyes bright with anticipation of the bride's no doubt speechless rapture as she in her turn beheld the same item when she unpacked it. Speechless was right, said Virginia. When the happily awaited letter of thanks was opened it read: *Dear Aunt Jessie — Thank you do much for your magnificent gift. I am sure no girl ever had a finer trousseau. You were very generous to send it and I am very grateful. With love, Ethel.* Well, what was wrong with that? Virginia would inquire rhetorically. Why was the dear old lady so disappointed that she cried? *Because,* said Virginia, that idiot girl never singled out one thing for itself — never said if the pink chiffon negligee made her look like a bonbon, never mentioned that the shoes and handbags were all meant to match, never said if she liked the blue suit better than the brown one, or if the sapphire velvet brought out the color of her eyes — never indicated one particular gift out of all that lavishness which appealed to her in a special way, never named a favorite item. And *that*, Virginia would conclude impressively, was being a Stingy Receiver.

So Mab said all the right things, and still Jeff's present had not appeared in the pile. She truly loved all her gifts, would not willingly have parted with any one of them — but it was always Jeff's present she looked forward to the most. It wouldn't be lumped in with Sylvia's, now that they were married. She knew there would still be something from him to her, as always. Even if war had already overtaken them, Jeff would have remembered to buy her present.

She could hear his voice on the telephone in the hall, talking to Bracken at the office

— low, unhurried, but with now and then the comic querulous note he sometimes brought into it, especially with regard to Hitler and the Germans. It was a long conversation, as Dinah had anticipated. Perhaps when he came in to lunch he would have to say that the party for tonight was off — Bracken's party at the Hungaria where the gypsy orchestra was, and the *Mr. Chips* film to follow. Well, she could bear that, if there was another crisis on. Newsmen had to watch the tickers in Fleet Street and the radio monitors, they were all used to that in the family. So long as she had Jeff's own personal present she could bear it.

Finally he came to join them, and their faces turned to him, grave and questioning, and he sat down in the empty chair at the table slowly, without meeting their eyes, still preoccupied by the news from Bracken. Gradually he became aware of a silence, and of the chaos of gift wrappings which foamed around Mab's chair, and of the fact that they were all waiting.

"Oh," he said, coming to by degrees, glancing round at them one by one — at

Virginia with her short crisp curls, so slightly greyed, and her slender body which never used the back of a chair, and her alert, humorous, heart-shaped face which seemed to change so little with the years — at Dinah, that porcelain figurine of a woman, so exquisitely dressed, with fading red-gold hair — at his own dear Sylvia with her honey-colored mane and eyelashes out to here, and her poised, dancer's grace — at Mab, their darling, whose level green eyes were exactly like those in the portrait of Tibby at home, her smallness and her dignity and her unchildlike comprehension of the terrible world she had come to live in. . . . "Oh, yes," said Jeff. "You thought I'd forgotten something, didn't you? Well, that's where you're wrong."

He took out of his coat pocket a small parcel, wrapped in white tissue paper. A ring? A pin? Perhaps a bracelet? Jewelry was something new for Mab, but she had lately discovered in herself a secret longing for something really nice of her own — a discriminating ambition born of being allowed occasionally to wear something of

Virginia's as a treat. If Jeff's present was jewelry, how had he known that she was suddenly old enough to appreciate it? No one else knew. Jeff always knew things.

"Happy birthday, Mab," he said gently, and reached across the table to put the parcel in her hand.

It was heavy, like the solid, satin-lined cases with springlids where Virginia's best pieces lived. Her fingers shook a little as she undid it, her heart was beating. Yes — it was — Asprey's name was on the outer box, there was always something a little extra about Asprey's — a flat blue leather case — the lid flew up — *a watch.* They heard the incredulous childish gasp. A small bracelet watch, with gold hands, on a bed of white satin.

"Oh, *Jeff!*" said Mab, and simply sat gazing at it, making no move to put it on.

"Of course there may be some difficulty with the family about your accepting jewelry from strange men," Jeff said with his straight-faced drollery.

He knew very well that it was not a gift for a child, and he had consulted no one, except of course Sylvia, who had at once said, Well, why not, everybody wanted a watch. But not even Sylvia had been there when he chose it, on the overcast, pregnant afternoon a fortnight ago with the blackout rehearsal scheduled for midnight. London had turned that grim exercise into a weird sort of carnival, gathering in holiday crowds of jeer at premises which had overlooked precautions or neglected to conform — singing songs with rude improvised verses about the ARP, frolicking in Piccadilly Circus and heckling the earnest Air Wardens to whom it was so serious a business. But underneath the apparent frivolity, the implications were still there. And everybody knew they could never hide the River from enemy bombers. . . .

Nobody said war nowadays. Emergency was the word. *In the event of an emergency.* . . . How long would Bond Street stand, Jeff wondered that afternoon with a long glance at Asprey's glittering windows as he turned in at their door to buy Mab's present. All that plate glass, he thought. Would London loot its shops when the glass broke under a raid? He would have wagered not. Meanwhile, Mab must have a watch, before it was too late. The first watch was always an event, and he wanted hers to come from him. Ticking out the days that were left of peace and safety in London. And he wanted no one else's opinion or advice on his choice. This was between him and Mab — and Asprey's. He took his time, and made his decision before he asked the price. There was only one that seemed to him just the thing, and this was it.

"Well, really, Jeff, you did let go all holds," Virginia murmured, but not with censure.

"Asprey?" said Dinah, and nodded her approval. "My first watch came from there too. I'll never forget it. I was sixteen, when Bracken bought it for me, and I didn't dare to wear it, because of the family — so he carried it for me, for months. It went all through the Cuban campaign with him. I didn't have it for my own until — oh, much later," she finished rather suddenly, conscious of their fascinated attention.

"Was it that one?" asked Mab, pointing

to the diamonded trifle on Dinah's wrist.

"No, it was on a chain," said Dinah. "You remember, Virginia, we wore them round our necks."

Virginia nodded, looking back. She had never heard about Dinah's watch, though she knew that her brother had had to wait for Dinah to grow up enough to marry him. The things you don't know about people you see every day, she was thinking. Like Bracken carrying Dinah's watch up San Juan Hill as a talisman. . . .

"One's first watch is very special, it matters a lot who gives it," said Dinah, and stopped again rather abruptly, wondering to her own surprise if perhaps she shouldn't have said that just now, and felt Jeff's eyes shift from her face to his plate.

"On our side we get a watch on our eighteenth birthday," said Sylvia, unconscious of undercurrents. "This is mine — from Stevie." She held out her wrist with pride.

"But we can't be certain any more how things will be, by the time Mab is eighteen," Jeff said quietly, looking at his plate. "I thought she might as well make sure of it."

There was a pause. They all sat watching him, without surprise or actual alarm, but with a sort of — alertness?

"What did Bracken say?" Dinah asked then.

"Nothing much. Don't — don't get excited, it hasn't happened." Once again his eyes travelled lovingly from face to face. "We may know tonight," he said.

"Know what?" That was Sylvia.

"There's something in the wind again," he said, almost as though he sniffed it. "Something brewing. A lot of activity here and there." His grave, compassionate gaze came back to Mab's anxious silence across the table. "Bracken says to tell you to hold tight," he said. "The party's not off, by any means. He'll be home for tea — he thinks."

"Well, in that case there's plenty of time to go shopping," Virginia said briskly.

"Aren't you going to put it on?" Jeff asked, for the open case was still in Mab's hand.

"You should put it on for her," Sylvia

advised, as the first course came in. "That makes it legal."

Mab, who sat between Virginia and Dinah, pushed back her chair and carried the watch round the table to Jeff, holding out her left arm solemnly for him to slip the bracelet into place. His hands were long and bony and very deft.

Quite suddenly, while his fingers were still on the bracelet, she had a surging impulse to bend and kiss them. An even swifter panic repressed it, and then, with the maids going round the table behind him and the others falling to on the food. Jeff raised her wrist and set his lips lightly on the watch where it lay, and turned away at once to help himself from the dish which appeared at his other elbow. Such tiny bones Mab had, he thought, giving his attention to the servers. Like a bird's.

"Thank you, Jeff," she whispered, and returned to her chair without looking into his face.

"If there's going to be a war — that is to say, a State of Emergency," Virginia was saying as she put butter on her roll, for she never had to think twice about gaining weight, "I fancy one of the things we should lay in is woollies, because we're sure to be short of heat again, like last time. So Mab and I will skip round to Fortnum's this afternoon and run amuck on Cashmere jumpers and skirts. We can also bring back something special from there for tea. Bracken will need it."

"I'll tell him," Jeff promised. "I'm going down to the Shop after lunch, so I can fetch him back here bodily if nothing — if there's no more news by four o'clock."

"*If!*" cried Virginia, and struck the table unexpectedly with a small exasperated fist, so that they all stared at her, astonished, and even the dishes jumped. "Was there ever a time when we made a simple plan without saying *if?* How long has it been since we accepted an invitation a week ahead without wondering if the state of the world would permit? I'm sick of living like this, from hour to hour! I'm sick of Hitler, they've got to settle him once and for all!"

"*Il faut en finir,*" Jeff murmured, for that was what they were saying in Paris last month when he was there.

"And let's hope they mean it," added Virginia grimly. "Because if they don't we'll have to do it alone. And don't think we couldn't, either. Hitler," said Virginia, erect and furious, "has got to go!"

"I guess that makes it unanimous," said Jeff, impressed. "Unless maybe the Russians."

"Temper," said Virginia by way of apology for her outburst, and shrugged. "It was thinking back that got me down all of a sudden — back to when Dinah got her watch to keep, and married Bracken — and I married Archie the same year. The *peace,*" said Virginia, marvelling at it. "Not just — no war. The peace of *mind,* the not *wondering* about anything, not trying to outguess anything — the feeling that it would all go on forever, like a summer afternoon. Before 1914, I mean — we had those dozen wonderful years before the war. But even in the Twenties, after the war, even with all the conferences and the running to and fro to Stresa and Locarno and all that — even then, you knew where you were for a week at a time —" She looked with compassion at Jeff and Sylvia

— and at Mab. "You can't remember," she said sadly. "Dinah knows what I mean. But you can't any of you remember what it was like, before Hitler."

"Well, I suppose I can in a way," Sylvia said sensibly. "Because he never mattered much to us in Williamsburg — not till after I married Jeff, anyway. Just lately that seems a thousand years ago. Jeff, did Bracken say anything just now about the Russians?"

"Oh, hell," said Jeff, begging off. "It's Mab's birthday!"

"Did he?"

"Well, maybe he did. Something's up."

"Our military mission is up," said Dinah. "Trying to get Russia to come in on our side if — Have we failed? Have they refused?"

"We don't know. But we will soon."

"By tea time?"

"Maybe."

Meanwhile for Mab there was a white cake with thirteen candles, and shopping at Fortnum's with Virginia. And there was the watch with little gold hands, which Jeff had kissed into place.

2

Because Mab and Virginia had skipped round to Fortnum and Mason's in Dinah's Rolls with a chauffeur to drive it, they were not much inconvenienced by the grandfather of all thunderstorms which broke without warning over London that afternoon. They arrived back home at tea time and spread out their purchases on the beds in Virginia's room for Dinah and Sylvia to admire — though the sultry heat which the storm had not dissipated made Cashmere seem somewhat far-fetched.

When they had waited tea for half an hour, pretending that it could be only the storm which delayed the menfolk, they began rather defiantly to stuff themselves anyway with the goodies provided by Fortnum's, and there was a certain comfort in it, at that. The tea was still hot in the pot, however, when Jeff and Bracken came in, damp from having had to run down a taxi in Fleet Street. The headlines in the evening paper they carried were innocuous — another peace move, this time by Belgium.

Bracken was tall and dark and lean, with the squared-off chin and hooded eyes of all the Murray men. He met his wife's anxious gaze with the deliberate blandness he assumed when things were not good, and which exasperated everybody and deceived nobody, dropped into a chair beside her and announced that his tongue was hanging out and could he have some tea.

"Mmm," said Jeff greedily, coming to anchor on the other side of Dinah at the tea-table. "Macaroons." He reached for one.

Dinah attended to their refreshment in a rather marked silence, noting once more that whereas in books people always lost their appetites under stress and strain, the worse things got the more her family wanted to eat, out of sheer nerves.

As soon as Bracken had entered the room Mab had said the right thing about his gift, and was waiting to show him the rest of her birthday loot. For ten minutes he devoted himself to her as though he had no other concern in the world, and reminded them that everyone must be dressed tonight at seven sharp so they could linger over dinner and listen to the orchestra before the film went on. Relaxed and charming in the big chair, having his tea, he finally glanced round with amusement at his attentive family.

"Let us be gay," he said, with the slanted, quizzical eyebrow they knew so well.

And they were, after that, because once Bracken had appeared in their midst it was always difficult not to believe that everything was under control. Mab had a glass of hock at dinner, and the roving violinist played to her, and the film made her cry a little, and altogether the evening was a pronounced success.

The telephone in the hall was ringing when they entered the house, and Bracken snatched it up, with Jeff standing beside him, while the others flowed past him towards the drawing-room.

"Almighty God," they heard him say quietly after a moment, and then there was a long silence while he listened, and Virginia's mind flashed back uneasily to an evening in New York long ago when Bracken's father had answered a ringing telephone which announced the sinking of the *Maine*.

Frozen in their tracks, they stood staring at each other, as though by their very immobility they could divine what was being said in the receiver in Bracken's hand. He had tilted it so that Jeff could hear too, but a slight crackling was all that reached the rest of them in the drawing-room doorway. They knew it was Jackson's voice from the office — Jackson the watch-dog, who slept on a cot among the telephones and tickers and short-wave radios.

And Virginia was thinking, I must get Mab out of London before the bombers came over, Dinah will lend me the car in the morning. And Dinah was thinking, Well, here we go again. And Sylvia was thinking, The radio — we've missed the late News. And Mab was thinking, Oh, don't let Jeff leave England now, he can do the war from here!

When Bracken finally set down the telephone his eyes held Jeff's in a long, significant stare.

"We'd better go right back down there

and watch this," he said, and Jeff nodded, his hat still in his hand.

"What is it *now?*" Virginia asked, with an impatience which almost blamed Bracken for whatever it was.

"At it again," said Bracken wearily, and slid an arm round Dinah's waist and moved them all into the drawing-room, though he did not sit down. "Jeff, let's have a quick one before we go."

Jeff went towards the tray which had been left on the sideboard with assorted bottles and crystal and cold food, and began measuring out Scotch and soda into tall glasses.

"Bracken —" Dinah appealed to his better nature, not to keep them longer in suspense.

"Well, I'd tell you if I knew," he said defensively. "All Jackson said was that Berlin is negotiating behind our backs for a non-aggression pact with Russia — well, we all know what their pacts are! — but the thing about this one is, *Ribbentrop is flying to Moscow to sign it!*"

They all stared at him as though he had made it up to scare them.

"But Ribbentrop built the Anti-Comintern Pact *against* Russia!" Virginia pointed out.

"But Russia is holding military staff talks with *us!*" Dinah spluttered at the same moment.

"Us have got caught in the middle again," said Bracken, taking his glass from Jeff's ministering hand. "It looks like," he added, and drank.

"But what does it *mean?*" Mab asked helplessly, looking from one to another.

"It means we have been double-crossed," said Bracken quietly. "If Russia undertakes to sit on her hands and not join in with us, there won't be an Eastern Front. So Hitler will go for Danzig, Poland will scream for help, and England and France will be at war with Germany — again."

"When?" said Sylvia.

"Before you can say Scat." Bracken drained the glass and set it down. "Well, no, not before Ribbentrop signs the pact. And even now the Russians could throw a monkey-wrench. Jeff and I are going down to the Shop to have another sniff round, but I advise the rest of you to take a lot of aspirin and try to get a night's sleep, this is going to be a rough week." He caught Mab in a protective arm, hugging her against his side. "Well, sweetheart, we had our birthday party, anyway, they can't ever get that away from us now!" Still holding Mab, he bent and kissed Dinah's upturned face. "Don't wait up," he said, for what seemed to her the millionth time since she married him.

Virginia followed her brother out into the hall.

"Bracken — no fooling, should I get Mab out of here early tomorrow?"

The light struck him full in the face as he paused to look down at her, haggard, handsome, with the swinging Murray carriage which was almost a swagger, and her heart cramped with love for him, for Bracken, the ultimate wisdom and authority in the long family story. Instinctively she reached out and caught at his coat with a small cold hand, and felt his close over it, steady and comforting.

"Don't scare her," he said. "Take it easy. It will footle along till

Wednesday, in Moscow."

"But people say the German planes may come over *before* the declaration —"

"Not tonight. Not even tomorrow," he said, and kissed her, and picked up his hat and brief-case and collected Jeff with a glance and they were gone, back to the tickers and the monitors and the cryptic, understated world of Fleet Street which sometimes knew so much more than ever appeared in the headlines.

As Bracken had foreseen, Tuesday produced nothing beyond world-wide shock and bewilderment — while they waited for Ribbentrop to arrive in Moscow. Everybody rallied slowly, and some one in France had the wit to raise the question if Russia had now joined the Anti-Comintern Pact, which caused a few snickers. And Bracken said to sit tight and let Mab have her Wednesday matinee, because the good Lord knew when she'd ever get another.

" 'Look thy last on all things lovely,' " said Virginia wryly. "Suppose the Poles should give in after all."

"The Poles aren't bluffing, whoever else may be," said Bracken. "They'll fight."

"One man," said Virginia through her teeth. *"Just one man,* gone mad! What about Camilla in Berlin? Are you going to bring her out now?" Camilla was the Richmond cousin, favorite of the fabulous Aunt Sally, wife to Johnny Malone who headed Bracken's European staff.

"Johnny's staying — for a while. She won't come."

"Not even a British bomb can recognize American neutrality in a Berlin shelter," Virginia objected.

"They'll both come out when our Embassy leaves — and it will eventually. The British wives are coming now, though it's not official yet."

"Then you do think America will come in."

"She daren't let him win this one," said Bracken.

When the British Cabinet had met on Tuesday it announced that the British guarantee to Poland would stand, whatever the Russian-German agreement might prove to be. No one was surprised at that except Germany, who had confidently expected the Western Powers to cave in in consternation. The Nazis never were any good as psychologists, said Johnny Malone reporting from Berlin by telephone, and he added that no one in Germany really expected war — they were saying in the Wilhelmstrasse that Hitler always got what he wanted without it.

3

Luncheon was going forward in Upper Brook Street before the matinee, when Ribbentrop arrived in Moscow at midday on Wednesday. Dinah's niece Mona Campion, who was a year younger than Evadne, had telephoned Dinah rather impressively that morning to ask if she might bring a guest to lunch, and was assured that everyone would be delighted.

There was no general astonishment when she swept in with Michael Keane in tow — both of them radiant and foolish and newly engaged. Michael was in uniform, expecting every minute to be recalled to his ship. Only an hour before, they had bought the ring which was on her finger, and healths were now drunk and a gala atmosphere prevailed, as though Hitler had never been heard of. Bracken, of course, was at the office, but Jeff had been given the afternoon off to accompany Mab and Sylvia to the theater.

Mab had always admired her cousin Mona for her rather Titian beauty and her royal self-possession — Mona was said to look like Dinah as a girl, but in Mona everything was underlined with a very modern, hoydenish vitality. Her hair and eyes and teeth shone with health, she moved like a colt, she spoke in italics, she dressed in strong colors. There was no one, Mab always thought, so *alive* as Mona, right down to her fingertips, never tired, never bored, never at a standstill.

To look at her now, you would think nobody had ever been in love before. She herself had just invented it, and happiness surrounded her like a spotlight. You would never know, to look at her now, that if war came, she would be driving an ambulance in London, no matter what came down, and that the man she was so in love with would be somewhere at sea in his ship, not heard from for weeks at a time. And it wasn't just putting on a front, Mab thought, Mona really was happy, and she had really forgotten all about the war.

But after the others had left for the matinee, Dinah and Virginia found out how much Mona had forgotten the war. Mona wanted to marry Michael now, at once, this minute, before he could be snatched away — and Michael wouldn't. They sat hand in hand in the drawing-room, presenting their case to Dinah and Virginia, because Mona said Mummy (who was Winifred, Countess of Enstone) was no use at all and only agreed with Michael.

"And what do you want us to say?" Dinah asked, ruefully aware that her own decision and Virginia's had been made so freely, without pressure, years before even the Kaiser was being a nuisance.

"I want you to help me make him understand that even if we had only twenty-four hours together, even if he was called back the next day, everything would be different if we had got married *first!*"

"Everything would certainly be

different," said Michael, not releasing his hold on her hand, "if I were posted missing, or lost a leg."

"But that's *old-fashioned!*" Mona pointed out. "If they bomb London and I'm out with the ambulance I stand about as good a chance of losing a leg as you do! We just don't *think* about that any more!"

Michael did not visibly wince, but his eyes sought Virginia's, dark and troubled and stubborn.

"If I had even a month in the clear now," he said reasonably. "But I'll be off this week, as sure as you're a foot high. Don't think it wouldn't be easier to do it her way — if there was time to get a license, even."

"My dears," said Virginia, striving for equanimity, "Dinah and I aren't qualified any more to say one way or the other. We never had to face the things you do."

"But if you did —" Mona hung on the answer.

"I'm old-fashioned too," Virginia confessed. "I still think the man is boss, and what Michael decided would settle it for me."

4

When the matinee party emerged from the
theater that afternoon they at once bought
the evening papers, which told them very
little. Bracken was quiet but undaunted at
dinner, where they were joined by Mab's
parents who had cut short their holiday in
France and returned full of hair-raising
stories about crowded travel conditions
homeward bound from the Continent.

Instead of reclaiming Mab from
Virginia's care, Irene's main concern was
now to make sure that Basil, who was at
their house in Sunningdale with his nurse,
should be moved at once to greater safety
at Farthingale. It was arranged that
Virginia should pick him up on her
way back and keep both children, with
Basil's nurse, and Mab's governess, in
Gloucestershire until — well, until things
Cleared Up.

Irene was anxious that they should leave
London tomorrow. She of course would

80

remain at their flat in Sloane Street with Ian, whose leave from the Home Office was not up until Monday, although he had been assured on the telephone that he would be very welcome there sooner. Lighting restrictions were to begin at once, he learned when he rang up his chief to report his return, and the first notice went out on the late News that evening. Ration cards were printed and ready to be issued, he told them — meat, ham, bacon, sugar, and fats would be cut at once. Evacuation from the cities of children on the Government plan when it started would interfere with all private arrangements for travel, which should be carried out at once, said Ian, eyeing Virginia severely.

"Ian, what are they going to do about pets?" Sylvia asked into a silence, and Mab laid a cherishing hand on Noel. She had been waiting for Sylvia to bring that up. Noel would be safe at Farthingale with her, but lots of other dogs would have nowhere to go.

"Pets can't be taken into public shelters," said Ian promptly.

"I know that," Sylvia replied equably.

"But you can't expect people to just shut them up in the house and go cheerfully off to the shelters, Ian. If the house is knocked down by a raid, the dog or cat even if it isn't hurt would be frightened out of its wits and would run and run and get lost, and the owner might never find it again."

Ian looked as though animal ARP was just one thing too many for him at the moment, and said there were plans, of course, to take care of all that, though it didn't come into his department. The best thing was to send pets to the country, if you felt that way about them, the same as children.

"But you can't explain to a dog, when you send it away," said Sylvia, who was not usually an obstinate girl. "They would pine much worse than children. There ought to be places in London where you could leave a dog during a raid and call for it again — safe places with somebody in charge who has been trained for the job."

"But you haven't got a dog," said Ian irritably. "And Mab's animal is accounted for, she never lets it out of her sight."

"I've got a bird," said Sylvia seriously. "He means as much to me as Noel does to Mab. Lots of people who have birds in cages won't want to leave them alone in an empty house, they would be even less able to save themselves from fire or —"

"Send your bird with Mab to Farthingale, then," said Ian. "She'll look after it."

"Ian, you don't understand. You aren't even trying. People count on their pets — people who can't leave London themselves and have no country house to send their pets to. A person's pet," said Sylvia, voicing a profound truth which was to dawn on other people much more slowly, "is part of his own morale, especially for people living alone. They will need something to be brave *for,* even if it's a dog or a cat or a bird. Whom should I get in touch with to find out what's being done about this?" she insisted, for she had felt sick all through her First-Aid course, and knew that she would be no good on an ambulance or nursing job.

"About *animals?*" said Ian, rather

incredulous still, and —

"Yes," said Sylvia, looking back at him levelly. "About animals."

"Ask the nearest vet," said Ian. "Or ring the League of Something-or-other."

Later that evening, when Jeff and Sylvia were alone in their room getting ready for bed, she said reluctantly, "Have I disgraced you, wanting to save the dogs and cats? Ian was very annoyed."

"Well, somebody ought to save them," said Jeff in his unargumentative way, pulling off his shoes. "The RSPCA must know what's afoot. Just start ringing up in the morning till you find something to join."

"You don't think it's silly of me? I mean, everyone's worrying about the children and the old people —"

"So somebody else should worry about the animals," said Jeff.

"It's the sort of work I might be able to do," she said, still doubtful, for to her own dismay she had not so far found her niche in the volunteer services.

"Then what do you care what Ian thinks?" Jeff inquired sensibly. "There must be somebody wrestling with that problem, who would be glad of some help."

"It was Midge's idea," said Sylvia, and got into bed with a sigh of relief and a glance at the cage on the table in the corner. Midge was an olive and gold canary with a highly trained Roller song, muted and sweet, never shrill, never tiresome. He was finger-tame, ate anything that was going, and had never known fear. He liked a good thunderstorm to sing to, regarding it as some kind of orchestration arranged to set off his best notes. Sylvia said that an air raid would doubtless do him just as well, as an accompaniment.

At a little after two A.M. the telephone rang, and while there was an extension in Bracken's bedroom the bell ringing in the hall woke everybody up, especially Mab. And when Mab sat up in bed, alert and listening, Noel on his cushion in the corner roused at once and sat up too.

Lights came on, the bedroom doors opened, and people looked out at each other with white, silent faces. Bracken's door opened last, and he was not surprised to see them all there, waiting.

"Jackson says the word has just come through from Berlin," he said quietly. "They have signed."

No one spoke, but Sylvia's hand closed on Jeff's sleeve, and Virginia laid a reassuring arm across Mab's shoulders, drawing her closer. Dinah came through the door beside Bracken, tying the cord of her dressing-gown.

"You'll want something to eat before you go back to the office," she said to him, her head down. "I'll make scrambled eggs for everybody, while you dress. We might as well, we won't sleep now."

Lights came on ahead of her, down the stairs. Mab and Virginia followed her, getting into their dressing-gowns as they went, with the spaniel pattering behind. Sylvia stayed in their room with Jeff while he dressed, and they were the last to appear, just after Bracken, both men shaved and immaculate and composed, if a trifle grim.

Mab had laid the table. Virginia had made the tea and toast. Dinah produced a platter of bacon and eggs. Unbelievably they all sat down and ate. Only Mab refused the eggs, nibbling at a piece of toast and sipping her tea with milk. Only Sylvia had to force the food down her throat against an aching lump which threatened to burst and choke her.

"They're trying at the Shop to get through to Johnny in Berlin," said Bracken as he ate. "No doubt he is trying to get through to us. This will have shooken 'em up at the Taverne, where the correspondents hang out. Of course as long as the British Ambassador is still in Berlin there's some hope. The House is meeting this afternoon, and then we may know what his plans are."

"Do you think he'll confide in us all?" asked Virginia.

"My dear, when the British Ambassador to Germany asks for his passports, that will be news and we shall hear about it, never fear."

Still understated and collected, Jeff and Bracken departed for Fleet Street, and their womenfolk trailed wearily back to the dishevelled bedrooms and lay down to wait, if not to sleep, while the windows greyed into another muggy dawn and the city of London awoke to its headlines.

Soon after that the telephone was ringing again, and Dinah stilled it, answering from her room. It was Irene, urging that Virginia start at once for Farthingale with the children. Dinah explained that Bracken would be in the House that afternoon, and would report home as soon as Chamberlain had spoken.

"You surely don't think the P.M. can wangle *again!*" said Irene crossly, and hung up.

While they sat around the table in Dinah's dining-room having a second breakfast, heavy-eyed and rather silent, but fully dressed now and tidy, Mona rang up to say that Michael had gone to join his ship without even time for more than a telephoned good-bye, and Dinah asked her to lunch.

"I suppose the Navy is gathering at Scapa Flow," she said, returning to her chair. "Last time it was submarines we worried about. This time it will be planes carrying bombs."

"I can remember," said Virginia eerily, "a day when they drew the flat outline of a battleship on the ground at the Hendon air show, and a plane going about forty-five miles an hour flew over and hit it with a plaster-of-Paris bomb from a thousand feet up, and we all clapped and thought how clever it was."

"Yes, well —" Dinah agreed vaguely. "I suppose now we had better start putting things together here. Ian says we shall be blacked out soon, no matter what happens. There's a grim little Home Office pamphlet about ARP in my desk — not that I don't know it by heart, but we might as well run through it again —"

Unemotional and efficient, they checked the pamphlet's requirements. There was no last-minute scurry, for Bracken had already had a comfortable refuge-room built in a reinforced corner of the basement, equipped with electrical outlets, and furnished with bunks and bedding, heavy tables and easy chairs, storage for drinking-water, even a rug. Then Dinah had assembled in it some useful extras such as candles, First-Aid kit, electric kettle and small spirit-stove, spare radio on a battery, books, tinned food, and bottled drinks.

It was time now, Dinah decided, to hang the dark draperies which were ready to go inside the fitted blackout blinds at the windows on all floors of the house. "I will not live like a mole," she had said when they were ordered some months ago. "We must be able to have all the light we want inside."

Virginia was leafing through the pamphlet for the hundredth time.

"What a swot these incendiary bombs are going to be," she grumbled. "Have you got all the bits and pieces to cope with them?"

"In the cupboard in the passage."

" 'Two buckets, one full of sand, the other with about four inches of sand in it, and a shovel with a pole or broomstick lashed to it to lengthen the handle,' " Virginia read out ponderously. "You throw the sand from the full bucket on to the bomb to smother it, and then — *with the shovel lift it into the other bucket!*' "

they chanted in unison.

"It's not possible, of course," said Dinah cheerfully. "But here are the buckets and the sand *and* the shovel! Not to mention a stirrup-pump as well."

"But I thought you weren't supposed to put water on them."

"Oh, Virginia, how do we *know?* And if we've all gone down to the shelter who's going to be mucking about with buckets and sand? Sylvia says it's exactly like a first night without a prop rehcarsal!"

Mab drifted about in Virginia's wake, being as useful as she could, feeling an uncomfortable detachment. These preparations were for other people's safety, after she had gone back to Farthingale. Children would be no use in London, she knew, but nevertheless it was a guilty knowledge that one was oneself exempt from the immediate emergency only by one's lack of years. That is, if they got away in time, before it began.

She was humiliated to find that she wanted to go *now,* at once, that she dreaded being caught in the general evacuation undertow, and that she was —

yes, *afraid* to stay in London. To discover that one was a coward, Mab thought, handing up curtain rings to Bracken's manservant on a stepladder in the drawing-room, was really the last straw. To know this sick churning in one's insides, to long to start packing a bag, to watch the clock, to prevent oneself by main force from asking when they were going to start — But Bracken didn't intend to let them run any risk. . . .

Her hands were cold and clammy, and she took great care not to touch Gregson's fingers as she handed things up the ladder, lest he notice and suspect that she was afraid. Gregson had been in the last war — all through it, twice wounded and gassed. Gregson knew he could stand fire. Gregson was brave. . . .

Sylvia looked in at the drawing-room door with her hat on.

"Oh, there you are," she said. "Would you like to come round to Cromwell Road with me and see about the animal ARP? I've been talking to some nice woman on the telephone, and she says I can put my name down to be an Animal Guard. I thought it was worth looking into —"

Mab accepted with relief. It was always comforting to be with Sylvia.

As they walked through the streets on that Thursday morning they felt the tempo of London quickening all round them. Men were at work reducing the traffic signals at the corners to thin colored crosses. Men were painting white lines along the curbs and traffic islands. Museums were loading their treasures into vans which would take them to prepared hideaways in the country. Police notices in unemotional black and white had gone up on walls and windows about masking your house lights and screening your motor lamps. And — this brought a sinking sensation when they realized it — live ammunition was being stacked around the A.A. guns in the parks.

And yet London was strangely calm, they felt, watching the unhurried, methodical workmen. Not just resigned. Not hopeful that it was all just another false alarm, either. But steady. Not the desperate composure of will power, like last September. Now there was a deep, unreasoning, illogical serenity. The British had put their foot down. And only by the periodic, inevitable secret wave of nausea in each individual midriff, resolutely downed unmentioned, did their nerves betray them.

Sylvia bought the noon edition of the *Standard* and they read it in the bus. The American Ambassador was advising Americans to leave England at once, and there was a rush for bookings on the SS *Washington* sailing at midnight.

"I'm glad that doesn't mean me," said Sylvia. "They'll pack in like sardines, the way it was last year before Munich."

"But you are an American," Mab said almost with envy. "And so is Jeff."

"Foreign correspondents are a kind of maverick," Sylvia remarked with a certain pride. "They're hired to break all the rules. To break their silly necks too, if necessary. It says here that volunteers are still needed to take charge of children in the evacuation — which may be ordered at any time now. That's the sort of thing I ought to be doing, you know — instead of fretting about mere dogs and cats."

"The children will get along," said Mab unsympathetically.

"That's the way I feel," Sylvia agreed gratefully. "They've been organizing to deal with the children for months, I tell myself. Well, anyway — we'll see what's going on about the pets before I give up on it."

When the House convened that afternoon at Westminster, Bracken was in the Press Gallery, noting tension but not gloom. The Prime Minister in a quiet, rueful speech admitted that there was imminent danger of war, but reiterated the pledge to Poland. Winston Churchill was not in his accustomed place, which indicated that he had not yet returned from his holiday in France. They would have Churchill back in the Government, everybody said, if Anything Happened. The House, having met and issued its warning and its reassurances, adjourned till the following Tuesday the twenty-ninth.

Mab and Sylvia returned at tea time to Upper Brook Street, full of information about the animal ARP, which was indeed glad of another volunteer, and enthused by an irresponsible detour to the Radiolympia Show, where they had been entranced by the miracle of television, which would be like having a tiny camera theater in your own living-room, they explained, as easy to turn on and off as a radio. For only thirty-two guineas, said Sylvia, and not taking up any more room than a sideboard — and Dinah hadn't the heart to remind her that all television entertainment would cease instantly once war was declared.

Jeff turned up for tea, having done his own tour of the London streets and handed in his story. There was the usual patient, undemonstrative crowd in Downing Street, he said, watching the Foreign Office and the Prime Minister's residence. There was increasing activity at the War Office, where poker-faced generals still wearing mufti came and went. The King was back at the Palace from his holiday in Scotland. The Fleet was admitted to be at war stations. All leave was stopped, and everywhere key men were disappearing quietly from their offices and clubs and homes.

"Take it easy," said Bracken again to Virginia, when he came in for dinner. "We're all right over the coming weekend apparently. Somebody is still trying. Ambassador Henderson for one, in Berlin. We got hold of Johnny on the phone there, to our intense surprise — had quite a chat. He says the British Embassy has begun to burn its papers. Well, they did that last year too, before Munich. Most of the British journalists have left for the Danish frontier. Warsaw is said to be gay and defiant, with beautiful weather — but Johnny thinks the big story is still in Berlin. It's a very baffled Hitler — up against a fed-up world. The question is, Will he be able to take it in now that he cannot accomplish another Munich compromise?"

Jeff was broadcasting to America at midnight, and they were going to try for one of their three-way roundups, bringing in Johnny from Berlin and also the man at the Paris bureau. Beamed at New York, Jeff's broadcasts were not received over the English wave-lengths, so Dinah always joined Bracken in the little studio at the

BBC and heard Jeff through the earphones. She arranged to meet them there tonight as usual.

During dinner Jackson at the office rang up to say that a cable had just been received from Evadne in New York. After two postponements because of her enchantment with life in America while Stephen and his father worked on the new show, they were sailing at once for England — there was no difficulty to get passage in that direction. Bracken dictated a cable right back insisting that they wait for an American boat. Returning to the table, he met Virginia's anxious eyes with a smile.

"That settles that," he said. "They'll be coming straight into it. I just happened to remember the *Lusitania*."

Sylvia began to wonder if Evadne might be disappointed in her for trying to save the animals when children and old people would be in need of help. Evadne had the strength of character to come back from Williamsburg when she didn't have to, because of her warden's post in Bayswater. That brought Stephen into the war zone with her, and the new show would have to wait. Stephen wouldn't just sit around while Evadne worked at the post, he would get that mobile canteen going, and, if there were no theaters in London, he would organize entertainment for the forces. . . .

They were all in it, up to their ears, Sylvia was thinking. Dinah went every day to the WVS office in London, Mona had her ambulance, Jeff would be out chasing the fire engines — they would all be on a job when the bombs started coming down, and they would have a right to expect Jeff's wife to do something constructive too. And the papers were saying that animals who had no place to go were better destroyed. . . .

Midge could go to Farthingale with the children to be really safe, but he wouldn't understand that, he would want to be with her, and she had to be with Jeff in London. The people at the animal ARP had welcomed her, and she had committed herself for training and brought back their leaflets.

There were plans for animal ambulances, she had learned, which in most cases would consist of private cars dedicated to the task. There were to be shelters for pets, underground or properly braced, with two exits, and intelligent humans in attendance; separate pens for each dog and cat, space for separate bird-cages, an identity tag for each inmate, registered and numbered so that it could always be traced. . . . Midge already had his luggage tag for travelling, with her address on it. Everybody must have a tag like Midge's now. . . . There wasn't to be any charge, because it was the people who couldn't afford to pay who would need it most. There had to be free food — I could buy a stock of food, Sylvia thought, and they wouldn't have to bring it with them — often there mightn't be time — and there will be strays, the woman said. Even without tags, the strays must be fed. There was still so much to do before it started, before rationing began, and they needed contributions terribly, and fortunately she had some money of her own. . . .

But she wondered if it looked as though she was funking it, working with creatures who had no souls and couldn't tell their trouble. Maybe it was funk, not to face the human fright and pain and blood. At least Mab seemed not to think less of her this afternoon, when she finally chose her war work and signed up as an Animal Guard, though it was often hard to tell what Mab thought behind that unchildlike composure. Apparently Mab had more courage than Jeff's wife, who found herself sick and shaky with what must be sheer cowardice when everyone else was so collected and sure where their duty lay. Even Mab was brave, thought Sylvia — and it was humiliating to remember, unfairly, that Mab would be sent to Farthingale before it began. . . .

When Dinah set out for the BBC to hear Jeff's broadcast, Mab and Virginia decided to try bed, but Sylvia was still mooching about in the drawing-room, where Midge's cage stood covered in a corner, when they all returned after midnight. Bracken said he had given up sleeping for the duration, and they sat a while with drinks and sandwiches, discussing the telephone conversation which he had had with Johnny before the broadcast began. The Taverne, where the correspondents gathered in Berlin, was reduced to its neutral customers now, after having drunk the Russian Pact in with champagne the night before as a gesture of defiance and to relieve their feelings; neutrals and the smirking German editors who were now suddenly denying everything they had been taught by the Nazis to say about Russia for six years, in a brazen overnight about-face fantastic even for the mindless hirelings of Goebbels. By dawn some of the Taverne arguments had turned pretty nasty, and some of the less-neutral, like Johnny, had had to take a turn in the Tiergarten to cool off. He would never forget Camilla's face when he got home, Johnny said, roused out of a belated sleep to hear his latest news. "Sitting up in bed jawing *me!*" he reported with something like a snicker. "I had to remind her that *I* hadn't gone to Moscow!"

They smiled rather feebly at the story, and their own dawn, twenty-four hours later, was greying the streets outside. Johnny thought the Berlin rumors last night of an immediate march into Poland were premature, because the German people hadn't been sufficiently worked up to it. The Germans were awfully happy so far about the whole thing at Moscow, Johnny said — too happy even to feel sheepish, for the terms of the Pact precluded a Soviet alliance with Britain and France now, and banished the carefully nurtured German nightmare of encirclement. Now there could be no Eastern Front — except of course Poland, which didn't count.

Johnny said the bar at the Adlon where he and Camilla lived was very lonely tonight with the British gone. He had been hanging out there with an American just out of Warsaw — some sort of Unofficial guy, just a Tourist, Johnny explained in his code voice which capitalized the vital word ever so slightly — one of those professional Globe-trotters on Holiday, as you might say.

This American said the Poles would fight like hell, *he* bet, and even then he gave them about a month, without help. They were too charming, and too confident, and too old-world, and too bloody ill-equipped. And by the way, said

Johnny, ask Virginia if she remembered anything about October, 1918.

Virginia would naturally remember several things about October, 1918, but she had gone to bed for once, and Johnny had not told them what sort of thing she was supposed to remember. Something about the American in the Adlon bar, apparently. Not much to go on. They speculated on it briefly, with yawns, and went off to lie down a while, if not to sleep, before the new day caught up with them.

5

"Of course I remember October, 1918," said Virginia at breakfast when they put it to her. "They went right on getting killed. What else do you want to know?"

"We sort of wondered if you recalled any Americans," Jeff said mildly.

"Quite a few. Why?"

"We don't know why," Bracken admitted. "Johnny was trying to get something across last night on the 'phone.

104

He's met up with an American tourist type
— he says — who is in and out of
Warsaw, and then he said to ask you."

"Intelligence man," said Virginia, not
batting an eye, pouring out more tea.

"Probably," Bracken conceded with
respect.

"What's his name?"

"No names," said Bracken.

"I see," said Virginia.

And then, though her eyes were on her
teacup and she did nothing so obvious as
catch her breath or change color, Bracken
could have sworn that she thought of
something. He waited, while a silence
spread.

"Well, it's not much to go on, is it,"
said Virginia, her eyes still lowered, and
they agreed it wasn't and went on waiting.
"There were dozens of them," she
remarked, and lifted her cup. "Most of
them I wouldn't know now from a hole in
the wall. Why? Is it important?"

"Hard to tell. It could be," Bracken
said cautiously.

"He'll get himself killed, no matter who
he is, mucking about in Warsaw, once the

fun starts," said Virginia.

"The American Embassy has taken a villa outside Warsaw as a refuge in case of air raids," Bracken said. "No flies on Biddle."

"Well, so they have here, at Epsom or somewhere," she agreed. "And will the German bombers know Biddle's Embassy villa outside Warsaw from anybody else's villa when the time comes — or will they care?"

"Remains to be seen," said Bracken, handing his cup for more tea. He perceived that there would be nothing more forthcoming now, and when Virginia remarked that believe it or not the annual cricket party at Farthingale village was tomorrow and she had to be seen there as usual, he allowed Johnny's mysterious American to sink into temporary oblivion.

"You'd think they'd call the cricket off this year," Sylvia remarked.

"What, and let Hitler have the satisfaction?" Virginia demanded. "They begin to plan these August festivals in January. This one has already sustained the march into Prague and the death of

Albania. We aren't going to miscarry now!''

"But surely everybody's called up," said Sylvia.

"Regulars and reservists, yes. But there are still enough old crocks and schoolboys to make a team, and the village expects it. They could never do it without Mab and me, though, so we'll be off right after lunch, if we can have the car."

"Certainly, take the car. But there's no real rush yet," Bracken said.

The morning papers lay beside him, folded so that only one headline was visible. *Hitler's Midnight Conference,* it said. Next to that there was a column about all Warsaw digging trenches, even expensively dressed women swinging picks and shovels in the dramatic eleventh hour effort.

The breakfast table party broke up reluctantly, and Virginia kissed her brother and Jeff good-bye with a secret dread of what might happen in the interval before she saw them again. Telephone service to the country areas was curtailed and belated even now, and once down in

Gloucestershire she would feel cut off and out of touch. Except for the children, she would have much preferred to stay in London.

Putting the last overnight things into her bags for the drive to Farthingale, she felt the same uneasy finality — when would she see Upper Brook Street again? The uncertainty, the depression, the sudden preciousness of commonplace things and everyday people took her mind back again to 1918. October. There had been dozens of Americans, yes, and one of them was now in and out of Warsaw where the bombs would fall first. Intelligence work, if that was it, was no joke nowadays, even for a neutral. Worse than ever before, because bombs didn't care about neutrals, for one thing, and much good Ambassador Biddle's suburban villa would be once the Nazi planes began on Warsaw. . . . October. . . . Twenty-one years ago, less a month.

Virginia stood by the window of her bedroom, looking out at the muggy, drizzling London day.

What weather, she thought, trying not

to think of the other thing. Beastly day for the drive home. But you don't know if he is still alive, she thought. He went back into the Line that October. You don't know if he was still alive when the Armistice came. But if he is — Intelligence is just about what you might expect Tracy Marsh to be doing. . . . Did they say my name last night, there at the Adlon or whatever it was? Camilla would hear, and wonder. Camilla was a kid VAD in 1918, preoccupied with her own unhappy affairs, which had nothing to do with stray American wounded passing through the hospital where they both worked. Anyway, it couldn't be. . . . But then why did Johnny say to ask me . . .

In Dinah's town Rolls, with the aging chauffeur to drive it, Virginia and Mab and Noel the spaniel left London in the early afternoon, going round to pick up Basil and his nurse — who was fortunately a sensible woman, thought Virginia, and was doing her best to prevent him from growing up a self-satisfied prig like Ian.

It was a mild day of clouds and sun, with showers, and except that they kept passing lorry loads of Air Territorials going somewhere in a hurry, England looked entirely peaceful and normal. Mab found Virginia a little absent-minded during the drive, and supposed that she was thinking of the people they had left behind them in London, for Mab hated that part of it too. Sylvia was grown up and Sylvia was brave and so Sylvia had the right to stay with Jeff. Dinah stayed with Bracken. Irene stayed with Ian. And in Berlin, Camilla stayed with Johnny. Children and grandmothers were spared the awful glory of sticking with a husband no matter what happened. You said Good-bye to Jeff, you felt his lips briefly on your cheek, his coat was rough and warm under your hands, and then the door closed behind him and Bracken, off to Fleet Street and the tickers. But Sylvia would be there when he came home tonight. And when the bombs came? But Sylvia was brave.

Virginia bought a local afternoon paper at the end of the journey to Gloucestershire. It said that Hitler had sent for the British Ambassador, which might be interpreted as a good sign. It said there was a feeling of relief, however faint, through the country. While negotiation existed, a chance remained. Anyway, the *Echo* concluded, the Nazis had miscalculated the effect of the deal with Russia. Instead of caving in, Britain and France were more determined than ever to see the end of a situation full of unpleasant surprises, intolerable tension, and suspense. Everybody was sick of Hitler. One way or another, Hitler had to go.

They arrived at Farthingale at sundown unreasonably tired, to find the elderly parlormaid and the ancient gardener coping with blackout preparations in the drawing-room. Virginia threw down her hat and stood facing the great west window where the tea-table was always laid. Fitted plywood shutters — black sateen curtains on extra rods — in Gloucestershire!

"Oh, *what* a swot it's going to be, blacking out every night!" she cried in despair. She had felt rather foolish last spring having part of the cellar reinforced to construct a refuge-room — but now it was done and ready, like the blackout arrangements. Tomorrow it must be stocked like Dinah's with emergency stores. . . .

Basil was asking in a whining voice for the seventh time if Mummy would be there in the morning. Virginia rounded on him.

"Nobody will have their mummies with them pretty soon!" she said a bit sharply. "And most people won't even have their grannies!"

Basil was tactfully removed nurserywards by his nurse, who knew her way around the house from previous visits.

"That reminds me, madam," the elderly maid Melchett remarked with some reluctance and an anxious smoothing of her apron. "Lady Laverham rang up and I was to tell you that we have been alerted for the reception of the children from Birmingham."

"Good Lord, *when?*"

"That's not definite yet, madam. She said the people from the Bank that is booked in there at Cleeve are expected too. And there's been a gentleman here

112

again about the billeting, and I let him look at the rooms. That's the third time.''

"All right,'' said Virginia, resigned. ''Let 'em all come. But first let me have a nice dry Martini, very cold, and a dish of salted almonds.''

As Melchett left the room on the errand and the gardener eclipsed the westward window with his blackout rehearsal, Virginia turned away to snap on a table lamp, which illumined the small satirical smile on her lips. It sounded like praying, she thought. Please God, let me always have a nice dry Martini *first*.

"Gran.''

"Yes, darling.'' She noticed with compassion that Mab had not sat down either.

"I haven't got a job. In the war, I mean.''

"Later, darling.'' Virginia sighed. Thirteen.

"But everybody has to do something,'' said Mab, standing helplessly in the middle of the rug. "And with the Bank people billeted here in the house we won't have any of the Birmingham children —''

"Thank God," said Virginia piously. "The village will be full of them, never fear. We'll have to have working-parties to make warm clothing, and stuff for the new babies which are sure to arrive. You can knit and sew quite nicely, so you can help with that. And something must be done for their entertainment, I suppose, because the cinemas will all be closed."

"Shall we get bombs down here, do you think?" Mab asked, trying to sound academic and detached.

"Theoretically, no. We are a reception area. But they'll try for Cardiff and Birmingham, and the observers' post on the hill beyond Cleeve will catch it — which takes them right over our heads." Virginia conceded wearily, and came to lay her arm around the small, lonely figure in the middle of the room, as a different window, on the south, went dark in its turn. "We're all groping, Mab, if that's any comfort to you. Nobody knows much more than you do about what's going to happen. And nobody's any braver than you are, either. Does that help?"

"But the people staying in London —

they have to be brave —"

"They have to find courage," Virginia said. "It's not quite the same thing. Deep down inside, everybody's scared, believe me. It's how you behave in spite of being scared that counts."

Melchett returned with a pale stemmed glass on a silver tray beside a dish of almonds. She cast a disparaging eye on the gardener's achievement, and when Virginia had taken the glass Melchett set the tray on a table and went to tweak the dark masking draperies into more seemly folds in the gardener's wake.

"We turned out the whole house, madam, while you were away," she announced. "Upstairs and down. Might as well start the war with everything tidy and shipshape, I said to Ivy."

"Well, yes — why not," Virginia agreed, sipping. "That was very thoughtful of you, Melchett."

"There wasn't time, the other war," Melchett reminded her, snapping on more lights. "But this one keeps hanging fire, you might say. We may as well get down to it now, it's the only way to teach 'im."

6

The cricket party took place the next day in perfect weather, proceeding with a sort of dogged frivolity along its usual course. Everything went off exactly as planned under the firm guidance of Charles Laverham, who was one of those so lightly referred to by Virginia as old crocks, and who as lord of the manor of Cleeve since the last war was confidently relied upon to see that the next one was not allowed to spoil the fun.

And still the slow-motion crisis dragged on, with the whole world balanced on the knife-edge of rumor and suspense. As the days ticked by, Ambassador Henderson flew to London, and flew back to Berlin. Hitler was said to be locked in his room, fuming and dangerous — and possibly hesitant for the first time. The obstinate, battered hope that not even Hitler could face the consequences would not quite expire.

But when on Thursday the BBC announced that evacuation of the children would begin early on Friday morning,

September first, "as a precautionary measure" everyone felt again the familiar sick crunch in the middle and recognized it for plain old-fashioned Fear. Somebody in Whitehall knew something — smelled something — sensed something. "It's no good their saying now that war is not inevitable," Virginia muttered. "Somebody is already sure."

All over England that Thursday night the pitiful travel-kits of the children were checked through again, packed and re-packed for the zillionth time — toothbrush, face-cloth, change of underwear (if possible), extra chocolate, some comic books or a favorite toy, gas-mask — the inevitable gas-mask. . . . All over England the children were sleeping in their own beds for the last night for who knew how long, and parents creeping in for another look stood wretchedly wondering once more if it were really for the best to send them away.

These doubts mostly vanished at breakfast time on Friday, when the ominous words: *"There is grave news this morning. . . ."* Hitler had finally thrown the lever, and the German war machine had been rolling across the Polish border since dawn. Open towns and refugee trains in Poland were being bombed from the air.

England stiffened again, and resolutely surrendered its children to the trains and buses which were to carry them to safer areas in the countryside. There were tears. But most of those were on the faces of the people who saw them go.

As the news from Poland worsened during the day, and censorship and blackout were announced to begin at once in England, there still remained a question — the British Ambassador had not left Berlin — England was still not at war.

"If anyone had told me the day I left London that one week later we would still be waiting for the other shoe to drop!" Virginia exclaimed when Charles and Rosalind Laverham arrived at Farthingale for a nightcap drink and a conference late on Friday evening.

"Not much like last time, is it!" said Charles, who had been in the Household Cavalry then. "I stepped into the club one day for a quick one before dinner, and *Bang!* I was in France!''

''No radio then,'' said Virginia. ''Sometimes I almost thought this war would talk itself to death before it happened.''

''Too late for that now,'' Charles said. ''They're bombing Warsaw. You can't take back a bomb and say it was no such thing.''

''Then why aren't we at war?''

''My dear, we are.''

''It doesn't say so on the BBC.''

''The House is sitting. We'll get it on the late News tonight, no doubt.''

They all glanced at the radio, which was playing what the BBC called ''light music'' softly in a corner. It was seldom turned off any more, but it seemed to tell them very little.

''Well, we were lucky today at the reception center,'' Rosalind said, stifling a yawn. ''Fewer children than we expected. I wonder how many other places could say the same. Somebody must have got our missing ones, which would swamp them. And it may all even up tomorrow.''

"Thirty-nine babies in that nursery school that's taken Overcreech House," said Virginia with a shudder. "One matron, and how many girls to help?"

"I couldn't see for babies. Not enough, you may be sure."

"Have your Bank people arrived?" Virginia asked.

"Only five or six, so far. The advance guard. I thought I just couldn't bear it last year when Charles arranged with the Bank to take over Cleeve, and they started putting in fitted basins and electric fires and partitions and blocking out windows. But I see now it was all for the best. The Bank is at least adult!"

As Charles and Rosalind had occupied the Dower House since 1917, the dislocation at Cleeve was relatively slight, except for the heart-breaking alterations to the elegant seventeenth-century manor house which had been completed during the past summer so that it could house offices, a canteen, and the loftier personnel. All the spare rooms at the Dower House and at Farthingale, as well as at the village inn, had been taken as billets for the smaller fry, some of whom had already arrived, escorting the lorry loads of records and files. Secretaries, typists, file clerks, and other underlings were arriving tomorrow. And in the village they would be expected to cope with more children, and more pregnant mothers with the ominous pink cards which meant that anything could happen any minute.

"Perhaps the delay on the declaration here is to get our children away before there is any excuse to bomb our railways and reception areas," suggested Rosalind, who was never afraid to face facts.

"That will take three days at least," Charles said. "Have you heard anything direct from London?"

"Three minutes on the telephone with Bracken yesterday," Virginia replied. "We try not to use it, of course. They can't get Berlin now, except by short-wave and only some of the time. They don't know if Johnny will be allowed to go on broadcasting from there. I wonder if his American has disappeared into Warsaw again as Bracken thought."

"What American?" Charles asked,

and Virginia's eyes came to rest on him, puzzled and grave.

"Do you remember Tracy Marsh?" she asked, and Charles's reply was just a fraction of a second slow, and then all he said was, "Yes."

"He *was* Intelligence, wasn't he, in 1918 — behind that bona fide captain's uniform?"

"What makes you think of him now?" asked Charles.

Melchett came in with the tray of glasses and sandwiches which she placed on a coffee-table in front of Virginia beside the tray of decanters, and went away again. At a hospitable gesture from Virginia Charles rose at once to deal with the drinks, and while he measured and poured the silence lengthened.

"Oh, all right," said Virginia with a sigh. "I mustn't ask questions about Tracy Marsh — even now. Have you ever heard from him since he left here before the Armistice?"

"Soda?" said Charles, her glass poised at the syphon.

"Just a splash, dammit." She accepted

the glass from his hand and glanced at Rosalind. "I thought Charles was out of it for good," she complained. "Is he going to clam up again this war too?"

"There aren't enough of them who can remember what he can," Rosalind said with her unshakable serenity. "Too many of them died. So they want him back."

"I'd have you know I'm an extremely valuable antique," Charles said with dignity, presenting his wife with her glass. "Beginning Monday, I am to be mounted in a glass case in an office in Whitehall — or its evacuated equivalent."

"Oh, but Charles, we need you here!" Virginia cried in dismay, for it was always Charles they ran to about the wardening and the observers' post and the gas-lectures and the billeting and the clinic and the maternity home — well, Rosalind there, but behind Rosalind, Charles, steady and patient and kind and *knowing;* even without a war they couldn't get along unless Charles was at Cleeve to be run to.

"There are things still imprinted in the mouldy recesses of my aging brain," Charles explained, "which may conceivably be of some use to a Government which finds itself at war with Germany — again.''

''But — is Rosalind going up to London with you?'' Virginia looked from one to the other with compassion, for the Laverhams were never apart.

''No. She's got things to do here. A good many more things than she had before I was called back.''

''Well, I do call that hard luck,'' Virginia said to Rosalind. ''I do think, at Charles's age —''

Charles bristled.

''I'm no older than Churchill!'' he said.

''Will he come back now?''

''Bound to. Can't run a war without him at the Admiralty. Even Chamberlain knows that.''

''Well, this *is* like old times,'' Virginia said thoughtfully. ''And there's Oliver in London gone into wardening because the War Office doesn't want any gaffers from 1914.''

''The term is dug-outs,'' Charles corrected gently. ''Remember Buffy?''

''Yes, of course. Good old Cousin Buffy in the Hussars!''

"At the War Office now," said Charles. "Not such an ass, you know, if he *is* my Uncle Aubrey's son. I've got him to thank for this. And you can tell Oliver from me that the wardens may have most of the fun before this is over."

"Suppose we get thousands of German planes all at once in a colossal raid to start with," Virginia suggested.

"Not practicable. They'll come a few at a time, all day long. Nights too. No time to clean up the mess. No sleep. Hoping to wear us down."

"Charles, darling, how do you *know?*"

"I don't. Just guessing." He retired hastily behind his glass. "Nobody knows anything yet. Anybody says he does is just throwing his weight around."

"Charles, would you answer just one question, yes or no?" Virginia leaned forward, fixing him with an innocent, appealing gaze. "Have you any reason to believe that Tracy Marsh is still alive?"

Once more that fraction of a second's delay occurred. Then Charles said, "I have no reason to believe that he is dead."

"And could he be in Warsaw now?"

"I suppose he could."

"But he's not a lot younger than you are!"

"Not a lot. Maybe he hasn't got a game leg."

"I suppose we'll never know now," said Virginia, looking into her glass, and the Laverhams exchanged glances, for everyone had done a good deal of wondering about Tracy Marsh twenty-one years ago when he was in London, wounded, after Saint-Mihiel, and when he vanished again across the Channel a month before the Armistice.

"Didn't you ever hear from him?" Rosalind asked sympathetically.

"No. No, of course not, I — meant it to be that way. That is —" Virginia flushed and floundered before their eyes. "— I mean, I never expected to," she finished lamely.

"This is the BBC Home Service. And here is the twelve o'clock News," said the radio crisply into the quiet room, and Virginia rose at once to turn up the volume.

There was no declaration of war.

They sat looking at each other incredulously. Chamberlain had spoken briefly and belatedly in the House, announcing the delivery of a last warning to Hitler by Ambassador Henderson in Berlin. *"If the reply to this is unfavorable, and I do not suggest that it is likely to be otherwise, His Majesty's Ambassador is instructed to ask for his passports. . . ."*

"Very odd, isn't it," said Charles at last. "There wasn't even any mention of a time limit for Hitler's reply."

"Charles, do you *honestly* not know what's going on?" Virginia said uncertainly.

"No more than you, my dear."

"B-but that glass case in Whitehall —"

"Ah," said Charles. "But I'm not in it yet."

"Well, in that case," said Virginia, "let's all have another drink."

Although they had been spared the additional turmoil of evacuated children and pregnant mothers at Farthingale and Cleeve, owing to the Bank billeting, both Rosalind and Virginia had served at the reception center in the village and it had been a long, tense day. They were all glad to sit a while, nursing their tall glasses, in a midnight haze of fatigue and bodily comfort. Old, old friends since the turn of the century when Charles came back from South Africa with a V.C., and Rosalind and Virginia were débutantes in a world where that meant something pretty special, they clung now to their mutual memories, and their love for each other's company enfolded them warmly in a brief illusion of peace and security.

Like every other old soldier, Charles was in a speechless private rage of his own. They had seen to it once, in Belgium, at enormous cost. And now the same old enemy was on his feet again and coming for them. Less than a generation — and the Somme and Passchendaele and Verdun had all gone for nothing. Once more, the main event was London and Berlin.

And this time it would have to be finished. This time there must be no Armistice, while the German Army marched home with banners. This time Berlin must be taken. Germans had always had the gift of offence. But now the

128

Germans weren't people any more. They were robots. You cannot reason with a robot, and he has no honor. You can only smash him before he can smash you. And you always have to start from behind. He is always readier to attack than you are, because none of the things that matter to you — this kind of room, this kind of women, confiding, casual children, the gentle routine of country life and little luxuries — none of that is comprehensible to robots. And before it could be demonstrated — again — that England could be pushed just so far, the very thing that England strove to defend must be sacrificed again, in the hope that it could be saved again. We beat 'em once, and we'll beat 'em again, the old soldiers said. But before that . . .

Morbid, unaccustomed thoughts for Charles, who presented to the world a deceptively stolid Guardsman's countenance. In view of the standard British joke that the War Office is always preparing for the last war, the off-hand way in which he had been summoned to London, at a time when most of the dugouts from 1918 were a drug on the market, was to him a sign that this time they were really up against it. And as for Tracy Marsh — if he was in Warsaw now, and if he ever got out, he, Charles, would give his game leg for a chance just to listen to him.

A sound at the door turned their heads towards it. Mab stood there, apologetic in a dressing-gown and slippers, and purple shadows under her eyes.

"I couldn't sleep," she said. "I got terribly hungry —"

Charles rose instantly, holding out welcoming hands.

"Come and join the wake," he said. "You can have all the sandwiches."

"Suppose I pop down to the kitchen and warm some milk," said Virginia, rising too. "Wouldn't you like a cup of Ovaltine?"

"I can get it," Mab said, holding to Charles. "Melchett's gone to bed, I expect."

"I'll do it. You sit down here with Charles and Rosalind."

It's worse for the young, Virginia was

thinking on her way to the kitchen. Suppose you were thirteen, and had never seen a war, and had to keep a stiff upper lip. Suppose you were Mona, and in love. What will they all have to bear before this is over! We had our fun, we had the last of it, before the other one. And what can we do now to help them? *Ovaltine!* And love. Lashings of love, for all of them, even the ones out of Birmingham — especially the ones out of Birmingham, God help them. . . .

Saturday produced glorious weather, and the atrocity stories began to come out of Poland. While evacuation proceeded methodically in England, the trains full of women and children leaving Warsaw were bombed, creating chaos and horror. And England had not declared war.

"We're right to wait," Virginia said, white-faced, laying aside the newspaper. "We're right to get ours out before he can get at them."

Driving into the village after breakfast to the Parish Hall which served as the reception center for evacuees, Virginia joined Rosalind who was already there, surrounded by her lists and billeting vouchers and accommodation forms, in a group of competent women who were dealing with small crises left over from yesterday and preparing for new complications which would begin with the first busload expected before noon today.

"Hullo," said Rosalind, looking wrung out but composed. "Charles got off to London early this morning."

"Today? I thought —"

"They 'phoned through and wanted him at once. Things are speeding up."

"There's no real news this morning."

"The House meets at three. It will come then."

Meanwhile, rumor invented reasons for the delay, especially in the pubs. Paris was wobbling, they said — there was something sinister going on at the top in France. Mussolini had stepped in — Russia had tripped up Hitler already — Roosevelt was going to do something — there would be another Munich — they had discovered too late that there was no way to get help to Poland in time — the first raid over England would come without warning before the declaration could be made — there was a Ray — there was a new gas — something sensational in the way of defence from bombing would be revealed. . . . "I am not going to believe anything unless I hear it on the BBC," Virginia said firmly.

Some things they did know, even down in Gloucestershire. There would be no more weather forecasts in Britain, but it was the most beautiful day of the whole year. The observers' post on the hill behind Cleeve was fully manned, on duty round the clock, and the Specials were out on patrol. The wardens' posts were at full strength, with somebody always on the telephone, with maps hung and gas-masks and decontamination suits smelling up the passage. One glanced up instinctively at planes in the sky and thought subconsciously, "Ours." One saw cattle grazing in a field, ancient horses living out their placid existence in a mechanized age, and thought of low-flying German planes with machine-guns. . . .

The district medical officer arrived at the Parish Hall with his grisly supplies —

sealed dressings, bottles of Dettol, bandages and lint and splints — not much of it, really — how much would be enough, in Gloucestershire? More children arrived, dismal or over-excited as the case might be, and more pregnant mothers with those sinister pink cards. . . .

At the back of everyone's efficiency and good humor there lurked a common rage — that bloody awful little man called Hitler. . . .

Working side by side, unemotionally, doggedly, right through lunch and on to tea time, Virginia and Rosalind got the new consignment from Birmingham off to its lodgings before the blackout, without anything which could be called disaster. Nothing was born on the spot, Virginia remarked with visible relief, and nobody threw up on the floor. And when they parted from each other with weary smiles the knowledge that they must not use the telephone for nonessential chat gave them a lonely cut-off feeling. The loss of Charles's week-end at home was a blow. Things must be in a bad way indeed, to overcome official reluctance to make use of that generation which was so terrifyingly scarce, even in Charles's exalted field.

She arrived back at Farthingale to learn that in her absence four female secretaries and four typists ditto had taken up their quarters in the house, and she went upstairs to make them welcome. She found them much as she had expected — well-dressed, personable girls, tired to death, a little on the defensive in these strange surroundings, anxious to please, and perhaps somewhat awed at sight of her. As usual there was on among the lot that stood out.

"I never thought anything nice could come of this war," said the secretary whose name was Anne Phillips. "But living in a house like this one will make up for a lot."

Virginia, who loved the house so passionately herself, at once warmed to the girl.

"Come downstairs and have a look round before the blackout," she suggested. "You're to have the small drawing-room for your own use. Don't feel that you have to coop up in your bedrooms all the time."

"*Two* drawing-rooms in the house?" Anne exclaimed, impressed.

"Well — card-room, music-room, back-parlor — whatever you want to call it. There's a piano in it, and a radio of course. It's on the left at the foot of the stairs. Come along, I'll show you."

Claudia Merton, who shared the bedroom with Anne, said she'd rather get settled first, thanks, and Anne followed Virginia downstairs, walking lightly, trailing one hand down the polished banister. She was a frail blonde with enormous eyes and a generous mouth. Her silk-clad ankles looked breakable, like a deer's. Virginia wondered if she had ever had quite enough to eat, but her voice was well-placed and her vowels were unself-conscious and correct.

"I've always dreamed of a house like this," Anne was saying as they reached the lower hall. "And to think it took Hitler to get me inside one!"

"I'm sure he never meant to oblige you," Virginia said.

"And wouldn't he be furious if he knew!" They laughed together, and Anne admired the little parlor set aside for their use, and then paused on the bottom step on her way back to finish unpacking. "I hope you won't mind Claudia's bad manners," she said unhappily. "Her boy's been called up, and she's taking it very hard. It makes her seem cross."

"And how about your boy?" Virginia asked kindly.

"I'm lucky. I haven't got one."

She skipped away up the stairs, with a graceful little wave from the top. What a nice child, Virginia thought, and forgot all about her.

Not until evening did the Prime Minister announce to a troubled, unruly House that there had been no reply from Hitler and that no further conference could take place while the invasion of Poland continued. Although there was still no formal declaration of war by Great Britain and France, a time limit was now implied. The House was to assemble tomorrow for its first Sunday session in modern times.

The prolonged agony of delay and seeming indecision caused only exasperation when the late News was read by the BBC.

"What are they *doing!*" cried Virginia, switching off the radio and rumpling her hair with the same impatient hand.

"It seems as though they don't know what to do," Mab said, longing for Jeff's opinion, which was only as far away as the telephone one could not use.

"They know well enough. We shall be a laughing-stock if this goes on. I've got to talk to Bracken!"

"It's like the crocodile's clock," Mab remarked thoughtfully, and Virginia sent her an inquiring look. "In *Peter Pan,*" Mab explained, "You hear it ticking. You know it's coming. Finally you only want to get it over with."

The telephone rang, and they both rushed to it. It was Dinah, low-voiced and hurried, slipping in one little three minutes from London. A cable had come to say that Evadne and Stephen were sailing today. On an American boat, so Virginia needn't worry, Hitler wouldn't touch that.

"How do we know he won't?" asked Virginia grimly. "Tell us more, we're starving for news."

"We don't know any more here,"

Dinah said wearily. "Unless at Whitehall, and censorship is on even there. I must talk fast, let me see — there was a violent thunderstorm tonight while the House was still sitting, and everybody thought it was the first air raid. You're supposed to laugh at that."

"Ha-ha," Virginia obliged mirthlessly. "Go on — quick."

"Churchill was in the House tonight, and Lloyd-George — like 1914 over again. All the barrage balloons are up over London and everybody is standing to. Mona is with her ambulance, helping to empty the hospitals of movable patients to make room for an estimated fifty thousand casualties a week — that figure is based on what happened at Barcelona and Warsaw. Yes, I know, our defences are better! Sandbags everywhere now, and plate glass windows all taped in pretty patterns. Theaters closing, people out of work. We can't go on like this, it will come tomorrow morning. — There go the time-pips, I'll have to stop —"

The connection ended.

As Virginia hung up, the door of the

small parlor opened across the hall and the Bank girls came out, having listened to the News on their radio there.

"What *does* it mean?" asked Anne from the foot of the stairs. "Are we going to back down?"

"That was my sister-in-law calling from London," said Virginia. "They don't seem to know any more than we do."

"It would be ten times worse than Munich," said Anne. "We can't hold up our heads if we don't do something now."

"Tomorrow, I think," said Virginia. "About noon."

She watched them trailing up the stairs. The one who was taking it badly mopped at her eyes, and Anne laid a consoling arm around her waist.

Then it was Sunday morning — September third — bright warm sunshine — a blaze of autumn color in the gardens and the parks — green, tidy England — ten o'clock, and keep your radio turned on for an announcement at eleven — as though anyone's radio was ever turned off, any more — eleven o'clock, here it comes — Bow bells, the BBC signal that a special bulletin was due — bells, like a wedding. . . .

Virginia gathered the Bank girls in the big drawing-room with the family. "We'll swallow it together," she said. They found places on the edges of the chairs and sofas, only Anne seeming at ease as a guest. Claudia Merton sniffed audibly and blew into her handkerchief while they waited. Basil was there, restless and oppressed, with his sensible nurse. Mab was there, silent and withdrawn in her young dignity. Miss Sim the governess, returned only yesterday from Scotland, sat upright in a corner with her knitting. Virginia lighted a cigarette. . . .

At eleven-fifteen the familiar schoolmasterish voice of the Prime Minister emerged at last from the radio: *"I am speaking to you from the Cabinet Room of Number 10 Downing Street. This morning the British Ambassador in Berlin handed the German Government a final note stating that unless we heard from them by eleven o'clock that they were prepared at once to withdraw their troops from Poland a state of war would exist between us. I now have to tell you that no such undertaking has been received. . . ."*

"Well," said Virginia quietly when it was over, "now we can hold up our heads, Miss Phillips. Now we are at war. Don't anyone go away, I'll only be a minute —"

When she had left the room they sat almost motionless and silent, obediently waiting for her to return. She was followed by Melchett wheeling a trolley on which were frail stemmed glasses and a bottle of champagne in an ice-bucket.

"Dutch courage," said Virginia, watching while Melchett popped the cork and began to fill the glasses, and the girls, wide-eyed and speechless, were almost as stunned by the elegance of champagne at eleven o'clock on a Sunday morning as by the declaration of war.

So they drank to victory, while the BBC read out again the air-raid instructions and precautions they already knew by heart.

And Virginia thought of Jeff's mother Phoebe, who by a miracle had survived when the *Lusitania* went down in 1915 — but Evadne was on an American boat, Hitler would never touch that. And she thought of Dinah and Sylvia, who would stick with their husbands in London, which might at any moment now become the firing line. And of Camilla in Berlin, sticking to Johnny, which would be much worse. And of Charles and Oliver, who could remember a war in South Africa, to say nothing of the one in Belgium, and who were too old now for fighting, praise be — at least, for the sort of fighting which was required of them in all the previous, predictable wars. . . .

Most of all, Virginia thought about her only son Nigel, who had grown up so like his father, even to being a barrister with chambers in the Temple — a rather dim and stranded copy of his father, since the sudden death of his young wife after only two years of marriage. They thought it was just a cold — then she started to cough — and then it was pneumonia and she was gone. No children — nothing for Nigel to go on with. Nobody saw him any more, he was at Winchester about a will case the week Virginia and Mab had left London. Since then he had rung up once or twice, but he was always bad about writing, and now it wasn't the thing to use the telephone. . . .

She supposed she would hear soon, what Nigel meant to do about the war. At thirty-one he would hardly be called up, not at first, and he had no mechanical sense even about a car, he would never be any use to the Air Force. There was no demand for enlistment now, except in civil defence, and he was already wardening at the Temple. Nigel had gone into himself with his heart-break, which was hard for her to get used to, but it seemed best to let him alone. Archie would have known what to do about his son, Archie would have helped him through it when poor Phyllis died, Archie would have turned sixty now, if he had lived, but Archie was safe, Archie was out of it, they would have to do without him this war. . . .

7

Sylvia had gone out with Jeff that Sunday morning in London to watch the orderly, self-contained crowds in the streets. A warm sun shone there too, women wore bright summer frocks and no hats, young men had left their collars open. Everyone carried the little brown box which held the gas-mask. There were almost no children, almost no dogs.

News of the actual declaration of war was called out to them from a window in Stratton Street by a fellow reporter who had just heard it on the radio. He came down and joined them, young Denis Arnold, hatless and grave, with his gas-mask slung over his shoulder, and they all drifted westward toward Buckingham Palace, where in 1914 a shouting, singing crowd full of ignorant enthusiasm had surged.

Today there was no visible change in the face of London as the eleven o'clock deadline passed. No one was taken by surprise, everyone had a fair idea of what it would mean, no one seemed to look backward with regret. But there was no bravado. It was like having a tooth out. You didn't argue with the dentist at the last minute, you screwed yourself up to it. England was now of a mind to have the tooth out and be done with it.

The three of them were at the edge of the crowd around the Queen Victoria Memorial in front of the Palace when the promised "Warbling Note" of the air-raid warning began, about eleven-thirty. So far as Sylvia could see, no one turned a hair, and after the first upheaval in her own middle she felt Jeff's fingers close tight around her elbow.

"There they come!" cried a woman's voice lightly behind them in Mayfair garden-party tones, and Denis said, "B'God, they aren't wasting any time!" and laughed.

Wardens wearing helmets and armbands, and police on bicycles with TAKE COVER signs hung round their necks appeared from nowhere, shepherding everybody towards the shelters in St. James's Park. No one hurried very much.

"Five to ten minutes, between warning and raiders," Jeff was saying. "They must have been already on the way —"

The shelter entrance, with its stout wooden railings, was not crowded, and there was room on the benches inside for a third again as many people. They sat down and lighted cigarettes. The lighter in Jeff's hand was steady, and Sylvia glanced up at him under her lashes and away. His heart had stood up to Prague last year, and more recently to the long days and nights of sleepless waiting. But would it weather a London air raid without going into the wild overbeat that left him prostrate and unable to stand until it had passed? She had never seen him during an attack, for he had not had one since their marriage, but he had told her in a few brief graphic words what could happen.

"I wonder if Bracken is already inside the House," she allowed herself to say, after the first puff.

"Sure to be," said Jeff. "They would have set out for there as soon as Chamberlain finished speaking."

"Good shelter there — they'll all be in it, wise-cracking," said Denis, and she supposed she looked a little green under his kindly eyes.

Jeff was gazing thoughtfully towards the entrance of the shelter, guarded by a helmeted warden.

"Do you think if we showed our Press

cards he would let us see what's going on up above?'' he suggested, and Denis said, ''Worth a try,'' and Sylvia only just prevented herself from saying, ''No — stay here with me.''

But it was all very new and serious to the warden, and he refused to let them pass.

The Alert didn't last long, and the All-Clear sang out its high, sustained note before noon. A mistake? Or had the raiders been turned back at the coast? Everybody trouped up the steps again into the sunshine, feeling excessively jolly, as though the tooth was already out.

The three of them had a late lunch at the Savoy, which except for sandbags was exactly as usual, and by then speculation about the delay in France had become embarrassing.

''It does make you think,'' said Denis rather hollowly, ''about those ugly rumors that something very queer is going on at the top over there.''

But when they got home for tea Bracken was able to reassure them. The declaration had come through from Paris at last. The

French had not ratted after all.

They listened to the King's broadcast at six, sweating it out with him, word by difficult word, and then Bracken handed round drinks. As usual the nervous reaction made them hungry, and dinner was a little early.

Bracken was finally showing the strain of tension and loss of sleep, and Dinah persuaded him to go to bed early and let Jeff handle the Sunday midnight broadcast to America, when they hoped also to call in Johnny from Berlin. Jeff promised to ring up the house if anything sensational developed, and then took up the vigil at the BBC, with the intention of returning for a last look round at the Fleet Street office after his broadcast. They were not to be alarmed if he decided to sleep there on one of the cots which had been set up several weeks before.

Before he set out, and Bracken went wearily to bed on Dinah's orders, they knew that Churchill was back in his old room at the Admiralty — and that when the signal went out to the Fleet: *Winston is back,* there were happy cheers. They knew too that Poland was standing fast under heavy raids, and the lack of bombs on London brought a guilty feeling, almost as though Britain had not fulfilled her duty and declared war. There was a story from Poland that Ambassador Biddle's suburban villa had been bombed, apparently without injury to himself or his family — the German airmen either had not known or had not cared whose it was, or that America was not in the war.

Because Dinah was engaged in what she called sitting on Bracken's head till he rested, there would be no one at the studio to hear Jeff through the earphones unless Sylvia went with him, and this he refused to allow, on the grounds that he had enough on his mind already. After he left the house she went wearily to bed alone except for Midge in the room they shared. There was a bad moment when a taxi at the corner ground its gears like the opening growl of the siren, and then she sank into a trance of exhaustion.

It seemed to her only moments later that she found herself sitting bolt upright in bed feeling sick, while the real, authentic siren wail filled the air again. It was two A.M. Monday morning and Jeff had not come in. She wondered if he was still at the office, where there was a shelter, or if he had been caught in the streets on the way home.

Bracken knocked on her door and set it ajar.

"May as well go down to the shelter, I think," he said calmly. "They may mean it this time."

Her hands were not quite steady as she pulled on a pair of slacks over her pyjamas and added socks and slippers. Tonight was going to be harder because Jeff wasn't with her — no one even knew where he was by now. There was going to be a lot of this, she realized, when they were not together. I mustn't be a baby, I mustn't hang on to him, think of the women whose men are away in the Army. . . . I must be steadier than this when it's my turn at the Animal Post, or I will be ashamed. That's tomorrow night. Tomorrow night I will be on duty, on my own. If Evadne can do it, so can I. But Evadne got it licked last year, training to be a warden. Evadne is brave. . . .

She collected Midge in his covered cage from a table in the corner farthest from the window, snatched up her gas-mask, and joined Dinah and Bracken on the stairs. Midge's gas-mask, she had learned from the animal ARP, would be a small blanket dipped in a solution of bicarbonate of soda and laid over the cage. The solution and the blanket awaited him below — unnecessary until the hand-rattles of the wardens should signal an actual gas attack.

Bracken saw them settled in and then, taking his gas-mask, returned to the upper floor and the street outside, where he encountered the warden on his beat and as an old friend was permitted to stay outside and watch while nothing happened. For nearly two hours Dinah and Sylvia sat in the comfortable basement room, drinking the tea Dinah brewed from the electric kettle, reading, or trying to, dozing, listening — there were no loud bangs, and the All-Clear was plainly heard.

"Maybe we really have got something that stops them," Sylvia said hopefully as they climbed the stairs again and met Bracken in the hall.

"Scouts," said Bracken. "Try-ons. Still working on our nerves. Well, so much for my nice early night."

The telephone stopped them before they reached their bedrooms and Bracken turned back and snatched up the instrument in the hall. Once more they saw incredulity and horror grow on his face as he listened — something worse than a Russian Pact this time. He thoughtfully tilted the receiver so they could be sure it was Jeff's voice at the other end of the line.

"It took 'em nearly a year to work up to that last time," he said. "Where will the survivors come in — Glasgow? She sailed from there, yes — All right, you come home now and catch some sleep, pack a bag and go up to Glasgow tomorrow and talk to survivors." He hung up and turned back grimly to the anxious women. "They have sunk a liner," he said. "The *Athenia*. Heavy loss of life. It's the *Lusitania* all over again. Well, my dears, the war is on, all right! It may last quite a while. I suppose we had better learn to go back to bed. Jeff's on his way here."

They separated silently, with reassuring smiles, closing the doors behind them gently as though there had been a death in the house. Sylvia replaced Midge on his night table and leaving her light on against the new nightmare turned the unseen pages of a book till Jeff let himself in quietly and came to take her in his arms. His coat smelled of tobacco smoke and outdoors and she buried her face against it.

"It's going to be a tough war," he said. "Well, we knew that. Sure you won't go down to Farthingale for a few days —"

Instantly she faced him, tousled and indignant.

"Now, Jeff, you know I'm booked to go round to the animal shelter tomorrow morning just as always —"

"All right, all right, I only asked a civil question," he said, half amused.

"I keep thinking about Stephen and Evadne," Sylvia said. "If they sailed last Saturday —"

"They're on an American boat. Hitler won't do anything now to bring America in."

"You can't tell what he'll do. It won't be very comfortable at sea right now."

"Honey, let's face it. Nobody's going to be very comfortable anywhere, for a while!" said Jeff.

"Except in America."

"Land of the free. How about going back there for a visit? You could take Mab with you, she's always —"

"Jeff Day, if I was willing to desert you, which I am not, I wouldn't cross the Atlantic now for a million dollars!" Sylvia told him with a shudder. "Whatever comes, I'll take it on dry land, and together."

"Maybe you're wise, at that." Jeff kissed her and put out the bed lamp and went to part the heavy curtains on the dark room and raise the window.

Moonlight streamed across the floor, and he stood a minute, leaning on the sill looking out.

"Come and look," he said, and she got out of bed and joined him at the window.

All she saw was bright moonlight over the housetops. He turned his head towards her uncomprehending silence.

"Notice anything?" he asked quietly.

"There's not a sound," she whispered.

"Look again. It could be a hundred — two hundred years ago. No lights — no traffic. I noticed, walking home tonight — a lot of London is just the same now as when Wren put up his churches after the Great Fire. When you take away machinery and artificial light, a lot of London is still pretty much the way our great-great-grandfathers saw it. London has gone back — 'way back — nobody's seen it like this since George III was King. And you know what? It's the loveliest city in the world tonight. And I wouldn't be anywhere else for a million dollars." He straightened with a sigh. "Make sure I hear the alarm," he said, and fell into bed and was asleep.

But Sylvia lay awake now, listening, wondering, watching the moon-shadows creep across the room — remembering the safe, dreaming streets of Williamsburg under other September moons, the silky, whispering night air, the wafts of sudden fragrance, the gay Negro voices, the unquestioning security. . . . Oh, God, make me brave, make me do the right thing here, don't let me disgrace myself. . . .

8

"Of course Evadne hadn't thought about Williamsburg all her life the way I have, before she went there," Mab said at breakfast on Sunday a week later. "It would be all new to her. But now she's *seen* it, with her very own eyes, and if we take a map and some pictures I can ask her —"

"Sweetheart, you get so carried away by Williamsburg, it's rather worrying sometimes," Virginia said, mindful of what she could only call a spooky letter from Evadne, all about Tibby's portrait being Mab, and Jeff looking like Julian's, as everyone knew, and the Mawes cottage down by the Landing which nobody but Fitz remembered any more. . . .

"Worrying how?" asked Mab with her upward, candid look, and Virginia found herself fumbling a little, which she was not accustomed to.

"It seems rather odd," she said lamely. "A place you've never seen, and yet sometimes you sound almost homesick for it."

Mab's eyes widened.

"That's exactly now it feels!" she agreed. "Like wanting to go *back*. How clever of you, Gran. It's as though I had been there as a very small child, too small really to remember, and yet — Are you sure I wasn't?"

"Quite sure."

"And yet it's as though I *might* remember if I saw it again. Do you think I could?"

"Remember?" asked Virginia uneasily, wondering if she ought to change the subject, aware that changing the subject was rarely any solution to the matter involved, divided between a wish somehow to get to the bottom of it with Mab and a doubt of the wisdom of encouraging her to dwell on her obsession even to discuss

158

it in cold blood. "Remember?" asked Virginia, with a slight frown on her serene brow.

"No, silly, see it again! Jeff used to promise I could go there some times — but now the war has upset everything," Mab sighed. "I suppose it will end eventually, and we can do as we like again."

"But when we suggested last year that you might go to Williamsburg *because* of the war you —"

"Oh, I couldn't do that," Mab said positively. "That's cheating. Not while you and Jeff and Mummy — everybody that matters — stay here, anyway. It's only — before the war began there seemed to be some sense in hoping to see Williamsburg for myself. And now you can't count on anything, can you!"

"I see what you mean," Virginia said gently, flooded again with pity for the young, trapped as she herself had never been in the old days, between uncertainty and despair. And she added with what she felt was base compromise with her own caution, "Williamsburg has been there a long time, through a lot of wars, hasn't it. It will still be there, when this one ends.''

"Well, yes, I suppose we can count on that!'' said Mab, more cheerfully.

To Virginia, who had not been in Williamsburg since she was a girl, whose life and love had been lived in Gloucestershire, and who at present was face to face with the second great war of her lifetime, what Evadne called Mab's Williamsburg complex did seem a trifle fantastic and remote. Some day, when Hitler had been disposed of, it might be possible to look further into this lifelong obsession with a background which Mab knew only through her bloodstream, the involuntary recognition of a tie which went back through Virginia herself to her mother who had married a Yankee and whose father was Julian's grandson. It was a hundred and fifty years, more or less, back to Julian's marriage with the woman in the portrait, only dimly recalled by Virginia, which had so startled Evadne by its resemblance to Mab. And even now, at the beginning of Hitler's war, Virginia found herself anxious to talk to Evadne about it, anxious to ask her — well, what?

The travellers were expected at Farthingale by tea time, having arrived at Southampton the night before, and disembarked into the blackout and a drizzling rain. Tripping over sandbags, running into policemen, biting their tongues by stepping off curbs they didn't know were there, falling into friendly taxicabs, reduced to whispers in the train under the light of the spectral blue bulbs which were all the railway allowed, they finally reached London and their flat in Bayswater, where they found Jeff and Sylvia waiting, with the blackout done and all the lights on and hot food ready.

Everybody asked questions at once. What sort of voyage was it, had they heard about the *Athenia* while they were at sea, how had the passengers reacted, did they see any submarines — had there been any raids in England, what did Bracken think about Poland, could they still reach Johnny in Berlin. . . .

"We heard Chamberlain's speech over the ship's radio on the second day out," Stephen said. "And then we got the news

161

about the *Athenia*. And then they cut off the radio and even took away the portables from the passengers, which I think was a mistake."

"Nobody was going to panic on an American ship so long as we were still neutral," said Evadne. "The Germans wouldn't have dared to touch it."

"If they knew it was an American ship," Jeff reminded them.

"They could hardly make any mistake about that! The crew painted American flags on the sides and the hatchcovers as we went. The flag at the masthead was spotlighted at night and we ran with all our lights blazing!"

"Weren't you scared anyway?" Sylvia asked.

"We said we weren't. We promised each other that no submarine would fire into a neutral ship, much less one that wore that flag. But the bar was a pretty busy place, I thought, and there was a certain tendency to sit around with lots of company. And when we got to Southampton and couldn't see a thing — I *listened*. Every taxi-motor cocked my ears like a bird-dog's!''

"Buses are the worst," said Sylvia. "I think they do it on purpose."

"And you've really not had any raids in England?" Evadne sounded almost disappointed, for the war was a week old.

"Wait," Jeff said. "Wait till Poland is finished. It won't be long now."

"But surely the Germans can't be doing all they claim in Poland," Stephen objected, having read the evening papers. "Nazis are only men. They must be dead beat, hot and tired and hungry. And their machines must run down. What are they using for petrol?"

"We've stopped talking like that over here," Jeff replied wearily. "They don't run down, neither men nor machines, they keep on going. They are at the gates of Warsaw. It's for real. They're *doing* it."

"Verdun held out," said Stephen, still arguing by the book of rules. "And Madrid. And there was the Marne, too."

"And Wellington won at Waterloo," Jeff agreed. "But all that was before Hitler."

"Aren't we doing *anything,* on our side?"

"Look, it's eight hundred and fifty miles by air from England to Poland," Jeff pointed out with patience which was a little overdone. "And you have to fly across Germany to get there. And the Polish aerodromes are already destroyed. No plane that got there could re-fuel and get back. Somebody should have thought of that."

"Then why don't we bear down on the Western Front?" Stephen insisted.

"That's for General Gamelin to say. He's in charge there."

"But the British are in France now —"

"Just arriving. And quick work too."

"Maybe General Gort will start something."

"Gort is under the French command. It's still Gamelin's show in France," Jeff said.

"Is he any good?"

"I ask myself," Jeff said.

On that Sunday morning Evadne and Stephen went round to the warden's post where she had trained last autumn, and found it occupied by the same tweedy Miss Piggott and her nephew Mr. Tilton, a dour young man with enormous spectacles. They seemed very glad to have her back, and their greeting was a little extra cordial to make up for having entertained doubts as to whether she would have the guts to return to England when she didn't have to.

For an hour or so they briefed her on the ARP developments while she was away, and discussed the strange exhilaration, which one must not give way to, of *not* being bombed. Miss Piggott was of the dark opinion that They Had Something Up Their Sleeves — with Something Worse implied. Mr. Tilton thought that London was sure to catch it as soon as Warsaw fell, which would be any day now. And when the Post Warden came in, a stout jolly type who might not have been quite sober, they boiled a kettle on the spirit-stove and had cups of tea all round and told funny stories — mostly apocryphal — about the blackout and the several dud warnings which had occurred in London.

Evadne was advised by the Post Warden, whose name was Smedley, to pop down to the country at once, before petrol rationing began, if she wanted to see her mother. The war would still be here when she got back, he promised.

It was nearly lunch time when they borrowed Jeff's two-seater, as their own car had been left at Farthingale, and made a quick tour of the West End before starting for Gloucestershire. The Sunday morning parks were full of relaxed people in deck-chairs, reading the Sunday papers, with their gas-masks in their little brown boxes on the ground beside them. Nearby, industrious people were filling sandbags from great craters dug in the turf. A.A. gun emplacements were fully manned inside their sandbag redoubts, and the ground crews of the barrage balloons sunned themselves in their little encampments on the broad green lawns beneath their serene silver charges. The paper strips which had been pasted on the plate glass windows of the big stores to absorb concussions made ingenious designs which had been planned and executed at some expense of time and labor. There were yellow gas detectors at the street corners, and the Palace Guard had come out in khaki, their towering bearskins and scarlet coats laid away for the duration. All of Whitehall, and the Cenotaph, and the entrances to hotels and clubs and stores were banked high with sandbags like the wardens' posts.

"You feel as though it's just a movie," said Evadne suddenly. "The whole of London has turned itself into a set for *The Shape of Things to Come.*"

"The theaters are closed!" Stephen suddenly realized it. "I knew I missed something! No cinemas, even. What will they do for work, all these people? Besides — everybody needs shows. They went to the theater all through the raids in the last war."

"I bet they aren't going to shows in Warsaw now."

"We're not in Warsaw. Anyway, Hitler can never get at London to bomb it the way he can Warsaw. The Channel is between, and a lot of neutral territory, let alone our own defence system."

"You don't think we'll catch it, then?"

"Sure we'll catch it! But we're not set

down in the middle of a flat plain at Germany's doorstep. England is still an island. That's bound to make it harder."

And England had never looked more English then when they drove to Farthingale that sunny afternoon. Petrol rationing was due at the end of the month, but today every roadside tea-house was busy, especially those with tables set outside in a garden. As they neared the end of the journey Evadne raised the question they had not yet solved.

"What are we going to do about Mab?" she asked at last. "She is going to ask a lot of queer questions about Williamsburg. Your mother was afraid it oughtn't to be encouraged."

"Let's see what your mother says."

"I suppose we must just give her the books and pictures we brought, and see what happens," she sighed.

"It's a harmless sort of game — I hope," said Stephen. "Give her something to dream about. Every kid needs that, especially now. How about the pictures of the portraits, though? Should she see those?"

"We'll ask Mummy first."

They had had the portraits of Tibby and Julian photographed in order to bring the disturbing likenesses home to Virginia, who had been away from Williamsburg so long. But they doubted the wisdom of allowing Mab to identify herself with Tibby Mawes, and the reproductions had been kept separate from the parcel of souvenirs they had brought for her collection, to which Jeff and Sylvia had been adding for years.

When they saw her again, running to meet the car as it pulled up at the front steps of the house, her knitted jumper and tweed skirt and her childish animation a little dispelled the look of Tibby which they had anticipated. It was when she was silent and thoughtful that the likeness to the painted face was most noticeable, and now her excitement at their return made her seem quite the usual kid of thirteen.

At first all her questions were about immediate matters such as what Jeff thought about the war now, and how was Sylvia, and had they seen any submarines, and when was Jeff coming down for a week-end's rest — and what was it like in London now, and had they heard any sirens, and was Evadne really going to be a warden with an arm-band and a helmet, and had Jeff stopped looking worn to a frazzle —

They told her about Jeff going up to Glasgow to see the *Athenia* survivors, and about Sylvia's job with NARPAC — the National ARP for Animals Committee — and how recklessly people had been having their pets put to sleep without waiting to see if it was necessary, and how bitterly many of them already regretted it. And they tried to tell how London looked, sand-bagged, paper-stripped, and blacked out for the raids that had not yet begun. They comforted Virginia with a description of the cosy warden's post in Bayswater, in the reinforced basement of a solid-looking house, its entrance padded against blast, furnished inside with some old but useful chairs and tables, an electric kettle, plain crockery, and a tin biscuit box — even a private lavatory, which was very posh for that neighborhood — and the jolly old Post Warden who didn't throw his weight about and didn't object if somebody happened to drop in at tea time, and was himself perhaps not always quite sober. . . .

And they in turn heard about Mona, sleeping with her ambulance nowadays, she said, and not hearing a peep out of Michael since he joined his ship, but not seeming to worry about that in her shining confidence that nothing could possibly happen to a man who was so much loved as he was — and about Nigel's dull warden's beat at the Temple, and about the evacuees in the village, and about the Bank girls in the house, who had proved to be not such a nuisance as you might think. . . .

Then Evadne produced the presents and pictures they had brought Mab and they watched with curiosity and dismay her complete absorption. Snapshots of a family picnic at Jamestown just before Stephen and Evadne left for New York she returned to again and again. The presence of the stone wall between the water and the grassy shore seemed to bother her.

"It spoils it," she said more than once. "You can't hear the River now. It's spoiled."

"Hear the River?" Virginia repeated, watching her, and Evadne glanced at Stephen and he shook his head.

"Yes, when the wind is up you could hear the River against the bank," said Mab, as though they ought to have known that without being told, and now Virginia's eyes met Evadne's and they both looked away quickly as though Mab might read their thoughts.

"We couldn't find a trace of the Green Spring house you wrote about," Evadne remarked then. "We saw the ruins of Jamestown church, but —"

"Green Spring isn't on the Island," Mab said quickly, and they all noticed the unconscious present tense. "It's over the other side of the road, before you come to the ford —" She hesitated, and frowned. "No — after you pass the turning to the ford. I can't be sure. The wounded were all over the lawn there after the battle," she added casually, and Evadne said, to test her, "What battle?"

"Jamestown," said Mab matter-of-factly. "It was the last before Yorktown, you know. Lafayette was there." Again she paused with a slight frown, her eyes resting on the pictures spread out before her, seeming almost to read from them the words she spoke. "Julian was riding courier for him. General Wayne made a fool of himself, it was almost an ambush — we had to fight and fall back, up the Neck after dark, and they moved the wounded in anything that would carry them — even wheel-barrows — the lanterns were like fireflies — the aides clanked about looking for each other and swearing — there was a smell of gunpowder over everything, and bloody bandages, and horse — it was hot, and some of the horses fell down and couldn't get up again, and the wounded in the wagons groaned and cursed and begged for water — there weren't enough surgeons, and they were all over blood, like butchers — it was a miracle how the officers kept themselves so neat, no matter what happened in the field — Lafayette's lace was always fresh — Julian was always

173

shaved and tidy — the British wore powder in their hair, even on the march — the French uniforms were all white, with colored pipings, and their flags — the French regimental flags were beautiful — when the French came to Williamsburg before Yorktown it was like a garden-party, everyone wore their best clothes all the time — the day Washington's army marched out at dawn to begin the siege we heard the drums as they went through the streets —"

The radio which had been playing light music quietly in the corner spoke suddenly with its usual authority: *"This is the BBC Home Service. Here is the News,"* it said crisply, and Evadne rose at once to turn up the volume. Virginia realized they had all been sitting motionless, hardly breathing, while they listened to Mab. She watched anxiously while the announcer's dreadful formula: *"The defence of Warsaw continues. . . ."* brought them ruthlessly back to the present, and she saw Mab come into focus without visible effort, unaware of what she had done before them all in those few moments of revelation. It was like sleep-walking, thought Virginia, and might have been difficult to adjust to if it had had some other awakening.

Here was the most complete evidence of Mab's secret world that anyone had yet witnessed, and while the announcer's voice flowed on, Virginia sat staring at the radio cabinet, pretending to hear, hoping that when the News finished they need not return to the subject of Williamsburg that evening. Memory was stirring in Virginia now, bringing up long forgotten family legends — had anyone ever told Mab, she was wondering, that Julian's Tibby was supposed to have been present during Jamestown Battle, must have seen the lanterns and heard the wounded? Jeff probably knew the story, he might have mentioned it to Mab long ago, so that it became embedded in her subconscious. . . . Fitz would remember it too, and might have told Evadne. . . .

When the News ended Mab had apparently forgotten where they had left off, and it was possible to divert the conversation, perhaps a little feverishly, while Evadne helped her gather up the pictures and postcards, and Mab made no objection to leaving it all behind in the drawing room when her bedtime came. Unconscious of having unnerved them all, she kissed everybody good-night and went upstairs.

Evadne went with her, casually, an arm around her waist, left her at the door of the room Mab was sharing with Virginia to make room for the guests, and returned at once to the drawing-room with the photographs of the portraits. Entering on a silence, she laid them without comment in front of Virginia, who at once said, "Good Lord!" and sat staring at them.

"I still say she could have read it — about the surgeons and the horses, even," Stephen insisted, striving for sanity. "She has memorized dozens of history books by now."

"She could have," Evadne conceded generously. "And what history book says that you could always hear the River against the bank when the wind was up?"

"Now, listen to me, the both of you," Virginia said firmly. "We *must* be sensible about this. Jeff might have told her about the River —"

"Except that he wasn't there either, before the sea-wall went in — which happened to be about 1900," said Evadne.

"He might have heard about it from somebody like Fitz, then, when he was there as a boy," Virginia argued. "Fitz goes back to 1900. Did you talk to Jeff about this while you were in London?"

"No. Frankly, I didn't have the nerve in front of Sylvia."

"Why not?"

"Mummy, you're losing your grip," Evadne said kindly. "Sylvia is Jeff's wife. And Tibby was Julian's. And Jeff is Julian. Somehow I came over all self-conscious about the whole thing. Mab is just a kid now. But she's going to grow up. We don't want to plant any ideas. Anywhere."

"Mother goes as far as to suggest it might be better if Mab never saw Williamsburg," Stephen said. "She feels it would be asking for trouble."

"Well, I don't know about that," Virginia sighed. "Do you think anything we do or don't do will make much difference in the long run? The trick has already been played on Mab. Call it heredity. We can't undo that."

And they all went off to bed, not knowing, because Evadne had been afraid to ask, that Jeff was the first to see that Mab was cast in Tibby's mold.

III.

Christmas at Farthingale.

1939

1

In view of repeated official warnings against bringing evacuated children back to London for Christmas, Virginia felt obliged to set an example and leave Mab behind when she made a shopping trip early in December.

Furious German threats of secret weapons and blood baths and even of an actual invasion of England had come to nothing at all, and there had been only false alarms in London so far. But when a week before she planned to start, Russia fell upon Finland there was a general impression that the somnambulistic pause in the war since Poland surrendered might be at an end.

One of the things everyone found hardest to bear was the loss of easy communication and travel. One felt utterly cut off. Virginia said she thought she would burst if she couldn't get up to Town and see and hear for herself what was going on and what people were saying.

"You can't but feel that somebody must know something if you only shake it out of them," she said to Rosalind, who drove her to the station the day she left, and who on her return would be released from their mutual duties to spend Christmas in London with Charles. "Just wait till I catch Bracken, he's been to Paris and Geneva, where Johnny and Camilla came to meet him, and it can't *all* be Hush-hush!"

"I suppose you can't blame people for manufacturing rumors to fill up the vacuum the BBC creates," Rosalind agreed.

"What now? That little man with the Ray again?"

"Now there will be five hundred bombers every fifteen minutes for twenty-four hours, to knock out our ports and railway centers," Rosalind recited solemnly as they drew up in the station yard.

"Wouldn't they get in each other's way? England's a small country." Virginia kissed her and stepped out of the car. "Who starts these things — fifth columnists? Thank you for the lift. Keep an eye on Mab, won't you. I'll get hold of Charles at once and bring him up to date on things here. And I'll be back Thursday, if you could arrange to meet me."

"I will. And bring me a siren suit," said Rosalind, waving her off.

Virginia found London emerged from its first buttoned-up tension of waiting for raids, and except for the blackout and the sandbags and the taped windows and the A.A. guns in the parks, the West End was pretty much itself in a weird sort of way. Theaters and cinemas were re-opening with earlier, staggered hours, and Bracken had got tickets for them to see *Design for Living* at the Savoy. Restaurants were busy and people got about somehow, even at night, when the moon assumed an importance it had not enjoyed for generations.

And yet to Virginia's loving eyes, London was tired, strained, and trying only to behave sanely while living in a bad dream.

Wearing a war correspondent's uniform for the third time in his life, Bracken had just returned from the Continent and British Headquarters near Arras, which he said was full of obliging lady spies in wait for foreign journalists at the Hotel Moderne. He had found Rheims prosperous and gay in the possession of an RAF bomber contingent. Johnny at Geneva said that Germany was dreary, bitterly cold, and severely rationed, and that despite Hitler's success in Poland there was little enthusiasm for the war.

"By the way," said Bracken to Virginia at dinner on her first night in Town, "it was Tracy Marsh in Warsaw."

"Bound to be," said Virginia without blinking.

"They seem to have lost him now, though. He went back there and has not been heard of since the surrender. He could have got out through Rumania with the remnants of the Polish Government, Johnny thought, but in that case he should have turned up in Paris by now. Ambassador Biddle is there, so I inquired on my way back, and they had no news of him. Everybody very cagey. Nobody knew what he was up to in Poland, or said they didn't. Must have been a Government job, though. Johnny said not to mention it. Biddle said the same. If he's alive, we can't help. If he isn't — we can't help."

"No," said Virginia, not looking at him. "Why didn't they use gas in Poland, do you think?"

"There was no necessity. German mechanized equipment was paralyzing enough. The Poles had cavalry instead of tanks — *horses*, mind you, against the Panzer troops! And a handful of old-fashioned planes against the Luftwaffe."

"Then you think gas might still be a last resort, if they couldn't win any other way."

Bracken hesitated.

"We can't assume they won't use it here, trying for a quick decision, if that's what you're asking," he said. "England is a different proposition altogether. They can't get at it, except by air."

"Yes," said Virginia, finding that she had very little appetite. "I see."

Bracken had no patience with the fashionable attitude that it was a dull war, and the bluff-krieg type of mentality pained him. He knew that good use was being made in England of the time during which the Germans failed to carry out their promised attack. And Virginia was impressed when she visited the various members of the family at their posts in London.

Stephen had gone out with a concert party to entertain the troops, and Evadne was alone at their flat, except when Mona used the spare room for a night, so Virginia stayed with her instead of in Upper Brook Street with Dinah and Bracken. Evadne's warden's post had stuck doggedly to its routine throughout the autumn, like all the others, in spite of some short-sighted criticism and derision by the sort of people who would be the first to demand service if the need for it arose. Virginia was made welcome when she went round to the basement to see how Evadne spent her hours on duty — Evadne was popular with her associates, especially with Smedley the Post Warden, who had always an eye for a pretty face and was thankful to have the place decorated by her cheerful presence.

Their uniforms had not come yet — they had only a black helmet, which Evadne wore cocked at the Beattie angle, and an armlet and a silver badge, won by a stiff course of First Aid and gas-lectures and a detailed knowledge of every house and fire hydrant and dead end in their sector. They were prodded out of their boredom by periodic practice drills staged realistically to test their memory and wits in supposed emergency.

"I don't really know which is worse," Evadne said, as they prepared for bed the first night of Virginia's visit. "Hanging about on duty, knitting, trying to read, making cups of tea, listening to tiresome stuff on my portable radio — or the mock raids they get up every now and then to relieve the stagnation. An umpire pops along to the post and says such and such a point has theoretically been bombed or set on fire, and we're supposed to get the right equipment there in the shortest possible time, and pretend to crawl into a burning room with our faces ten inches from the floor and bring out an unconscious casualty, or some such nonsense. You do feel such a fool, and there are solemn post-mortems with the umpire afterwards about what you did wrong and should have done instead. I've an idea the bombs aren't going to do what's expected of them either. After all, they haven't rehearsed it with us, they're going to have ideas of their own about exploding.''

''And how do you get an unconscious person out of a burning room?'' Virginia asked, taking an unwilling but fascinated interest.

''Haven't they told you? Tie his hands together and hook them round your neck and drag him.''

''I see,'' said Virginia, repressing a shudder.

''I manage all right with that one. But it's really too much for old Smedley, though he'd never admit it, and Miss Piggot is too fat. I think I ought to leave wardening and get a more useful job. That is, go into the ATS or the Land Army. And then I take another look at the collection of crocks at our post and decide to stay. I'm the only able-bodied one there, as a matter of fact. Tilton can't see a foot in front of him without his specs and he can't wear them inside a gas-mask, so he'd be next to useless in smoke, or even in the dark. You can't wear eye-black inside a mask, either, I suppose you know — if it ran and made your eyes water you'd be done. Now, *that's* a hardship, if you like! I feel very unfinished without it!"

"Evadne — I don't want to be embarrassing — but may I say I think you're wonderful?"

"Why, thank you, Mummy, it's nice to hear a little praise for a change," said Evadne, and put her arms around Virginia for a hearty kiss. "I'm lucky, really, because on our post we get along together very well. Some don't. The next one down the road is saddled with a woman who happened to see something of the war in Spain, and she never lets them forget it, besides a couple of foreigners who have had a bad time already and are sure to go to pieces. We may be a little on the dull side where I am, but we all pull together and nobody puts on any airs."

Virginia paid a call too at the Animal First-Aid Post, which was manned at all times as conscientiously as the human ARP. Things seemed if possible even more futile there as the long lull continued, but there was no slackening of effort in the paper work to publicize their plans and put a stop to the hasty sacrifice of pets which had gone on in the early days of the war.

They were established in the back room of a bookshop, where a half-dozen unpaid volunteers like Sylvia had furnished a corner for themselves with donated chairs and a table, and had made pens out of cardboard boxes, a few fruit-crates, bits of wire netting, and some empty second-hand bird-cages. They had collected assorted drinking bowls and feeding dishes which had seen better days in the kitchens and pantries of their friends, and had stored various kinds of food in all shapes and sizes of tins. They had a cupboard which housed a small supply of medicines and dressings and splints, and the local vet had given them instruction in how to use the remedies he had himself supplied. They had gone round the neighborhood with a notebook and registered all the animals for a numbered disc to be attached to its collar or cage, and they solicited donations shamelessly.

Virginia emptied her change purse on the table, and looked round the stuffy, ill-lighted room, crowded with improvised comfort for the helpless creatures who so far knew no apprehension, and felt a stinging in her eyelids.

"I don't want to sound ridiculous," she said. "But may I say I think you're wonderful?"

"Why, thank you!" said the girl who was sharing the shift with Sylvia. "It's nice not to be laughed at!"

Mona was doing her night duty that week. She had a little the best of it so far, Virginia thought, in quarters in what had been a pleasant upstairs café next door to the garage where the ambulances slept. Tin hats, gas-masks, and rubbery gas-repellent suits hung in redolent rows at the entrance. Inside, except for the cots and sleeping-bags which occupied most of the floor space, it was rather like a club, with a table full of magazines and books, a radio always turned on, a small canteen, a dart game, and a few odd chairs, none of them very comfortable.

The girl ambulance drivers, wearing the dark blue sweaters and trousers of the corps, were knitting, reading, and napping when Virginia looked in round midnight. Mona laid aside *Gone With the Wind,* which she said would last out the war if she was careful, and made introductions, and asked for news of Gloucestershire and America.

Enrolled in what might become the most exacting and hazardous service of all, Mona maintained stoutly that so far it wasn't a bad war, even including the occasional yellow signals which meant a stand-to, never knowing if this time it was real. And here too the monotony was systematically relieved by practice-runs with make-believe casualties who could never refrain from wise-cracks. A driver had to know her way through the blackout over a large district of London. It would be her duty to stand by the target fires with her car, waiting for a load while more stuff came down, and then dodge through the streets to the nearest hospital, and return as fast as possible to the scene of what was officially known as the incident, for another load.

"But when you can back a loaded ambulance while wearing a gas-mask, *in* the blackout, *with* the inspector sitting in the seat beside you, *and* not foul it all up, everything else is easy!" Mona assured her happily.

Virginia asked about Michael, because with the unexpected quiet on the so-called fighting fronts, everybody was hoping for Christmas leave for the forces, even in the Navy, which was bearing the brunt of things as usual.

"Lots of people are planning to get married on Christmas leave," said Mona, with a sigh. "I don't know — I haven't heard for a long time now. But if he does turn up, I'm not going to stand for any more nonsense!''

Nigel at his warden's post in the Temple was in fairly congenial company, but felt very thwarted and elderly and superfluous. Urged to come to Farthingale for Christmas, he looked haunted and unhappy and said he thought not, thanks. And then, reaching out to her with compunction, ''I'd be a death's head, Mummy. You'll do better without me.''

Virginia stood clasping his hand in both hers, and swallowed with difficulty before she spoke.

''Nigel, you oughtn't to be like this. I don't want to be tiresome — but it's time you stopped sulking.''

''Sulking!'' He stared at her, outraged.

''I'm sorry. One ought to be very careful about words.''

She kissed him, and went away, without withdrawing it.

From there she took a bus to Woolworth's and bought the small toys and trinkets for the evacuees' tree, and then she stopped at Dinah's WVS office, which was tidy and efficient and more philosophical than the rest, as evacuation still furnished them with plenty of problems to keep them from going stale.

"I feel very frivolous," she said as she rose to go without taking up more than a few minutes of Dinah's time. "Doing Christmas shopping while everybody else slaves at a war job. I've finished at Woolworth's and now there's only the family left to do."

"There's not supposed to be extravagance about gifts any more," Dinah reminded her firmly.

"I know. I thought some Fortnum goodies in bottles and tins for the store cupboards — warm things to wear — and things that are getting scarce like electric torches and batteries —"

"And hot-water bottles!" said Dinah. "And thermos flasks, if you can find them. And get yourself a siren suit, they're heavenly if you have to turn out in the night. All in one piece, with a hood."

"Rosalind wants one too, we wear the same size. Where's the best place to go?"

The conversation, though brief, became technical.

Before she returned to Farthingale, bitter cold set in, and Finland seemed the grim answer to the dreadful query, *What Next?* which had overhung them all since the Polish surrender. If Finland went under, which seemed inevitable, it would be the eighth small nation in two years to be obliterated by dictator tactics.

"This Christmas will be even stranger than last year," said Mab as they sat in Virginia's room wrapping toys for the children's tree on the night of Virginia's return from London. "Will any of the family be able to come away from Town, do you think?"

"Whoever does come will have to double up and sleep on sofas and what-not," said Virginia cheerfully. "Unless some of the Bank get leave to go home, which could happen, please God."

"Anne Phillips hasn't got much of anywhere to go," Mab said thoughtfully. "She said I could call her Anne. Before she came she lived with some kind of cousins that she doesn't seem to care about. I like her the best of our lot. I'd like to invite her to be one of our family for Christmas."

"If you like," Virginia agreed, for the girl's gentle humor and reticence appealed to her too. "But that means we will have to take in any of the rest of them that are stuck here, along with her."

"Wouldn't we have to anyway?"

"Oh, dear, I suppose so," Virginia sighed. "It can't be much fun for them either."

"It's funny how some of them just don't belong," Mab reflected. "Well, look at Claudia Merton, moping around about her precious Harold when he's still safe in England anyway — and then look at Mona, I bet there's never a peep out of her about Michael!"

"Miss Merton has been awfully good with the children in the village," Virginia pointed out fairly, for Claudia had coaxed and bullied and bribed the little evacuees into learning a Christmas play to be presented in the Parish Hall on the twenty-second, which was a Saturday. "She's taken endless trouble with those poor little snotty-nosed infants, I'm afraid I never would even have tried."

"Yes. I don't think they thank her for it," Mab said with her sometimes frightening penetration. "I think they'd much rather be let alone to bore themselves in their own way."

"Perhaps. But with the weather what it is now, though we mustn't mention that where Hitler can hear, they can't be turned outside to play and something has to be done with them or their hosts will go mad."

"Shall we all have to go to the performance on Saturday and applaud?" asked Mab resignedly, knowing the answer.

"Certainly we shall."

"Don't tell them that in London, they might not come at all."

"How *can* you?" cried Virginia, pretending to be shocked. "When the poor girl has tried so hard!"

"The vackies are all crazy about you," Mab reminded her. "And you never lift a finger at them."

"I do, I do! I've had countless working-parties to make flannellette nighties for them, and I've sat up with Rosalind devising a way to feed them better in batches, and we've swapped them round in their lodgings to get them satisfied and break up feuds —"

"But you don't *bother* them," Mab explained placidly. "For their own good, I mean."

"Because with an American income I can satisfy my conscience by buying them things instead," Virginia admitted ruefully, jerking a red bow in place on the knobby parcel a toy anti-aircraft gun made no matter how you wrapped it. "I hope we're right to give them these modern war-machines to play with. I can remember when one brought a whole model farm, tree by tree and cow by cow, for the young. Nowadays you set up a miniature war on the nursery floor — even to barrage balloons and barbed wire and dugouts. It can't be good for their what-you-may-call-its. Even the dolls are in uniform this year!"

'Yes, I'm glad I was young before it began," Mab nodded, looking down from her new teens. "I had a toy garden, remember — it would be fun to get it out again, just for old times if Sylvia comes."

And if Jeff comes, she thought secretly. She and Jeff had chosen most of the garden together — tree by tree, just as Virginia had said, and three-inch lengths of cream-colored balustrade and inch-square blocks of crazy-paving and a tiny sundial and wheel-barrow. . . . Bracken surely wouldn't send Jeff to Finland now — there was already a staff man in Rome and in Brussels — Bracken had recently gone to Geneva himself — and it wasn't as though the raids on London had started. . . .

Like everyone with any sense, Mab was quite aware that the raids would start some time. The war could not be won by sitting behind fortified lines on the Continent. And Germany never packed up, Bracken said. The Germans were used to hardship, they had known nothing else for twenty-five years. Germans didn't miss peace and security and freedom to do as they pleased with their lives, because they hadn't had it to lose, last September.

Bracken said it was childish of people to count on the Germans' cracking, or starting underground plots to get rid of Hitler. They believed in Hitler, and so far, said

Bracken, he had delivered the goods. The Germans would not give up Hitler until he was hauled out of the Siegfried Line by the scruff of the neck and beaten up on the Western Front. Mr. Chamberlain had recently told the House that the war might last three years, which would be September, 1942, and Virginia had at once recalled that when Kitchener said the same thing in 1914 he underestimated the Germans even then.

And what would it be like, Mab wondered, tying up a Red Cross nurse doll, for these Birmingham children in the village to go home after three years away, after they had got used to the country and had got fond of the people they were staying with? The little ones wouldn't remember anything else. After three years nobody would be able to remember exactly what it was like before last September — except as Virginia remembered the time before the Kaiser's war, like a different world. And after the raids came, they might not have homes to go to, their parents might not be alive to claim them, and their war-time hosts, many of them very unwilling still, might find themselves saddled forever with what began as an emergency duty.

Mab had seen the pictures in the weekly illustrated magazines of Warsaw after the German bombers had finished with it, and she understood that British cities might look the same in a few months' time. When the crocuses bloomed again, they said, Hitler would strike at England. March was his month. He always broke loose then. It was horrifying to find oneself dreading the spring. The uncertainty, Mab thought, feeling it like a cold draught down the back of her neck. The daily knife-edge of *not knowing.* It must have taken courage for Evadne to come back from Williamsburg to the warden's post in Bayswater. I couldn't have done it, Mab thought humbly. I'd have made some humiliating, transparent excuse and stayed safe in America. But then, I'm a coward. . . .

"Mona is hoping Michael may get leave for Christmas," Virginia was saying, for she felt the silence had lasted long enough. "Nobody knows where he has got to by now, of course."

"Will they get married if he does?"

"Mona would, like a shot. But Michael has other ideas. He's afraid of coming back maimed and useless. Most of them dread that as much as dying, I think, if they really stop to think about it. They used to say in the last war that everybody has their own particular secret nightmare — blindness, amputation, disfigurement, fire —"

"Or the roof falling in," said Mab, and her eyes were lowered to the tissue paper in her hands. "If I were ever in a raid that's what I'd think of first. I'd hate more than anything being in an underground shelter, for fear it would all come down on top of me."

"That's claustrophobia," said Virginia, deliberately unemotional. "Some people have it so badly they can't even bear going into a lift." And she thought, So that's what's been going on behind her face all this time. I knew there must be something — nobody could be as unconcerned as she seemed to be, but I thought she'd never give me a clue. They've got such *pride,* not to let you know they're afraid. We weren't like that, we'd have confided more and let ourselves be comforted. Or would we? How do I know how I would have reacted to all this, it hadn't been dreamed of when I was Mab's age. Even when the Zeppelins came over, it was nothing like this. Even when it happened in Spain, we never really thought of it in terms of London. It was all waiting — building up — for Mab. I must say something, I must keep on talking, what can I offer her, how can I help, I mustn't shirk this, perhaps she ought to be drawn out now that it's come up at last —

"Tell me more about London," Mab said steadily, closing the crack again. "What else have they done, in London?"

"Well, I told about the sandbags, didn't I, even round Eros's pedestal in Piccadilly — and the pillar boxes are all ringed with white and have yellow gas-detector paint on top. Curbs and traffic islands are checkerboarded black and white, it's quite gay, really, in the daytime. When you come out of hotels or theaters into the blackout the commissionaire says, 'Three steps, madam,' as though you were blind. There's no more evening dress, women go dancing in uniform, even in trousers. Everybody's likely to sing *Run, Rabbit, Run* as it gets toward closing time. The pigeons are still on duty, and the policemen. But the policemen wear blue steel helmets and gas-masks —"

"And the pigeons haven't got any," said Mab.

Virginia bit her lip. Nothing was safe to say any more. Had Sylvia thought about the pigeons? One gas raid and the pavement would be thick with dead pigeons. . . .

All because of one man — one bloody awful little man called Hitler. . . .

2

As Christmas drew near, there was a general exodus of the evacuees back to Town, in spite of Government pleas and warnings, and most of the bereaved country households found it hard to refrain from encouraging it, if only for a few days' respite from unaccustomed crowding, confusion, dirt, and dissension

— to say nothing of regaining a spare room for a relative on leave. There were children who preferred to stay with their sometimes embarrassed hosts, and were yanked back to London anyhow. There were wives who wanted to go back and whose husbands wanted them to stay away. And there were violent quarrels between parents who took opposite views on where the children should spend Christmas.

Virginia's thankfulness for her eight adult Bank guests increased when six of them proved to have devoted families and all wangled trips home for the holidays, while Claudia and Anne gratefully accepted the invitation to share the Farthingale festivities. It was the last feast while this abnormally normal interval lasted, before rationing and economy set in in dead earnest.

Bracken and Dinah elected to stay in London where they had so many friends who were doing the same thing, and send Jeff and Sylvia to the country for a few days. Jeff's mother Phoebe and her second husband Oliver found opposite numbers with London ties to cover their Red Cross

and warden jobs for the Christmas week-
end. Stephen was pinned down with a
Christmas show in the North and Evadne
was released from duty by Smedley, who
was in a visibly convivial mood, to join
him there.

Everyone's plans were of course hedged
thickly round with ifs and buts, and a
single raid could have thrown them all
endwise. The moon would be full on
Christmas Eve, which was a blessing for
those who wanted to travel, even across
London to a party, but at the same time
everyone realized that it might tempt
Hitler's bombers to open the ball over
England. It would be just like him, people
said, to try to spoil Christmas.

On Friday morning a telegram arrived
at Farthingale: *Homesick. Past-sick. A
sofa will do. Arriving tea time today.
Nigel.* And Virginia caught herself singing.

She had tried hard to be sensible about
Nigel, and it was difficult not to cling on
to him because of his likeness to his
father. Slender and fair, with a deceptive
gravity which had once masked a very
subtle wit, and which now since his sorrow

was without the relief of drollery which made Archie such an enchanting companion, Nigel embodied for Viriginia the very essence of all she had lost in 1918. Just to look at Nigel she found comforting proof that such a man as Archie had once existed. Nigel's choice of the Bar as a career, his manner of speaking even across a dinner table, his quick, legal turn of mind even on a joke, and particularly his profile in his barrister's wig, twisted her heart between memory and present joy. And to have him turn homeward at last, voluntarily and doubtless at some pains, made up more than a little for Evadne's second absence on Christmas Day.

Nigel arrived by the same train which brought Phoebe and Oliver, and having hoarded petrol for that purpose Virginia was able to drive the car to the station to collect them in the usual way. With them as they descended from the train was a tall boy in Air Force blue, whom Virginia identified after a startled moment as her sister-in-law Clare's youngest, Roger Flood, grown a foot since she last saw him, and carrying himself with the easy grace of his Campion uncles.

"I am a homeless orphan," he announced tragically, posing before her on the platform. "I got holiday leave all of a sudden and there is no one to care. Nigel said you might give me a dry crust and a straw pallet by the fire."

"Fool," said Virginia with affection, kissing him on tiptoe. "Where have all your rafts of relations got to?"

"Gone," said Roger, drooping dramatically between her hands. "All gone with the wind, to Scotland and Wales and who knows where!"

"Seriously," said Virginia, "does your mother know you're out?"

"She's in Edinburgh with brother Lionel," Roger explained, gathering up luggage right and left. "She said to ring you up and ask, but Nigel said that nowadays we mustn't use the telephone for idle gossip, so I just came."

"And I am delighted to have you, of course," said Virginia, making swift mental calculations about sofas and blankets and bathrooms and butter. "You can amuse the Bank."

"The what?" He stood still, dripping with bags.

"I've got two Bank secretaries left over — Anne Phillips and Claudia Merton. You're just the thing."

"I'll take Claudia," said Roger, starting for the car.

"She's spoken for, by somebody named Harold, who is somewhere in the North. And the other one is nicer."

"I say, that reminds me! Mona is getting married tomorrow!"

"That's wonderful!" said Virginia.

"She finally talked him into it," Roger said lightly. "He's only got a few days, and it's the last leave he'll have for ages, and almost nobody will be at the wedding, and it's only a Registry Office do, and they'll have to honeymoon at some hotel. None of that matters to Mona, she's determined to have him anyhow."

"She's in love with him!" said Virginia.

"She must be," said Roger, piling the bags into the car. "Dinah and Bracken will see them married, so it will be legal, and nobody is to send them wedding presents till later because they've no place to put them. May I drive?''

"If you'll try to keep it on the ground," said Virginia, getting in beside him.

Roger's nonsense had smothered other, more intimate greetings. Soon they were all gathered round the fire in the drawing-room inside the blackout, having tea with Mab. Virginia looked round at them with a rather tremulous smile — so many other Christmases, good and bad — and now they came to this one. And here again was Phoebe, with her firm dimpled chin and the white streak in her hair, who had come out of Williamsburg so long ago for the coronation summer — there had been two coronations since then, not counting Edward VIII — and had fallen in love with Archie's brother Oliver, and yet had married her Williamsburg cousin and borne his child, which was Jeff. Phoebe's life was far more improbable than any of the two dozen novels she had written, Virginia was thinking, not for the first time. And not for the first time she entertained a secret speculation about Jeff's part in it.

To let Bracken raise Jeff as his heir to the newspaper made perfectly good sense in the closely knit family tradition, to be sure. Handicapped with a rheumatic heart from childhood, Jeff could not have followed Oliver into the Army in any circumstances. But it meant that Jeff's daily life was lived in Bracken's spacious household and not in the small Westminster flat near the War Office which Phoebe and Oliver established when they finally married at the end of the other war. It meant that Jeff travelled abroad with Bracken and a tutor instead of receiving the English public school education he would have had as Oliver's stepson. It meant that Jeff and his mother met like this, as fellow guests and relations, not as a family unit. And it occurred to Virginia to wonder, not for the first time, about Oliver, whose only child by his first marriage had become an acid spinster shirking the war by living with some rather doubtful friends in the Lake District, where there was absolutely nothing to bomb.

It was conceivable that Oliver had been

robbed of a companionship he might have valued, as Jeff grew up. But to look at him now, the soul of contentment, sitting as he always chose to do within reach of Phoebe, his brilliant, caressing gaze often on her face, anticipating the moment she finished her tea so that he could take the empty cup away, or the moment she was ready for a cigarette so that he could supply and light it — Oliver was still after all these years a man devotedly in love.

And Phoebe? Not the maternal type, certainly, and honest enough to admit it — true granddaughter of Louise Day, whose children always recognized without surprise or resentment that nothing ever mattered to her, really mattered, to her dying day, but their father. Once more, Virginia gave it up, baffled again by the obvious satisfaction of all concerned with the arrangement as it stood. It worked. It didn't deserve to, but it did. Jeff had a job, Bracken had an heir, Dinah had a son, and Phoebe and Oliver had each other.

Just then, as though on cue, Jeff and Sylvia appeared, driving their little two-seater on petrol kept for the trip so they could leave it at Farthingale for the duration, going back by train. And soon it was time for drinks, and the two remainders of the Bank were brought in and introduced and given sherry in which to drink the healths of Mona and Michael, and the six o'clock News was allowed to go by unheard — because, Virginia argued, there was never anything you could call news anyway, outside of Finland — and an almost pre-war relaxation briefly prevailed.

"How well I remember the 1918 Christmas," Phoebe was saying dreamily through the smoke from her cigarette, looking like a very modern oracle. And the Bank regarded her with interest and respect, for it had barely been born in 1918, and yet she seemed almost as young as anybody. "Just think, Virginia — you and I can remember the first Peace Christmas from the old war."

"So can I," said Jeff unexpectedly, and his eyes went to his stepfather and found his eyes waiting, and they smiled at each other. "It was the first time I saw Oliver."

"I never heard about that." Mab's interest in the family history roused at once, and she went to stand beside Jeff. "What happened?"

"I was tickled to death," said Jeff simply.

"So was I," said Oliver.

Well, thought Virginia in intense surprise. And here I was under the impression that everybody but me had forgotten. . . . Right here in this very room, twenty-one years ago, she thought. . . . Phoebe dropping to her knees to greet the self-possessed little boy she had left in Dinah's care — and Jeff when he had kissed his mother, advancing confidently to her new husband without an introduction, his face alight with something like recognition, giving the tall man in the red-tabbed uniform both his hands, smiling, somehow *proud* — "It's Oliver," little Jeff said, as though the rest of them might not know. "My mother's married to him." And amid the general astonishment it was Oliver who gave them all the cue, casually accepting without any fuss that he was somehow already known to the child Phoebe had borne to another man while rebelliously loving himself in spite of everything.

But nothing came of it, Virginia was protesting silently to herself. We all noticed, but we all tried not to create hurdles in Jeff's mind by noticing out loud. Jeff already belonged to Bracken and Dinah, it never made any difference in their plans that he knew Oliver by a kind of instinct. Oliver taught him to ride, like a favorite uncle — gave him a dog — they were often together when Jeff was small, they must have talked about the bond between them as Jeff grew older, and about the newspaper, and Jeff's strange divorce of the blood. That year Jeff was so ill — Oliver often sat with him, brought him presents, read to him. What did they say to each other then, Jeff lying in bed, Oliver sitting beside it in a big chair — talking and laughing together — they must have discussed Jeff's destiny then, and faced it together. It was *Oliver,* Virginia discovered now in a blinding light — it was Oliver who stood behind Jeff, and somehow kept him straight on it!

Dear old dark horse Oliver, Archie's favorite brother — Archie would have known — Archie would have told me. But Archie wasn't there in 1918. . . .

"All sorts of things happened," Jeff was saying easily to Mab. "I learned how not to fall off a horse — much. I got my first dog. I had a lot of fun."

"You see, he'd been living in New York with Dinah during the war," Phoebe explained to Mab. "And that's no place to have dogs and horses. It wasn't Dinah's fault."

"I always had a very good time with Dinah," Jeff said instantly, and so he had, as far as it went.

Melchett came in to say that dinner was served.

Nigel, occupying what had been his father's chair at the end of the table opposite Virginia, felt once again the subtle enchantment of her company, and the love and contentment which was like a fragrance in the house she cherished as as though it was one of her children. How very fortunate it was for them all, thought Nigel, that the commodiousness and location of Farthingale had earmarked it for the lesser evil of the Bank billeting, and allowed it to escape the devastation which sometimes accompanied the less desirable evacuees like the Birmingham children and mothers who were lodged roundabout the village. She had given freely of her time and energy and resources to the almost insoluble problems of the evacuees. It was only fair that she should have a little peace at the end of the day, of course, but it seemed that fairness had ceased to operate for the duration, and so one could only call it luck.

Erect in her chair, smiling and serene, she looked nevertheless very fine-drawn and weary — as who didn't, he reminded himself severely, curbing again his lifelong tendency to sentimentalize his mother, when she herself would have been the last to encourage or even passively to endure it. But he wondered once more, while carrying on a comfortable conversation with Phoebe on his right, why no one had ever contrived to marry Virginia during the long widowhood which had begun before she turned forty. Doubtless the man who might have won that privilege had died on the Somme, or at Passchendaele. She was not the only woman of her generation to be wasted and lonely in the years between the wars. And now it was beginning all over again, and the cream would be skimmed off the new generation, just as things had begun to right themselves again a little, in England. And this time, even with American money to help out, the kind of life his mother had maintained at Farthingale would be finished, perhaps forever. . . .

At this moment she caught his eyes down the table and indicated the silent girl on his left, momentarily stranded by Roger's interest in something Oliver was saying. Obediently, Nigel turned to his left, and encountered the most enormous eyes he had ever seen — grey, black-fringed, with the lids deeply indented below the brows so that she looked as though she had just waked up, or had been crying. Anne. Well, she was young enough for last names not to matter now. Nigel had done no more in his turn to fill his life after his own loss than Virginia, and in his solitude in chambers and his inactive war job he had acquired a somewhat elderly state of mind for thirty-one. While he was trying to think of something suitable to say to her, Anne relieved him of the necessity.

"It's like a play," she said.

"A play?" he repeated densely.

"All this." Her small, embarrassed gesture embraced the whole house and its occupants. "Like — Noel Coward, almost."

"*What?*" said Nigel, rather horrified.

"Well, I mean —" Her generous mouth spread into a rueful smile. "To you it's an old story, you belong here. But to me, every day I live in this house is as though I had bought a ticket and the curtain had just gone up. You don't see what I mean, do you. You don't have any idea what it's like to somebody who — who isn't at home here."

"I think I do," he said slowly, giving it his undivided attention in his flattering barrister's way. "As a matter of fact, I was thinking something like that myself a minute ago — even though I am at home here. You mean it's a survival from another world — a museum piece."

"You certainly can't call your mother a museum piece," she said sensibly. "There was never anybody less obsolete. It's just as I told her the first day I came here — I've read about it, I've bought tickets to it, and now here I am living in it, only — I don't know my lines."

"And where did you live before you came here?" he asked, with the kindly interest he always showed to children and kittens and earnest young women he had never seen before.

"Wimbledon. With my cousins. It always sounds silly to say it, but I'm an orphan, and you needn't say you're sorry because I've been one most of my life and it's not sad any more. I was brought up by my mother's aunt, if you can follow that, and it's been very dull and dreary at times, but now that I'm earning my way I felt I ought to go on living there at least long enough to pay them back a little money for keeping me all these years."

"Surely not as many years as all that!" he protested, smiling.

"Well, it *seems* a long time," Anne said. "To all of us, I fancy. It's a small house, and rather crowded. You're a lawyer, aren't you. I suppose that's why one instinctively tells you the story of one's life, with some dim idea that you'll see to it that everything comes out all right."

"Is that your impression of the law?" He was amused.

"Well, yes — as soon as the innocent man puts himself in the hands of the brilliant K.C. he's as good as saved from the gallows."

"And what gallows must I save you from?"

"From Wimbledon, maybe." Her gaze faltered and dropped. "But you've already done that, without trying. It can never be as bad again, because once I was here."

"That's very charming of you," said Nigel, a little at a loss, unaccountably touched.

"I didn't intend to be charming," she said briefly, and "I say," said Roger on her other hand, "we're organizing a Christmas party for the Observers' Post on the hill tomorrow afternoon. There's no petrol, so we'll put the girls in the pony-cart with the food and the rest of us can go on bikes, and we'll surprise them —"

"Surprise them too much and we'll get shot at," said Jeff.

"Well, it's a very dull job up there with nothing to do," Roger said. "Cold, too. We ought to ginger it up a bit for them. Virginia says we can have some sandwiches and mince pies, and tea in thermos bottles. You'll go, won't you, Anne?"

"Yes, of course," she said quickly. "I've got some chocolate. I could give them that."

What a nice little creature it is, Nigel thought. Giving up her chocolate to a bunch of strangers on a cold job. I'll buy her the biggest box of Cadbury's best that I can find, with a pink ribbon on it, for a Christmas present.

"You'll have to carry out your errand of mercy in the morning tomorrow or get caught in the blackout," Virginia reminded them. "Because in the afternoon we're all going to the Parish Hall to see Miss Merton's children do their Christmas play."

And there was nothing to do, with Claudia sitting right there, but express polite enthusiasm and acceptance.

"Of course *if* we went afterwards and got caught in the blackout I could walk ahead of the cart with a torch and Jeff could follow behind with a torch —" Roger reflected wistfully.

"You'll go in the morning," said Virginia. "A pony-cart on the road after dark now is a good way to get killed."

In the old days when the family Christmas parties were really large, they used to roll up the rugs in the drawing-room and dance to the gramophone. Tonight they drank their coffee round the fire, content with conversation and the BBC Light Music till the nine o'clock News, which as usual told them nothing.

Roger sat on the sofa beside Anne, watching her knit, and asking rather personal questions about her life before she came to Farthingale and her plans if ever she was free to leave again. He seemed to find it extraordinary that she had no particular ambitions beyond keeping her job and possibly working her way up to a really good secretaryship, and maybe some day having a little flat of her own somewhere in London — Kensington, she thought, or Knightsbridge.

"Aren't you going to get married?" asked Roger, amused. "A pretty girl like you?"

"Well, now, whom would I marry?" she asked sensibly.

"Not got your eye on anybody? At your age?"

"What do you mean, my age? I'm twenty-six."

"Old enough to look round," said Roger.

"I have looked round. And saw nothing to get excited about."

"Maybe you weren't looking in the right place."

"What's wrong with wanting to be on my own? If you'd always had to share a room with somebody else you'd understand that even the tiniest place of your own would look like heaven."

"So you wouldn't have a husband as a gift! What are we coming to!" said Roger, his masculine *amour propre* bristling.

"I didn't say that," she denied placidly, her eyes on her knitting.

"Well, I must say, it's very discouraging," Roger complained. "Girls were never like this in my day."

And Nigel, watching them benevolently from Archie's chair by the hearth, thought what an attractive pair they were to look at, secret and smiling on the sofa, and how without the war they would never have crossed each other's paths or had a chance to find each other interesting. It's going to level things off a bit, Nigel thought. I suppose that will be good for us, in the end. Of course it's more than likely that she'll never see Roger again. I wonder, Nigel asked himself with some chagrin, if that would be a good thing.

3

Rather early the following morning Jeff left Sylvia still asleep and descended to the dining-room, where he found Oliver alone at the table eating breakfast.

"Bacon!" Oliver said, by way of

greeting. "Stacks of it! Can't think how she does it, we never see bacon in London and it's not even rationed yet!"

"Soon enough," said Jeff, helping himself from the hot plates on the sideboard, and sitting down on Oliver's left.

"Better than the last war. Rationing didn't start till 1918 and things had got into a terrible state."

"I wonder why we say the last war," Jeff ruminated. "It was anything but."

"It's not going to be the Great War, either, much longer. This one will be far greater, once it gets going."

"The late war," said Jeff experimentally. "The other war. The little war. The little, old war."

"The Kaiser's war," said Oliver. "And now Hitler's war. Render unto Caesar, why not."

"Caesar wouldn't own either one of 'em if you gave it to him, I'm thinking."

They ate in companionable silence for some minutes.

"Well, how does it feel?" Oliver asked then, lighting a cigarette. "And what did I tell you?"

"You told me I'd have a box seat for the next war, if I went ahead with Bracken on the newspaper," Jeff recited obediently. "And that I'd never regret it, and wouldn't change places with you then. And so I did, and I have, and I don't, and I wouldn't. But it feels pretty scarey, now that the time has come."

"I know. You haven't got a lot of other fellows doing the same thing at the same time, the way it is in the Army."

"Maybe that's it," Jeff agreed.

"It feels scary that way too," said Oliver, and Jeff looked at him with surprise and disbelief.

"You mean to sit there with your record, and tell me —" he began, and his quiet voice rose a half tone.

"Record, what's that worth!" Oliver waved away the double row of ribbons he was entitled to wear. "One is always sick with fright when the whistle blows. I can promise you one thing, though. When you've had your first bomb you'll be all right." And then, as Jeff only stared at him quizzically — "Oh, you won't stop being scared. There's no cure for that. But you can deal with it. You'll be all right."

"We've had some false alarms in London," Jeff reminded him. "And every time the siren goes — I —" He broke off, jabbing at a piece of toast with his fork.

"That's because they were only false alarms. Wait till it's happened once, Jeff, and *then* tell me you can't take it and I'll listen."

"You always listen," said Jeff humbly and gratefully. "And I always believe what you say — until now. I thought — since you must have been under fire so many times yourself —"

"You thought I might have discovered some magic formula?" Oliver shook his head. "There isn't one. Oh, in the old days of cavalry changes, once the troop was in motion behind you, you got a sort of battle-joy from sheer excitement. To stand still under fire is harder. To be a sitting duck, as you are in an air raid, is still worse. I grant you that. But after the first one — you'll know where you are, I'll guarantee it."

"Are you going to let Mother stay in

Town when the raids start?"

"What choice have I got?" Oliver spread his hands. "She nursed in Belgium — she was here under the Zeppelins — she knows she's as good a soldier as I am. Women," said Oliver, "can be braver than men. True, some of them go to pieces, and some of them don't even attempt to stand up to it. But by and large, if properly trained they're as steady as any man. Girls like Evadne and Mona — they'll show you."

"And Sylvia?"

"I know," Oliver said again, with sympathy. "It's hard. But don't quarrel with her about it. There are no non-combatants in this war. We'll be lucky if we can keep people like Mab out of it till they're eighteen at least."

"Will it go on till Mab is eighteen?"

"I'm afraid so."

"Five years? But London will be pulverized!"

"You'd be surprised how much high explosive it takes to knock out a city."

"Warsaw —?"

"Had no defences worth mentioning."

"I suppose you couldn't give me a glimmer about what's going on at the War Office?"

"I suppose not," said Oliver with a sweet smile.

"Are you going back to work there?"

"No. Charles will. I'm being sent round to lecture to the poor civilians."

"What about?"

"Gas, mostly."

"Evadne says there's one that smells of mouse."

"There is. As near as makes no difference."

There was another silence. Then Jeff drew an unconscious sigh and poured out another cup of tea.

"Well, I feel better than I did," he said. "That's always the way, isn't it, if I can have it out endwise with you."

"Anybody else would have said about the same as I have," Oliver told him, not naming any names.

"Probably. But now I've got it straight from the horse's mouth."

They grinned at each other affectionately.

"Oliver, sometimes I think I ought to

say —" He hesitated.

"It's all right, son, don't try."

That word, so rare between them, and only when they were alone. That word, to which Oliver had no real right, a word so carelessly used by men who were only good friends, like Stevie — when it came from Oliver, Jeff's throat closed, as always, and he could not speak. It had seen him through some bad times before now, and he heard it again with the same involuntary lift of the spirit, recognizing as his mother had done many years ago the strength and serenity of Oliver's soldier philosophy, which went so far beyond fatalism. You lived whatever was ahead of you and enjoyed it the best you could, in Oliver's book of rules — whether it was leading a cavalry charge in South Africa, or lying flat on your back in bed for a whole year to give a rheumatic heart a chance as Jeff had done at fourteen, or waiting like a sitting duck for bombs over London. There was always something to be said for most of it, and the main thing was, you weren't dead. It was a new challenge for Jeff — to be as good a sitting duck as Oliver had been a cavalryman.

"It's a funny thing," he was able to say at last. "My stomach turns clean over when the sirens go, but so far my heart hasn't jumped the track once."

"It won't," said Oliver.

"How do you account for it? Sylvia?"

"In a way, yes. She's made you forget it. Oh, you thought of it with your mind sometimes, but your subconscious forgot it. That seems the wrong way round, doesn't it."

"It makes sense," said Jeff. "In a goofy sort of way."

Mab came in then, looking less tense and self-contained than she had for weeks, and was delighted to find them still at table.

"Where is everybody this morning?" she asked happily as Jeff rose to pull out a chair for her and took her plate to the sideboard.

"Catching up on sleep, I expect." Oliver poured out her tea, passed her the toast and jam. "I meant to myself, but somehow I've got out of the habit of sleeping."

"This is fun," she said, as Jeff set a plate of bacon and eggs in front of her. "This feels more like Farthingale again. Has anyone listened to the News?"

"We clean forgot it," said Jeff guiltily with a glance at the silent radio in the corner.

"They're saying that we must expect Hitler to do something horrible just because it's Christmas. Well — not in so many words officially — but that's what they mean."

"Too cold," said Oliver. "Snow coming, I think."

"Sh!" said Mab. "He'll hear you! Jeff, will you have time after breakfast to look at the Williamsburg things Evadne brought me?"

"Time any time," said Jeff, sitting down beside her.

"How nice that sounds. Aren't you going to the Observers' Post expedition?"

"Not if you'd rather I stayed here," he said simply.

"And how long before you have to start back to London?"

"Tuesday morning."

"So soon?" she sighed.

"Look, Mab, I'm lucky to be here at all!"

"Yes, I know, I'm very thankful," she said seriously. "I've had nightmares you might have to go to Finland."

"I'm afraid the war would be over before I could get there now."

"Are they beaten?"

"Yes. They'll go down fighting, but they're beaten."

"And then what?" asked Mab.

"Holland, maybe. Maybe Switzerland. Or Belgium again."

"Before Easter?"

"Probably."

"I was only wondering if you would be here again for Easter."

"It will be Bracken's turn to come away, at Easter."

"The only time you can be sure of any more is *now,*" said Mab. "I'm going up and get the Williamsburg things this minute." She slipped from her chair and left the room.

"She hasn't eaten much," Jeff said. "And her tea has got cold." He found

Oliver looking at him. "I don't know," he said, to a question which had not been spoken. He rose and carried Mab's cooling cup of tea to the sideboard and left it there, took a cup from the setting further down the table and put it at Mab's place. "I don't know," he repeated, moving restlessly round the room. "She's always been crazy about Williamsburg, you know — like a sort of second sight. If there is such a thing as reincarnation, maybe that's what it is. I never encouraged her in it, honestly I didn't — well, one time I did promise that I'd see that she got there for a visit. But now I don't know. I'm not sure that it would be a good idea for her to go there. The veil is too thin. Oliver, I admit I don't quite know how to handle this. If I clamp down on it suddenly, dodge talking about it, forbid her to dwell on it any more — well, maybe that's the wrong way to come at it. But if I go along with it, as I have been doing, answer questions, confirm her ideas, and some of them are pretty uncanny — if I go on pretending there's nothing unusual about any of it, where does it end? I —"

"Jeff. Mab is growing up."

"I know that. I used to think maybe it was just a childish sort of game, something she might outgrow — but —"

"But now you know better." Oliver glanced at the door and lowered his voice. "Why do we worry about a war, with *this* going on under our very noses?"

Jeff stood stock still in his tracks, staring at the carpet in front of him.

"Oh, no —" he said, like a prayer.

"Mab isn't a child, Jeff. You must be careful."

"I am careful," Jeff told him unargumentatively. "I've been careful for years. But I can't just start avoiding her, all of a sudden. That would be — noticeable."

"So will it be noticeable like this, soon."

"To you, yes, but you —"

"To anyone, Jeff. You can't expect her to hide it, she's not wise enough."

"But everybody's used to Mab and me, it's nothing new, we've always — She's only thirteen," said Jeff.

"She's not going to stay thirteen. And

235

it's not just Mab I mean, Jeff."

"Oh, not me too, I give you my word, I — there's nothing but Sylvia for me, ever, we fell in love when we were kids, I could never —" Jeff passed a fretful hand across his face, as though to mask it even for a moment from the thoughtful eyes of the man at the table. "Now you've really got me worried," he said.

"I think you should be."

"Oliver, don't for God's sake sound as though it was my fault — I —"

Mab returned to the room, rather breathless, with her hands full of photographs and postcards.

"It's this Jamestown thing," she was saying, as she laid them down beside her plate. "When did they wall up the River bank with stones?"

"Before I can remember. Why?" He came slowly to sit beside her.

"Well, why on earth should they do a thing like that? The grass always went right down to the water."

"It did?" He glanced at her quickly. "They found the land was being slowly eaten away by the current. That tree stump sticking up in the water way out from the shore shows you how the bank had already receded before the wall went in."

"Jeff, what's the matter?" She had caught the preoccupation in his manner. "Was there something in the News?"

"I haven't heard it. Was there?"

"I don't know, I — just thought you looked sort of funny."

"I can't help that," said Jeff. "I've got a funny face."

"I like it," she said, and laughed, and laid one hand briefly along his cheek. "Tell me what you know about the house called Green Spring."

"They fit a battle there," Jeff obliged. "Lafayette and Wayne — before Washington came South."

"What's become of the house?"

"It's gone. Burned down, I guess. The chimney is supposed to be there, but I never found it. Probably wasn't looking in the right place."

"I bet I could find it," said Mab. "Evadne brought me the map I wanted — look, an old one, the way it was then.

This is the part I wanted to know about —"
She unfolded the map and laid her fingertip
north of the Capitol building. "She says
there's a paved road there now, with
motor courts and petrol pumps."

"Mm-hm."

"Jeff?" Her look was searching.

"I'm listening. What about your
breakfast? Virginia won't let you go with
us to the Observers' Post if you haven't
had some food."

"Couldn't you and I stay home? There's
so much here I want to talk about —"

"Don't you think we ought to lend
Roger a hand with this picnic?" he
suggested cautiously.

"All right, if you say so." She began to
fold up the map.

"*Good*-morning, all," said Sylvia at the
door, with Virginia just behind her.
"Look at the early birds. Any worms left
for us?" She went confidently to the
sideboard.

Jeff rose instantly and joined her there.

"We found a lot of black market
bacon," he said, and "*Jeff!*" cried
Virginia in furious denial.

The dining-room filled up. Nigel — Phoebe — Roger — the Bank girls, a little shy at sharing the family meals during the holidays instead of bicycling over to the canteen at Cleeve.

There was bustle and chatter over collecting the party for the Observers' Post. Eventually the pony-cart was brought round, drawn by a fat little horse left over from Evadne's childhood, and hampers were loaded into it, bikes were rolled up beside it, and everybody went away to bundle up, for it was biting cold, with a wind.

"Aren't you coming?" said Anne to Nigel, glancing back on her way to the door.

"Well, I —"

"You can take my bike, Sylvia has asked me to ride in the cart. Claudia can't go because she has to see to the children for this afternoon."

"I haven't been on a bike for years," said Nigel, with a certain wistfulness.

"You'd better get in practice again," Anne advised him. "Soon we can't get round any other way."

"All right," said Nigel, to his own surprise. "I'd like to come."

"Have you got overshoes, it's frightfully cold."

"Yes — I must have, somewhere. Mummy," said Nigel, using the little word without self-consciousness, "I used to have overshoes here, didn't I?"

"In the cupboard under the stairs, I should think. Do shut the outside door, somebody, as soon as you can."

The dining-room was suddenly very quiet, as the commotion was all drained away to the hall. Virginia, Phoebe, and Oliver were left at the table together in an empty silence.

"I'm only glad I'm not trying to be young now," said Virginia. "I'm glad I was young when it was easy."

"They don't miss it, because they can't remember how it was," said Oliver.

"That's rather like saying dumb animals don't suffer the way human beings do," said Virginia. "How do we know?"

Roger reappeared in the doorway.

"I say, Aunt Virginia," he said in a stage whisper. "Gary Cooper's big brother has just driven up in a Consulate car and says he knew you when. Shall we bring him in here?''

"G —?'' Virginia began, and something like a sunburst began in the pit of her stomach and spread to her fingertips. Roger had put a careless finger on the resemblance which left no doubt about the visitor.

She rose.

"Yes, bring him in here, he'll want a cup of coffee,'' she said, and rang the bell. And to Phoebe and Oliver, who sat gazing at her from their places at the table, she said quite calmly, "Do you remember Tracy Marsh?''

4

He filled the doorway, making Nigel look like a stripling beside him. He was not in uniform, and had left his overcoat and hat in the hall. His country tweeds had come from the right London tailor and were not new. In twenty years he had not put on more than five pounds, and he was always six foot three. His long, lined, humorous face was tanned — a used-looking face, Phoebe thought, observing for the first time the man they had all wondered about in 1918.

Having escorted him in, Nigel faded from view, and sounds in the drive soon indicated the departure of the picnic mission.

"Well, Tracy," said Virginia steadily, and advanced with her hand held out, "where on earth have you dropped from?"

He stood still and let her come to him. It made no difference to him that two people he had never seen before were also in the room with nothing to do but look on at his meeting with Virginia. Without a glance in their direction, sublimely unself-conscious he stood with her hand in his, looking down at her.

"I know I should have asked permission to come," he said. "But when we found I was headed for Cheltenham today, Charles said it would be all right if I stopped here on the way."

"Indeed it is," said Virginia, recovering

her hand. "And I suppose you can't say what brings you to Cheltenham."

"Sure, I can say," he drawled. "Man I've got to see happens to be there."

"You remember Phoebe and Oliver Campion," she said, walking beside him into the room towards the table.

"I remember hearing about them, but we never met, I guess."

He shook hands composedly, and Virginia said to Melchett, who had answered the bell and stood waiting — "Bring a pot of coffee for Captain — I mean, Mr. — what is it now, Tracy, General?"

"Colonel, I guess, will have to do."

"Colonel Marsh would like some coffee," Virginia said to Melchett. "Do sit down, Tracy, you must be perished with cold. How about some eggs and bacon?"

"No, thanks, I've had breakfast. Just some coffee would be nice." He sat down easily at the corner of the table, and Virginia removed the plate before him and brought a fresh setting from the sideboard.

"You'll stay to lunch, won't you?" she suggested as she did so, and his slate-grey gaze came up to her face.

"I didn't expect to," he said.

"Could we persuade you?"

"If I could make a phone call."

"Make a dozen," said Virginia, smiling down at him.

"It wouldn't inconvenience you?"

"Of course not, we'd be all delighted. You won't mind if the family tries to pump you, will you! Are you allowed to tell about Warsaw?"

"Some."

"And about Johnny and Camilla in Berlin?"

"Haven't seen 'em lately," he confessed, without elaborating.

"Have they got shelters and gas-masks and things in Berlin?"

"They're living at the Adlon. It's bar is better than its shelter. Between the two, I guess they're best off. So far."

The coffee came, and Virginia poured it out for him. Phoebe and Oliver exchanged glances and on the flimsiest excuses drifted away. Virginia sat with a cigarette, facing Tracy and his cup of coffee across the table.

"Well," he said, and the long laughter lines each side of his mouth deepened. "It took another war, but here I am again. It's amazing how you don't change."

"What did you expect? A doddering old woman?"

"I expected you to be different. And you aren't." His eyes ran affectionately over her slim figure, the short, greying curls, the heart-shaped, cleverly made-up face.

"You know I am, and I know I am, but thank you anyhow. Men have the best of it after forty. So I can truthfully say — neither are you!"

"Yes," he said. "I'm just the same." He glanced round the sunny room. "So this is Farthingale," he said.

"It's hard to realize we never met except in London."

"You showed me some pictures of it once — while I was in the hospital. I used to try to imagine what it would be like, instead of counting sheep at night. I knew where I was the minute I came to the entrance today. It's a beautiful house. I'm glad it didn't have to be overrun with city kids."

"I was fortunate. I got the Bank overflow from Cleeve."

"So Charles said. You stuck to what you told me — that day at the hospital. You didn't marry again."

"No. What about you?"

He nodded.

"You told me to. So I tried. It wasn't any good."

"I'm sorry."

"Maybe my heart wasn't in it the right way. She soon took with with an Air Force man who had more time to spare."

"Divorce?"

"Yep. She married him. Got a couple of kids now. Must be she knew what she wanted. Me, I'm back on the old beat."

"What *were* you doing in Warsaw, Tracy?"

"Snooping." He grinned.

"How did you get out? Bracken asked in Paris — Biddle didn't know."

"He knows now."

"It must have been pretty ghastly, wasn't it — in Poland."

"It was rough," he conceded.

"Will it be as bad here? In London,

I mean. Is it coming?"

She watched him light a cigarette — his lean, fine hands, brown from the sun. How had his summer tan lasted like this, into December? Where had he been, since Warsaw fell? Italy? The Mediterranean —?

"Honey, I'm not going to try to fool you," he was saying slowly. "You know as well as I do, this is a new kind of war. Spain was the test-tube. Barcelona — Guernica — that was the experiment. Then Warsaw. They're learning fast."

"And now Helsinki. What's next? London? Paris?"

"The Lowlands," he said with quiet assurance. "They want the coast, before they go for London."

"Holland? But, Tracy, the dikes — they can flood it. How long could Holland hold out?"

"A month."

"*Tracy!* What about Belgium?"

"A little longer, with a lot of help. Denmark they could take any minute by long distance telephone."

"But France?" she urged, feeling a draught. "Surely France will hold?"

"Yes, the French Army is all right."

Eager for reassurance, she missed the reservation, if there was one.

"I still don't understand the Western Front," she said, and as he made no reply, "I suppose we aren't supposed to."

"You always smelled so sweet," he said, apparently at random. "Even if I couldn't see you, after all these years I'd still know you were in the room now."

"Tracy —"

"Where's the harm?" he asked reasonably. "There's a war on, Virginia. Again. We're right back where we started from."

"Or where we stopped."

"You can't blame me, can you? You've no right to look so much the same. Women are supposed to age, as time goes on."

"Oh, Tracy, I have, I have! I —"

"And it wouldn't matter anyway. If you had."

"But Tracy —"

"You don't want the others to know, is that it? You don't want to be kidded about your old beau. You won't have to worry about that, I guess. I'm off to France very soon."

She looked up at him doubtfully, drawn as always, resisting still.

"It's what you said before."

"Almost. I said something else too."

"Now, Tracy, please, I —"

"I said — Let me come back, if I can."

A moment more she sat with her eyes on his. Then with a swift, impulsive movement she was standing beside his chair, his head held against her breast, his arms around her.

"I was wrong that time — I was wrong — I didn't think it would last — Tracy, I'm sorry — I spoilt your life — I'm sorry —" She was crying helplessly.

He shifted in the chair and drew her down on his knees.

"Now, now," he said. "Everybody has to learn the hard way, I guess. It could have been worse. I got here, didn't I?"

"It's too late —"

"Who says it is?"

"We've got another war —"

"What's a war? You never did this before."

She took the folded handkerchief from his breast pocket and mopped herself with it, while he sat with his hands around her waist, looking up at her.

"I'm behaving like a schoolgirl," she said unsteadily.

"Maybe it's time. Maybe it's time you acted young again."

With a faint, final sniff she replaced the handkerchief and removed herself from his lap. He let her go, but his hands lingered.

"I thought you must be dead," she said. "It was much worse not to know, after I began to suspect you were in Warsaw. And then Bracken said they had lost you —"

"Yep, I sure thought I was a goner for a while," he admitted cheerfully, with no further details. "Remember that, won't you, when it hots up here. Remember the odds. It seems as though each bomb was aimed at you personally, signed, sealed, and delivered. And then it lands a half a mile away."

"Tracy, what do you do about being scared?"

His slow smile spread affectionately.

"You rise above it," he drawled.

"I suppose I shall be afraid when the time comes," Virginia said thoughtfully. "I suppose I was last time, when we had the Zeppelins, but somehow I can't remember much about that. Isn't it odd how long ago it seems? We talked about invasion then, didn't we — more than we do now, I think. So far, my worst time this war was the week before Munich last year. By the time it really began I had grown a sort of callous. I hope it lasts."

"Oh, come," he said gently. "You've heard gunfire before. You'll be all right."

"One thing we didn't foresee last time, though," she went on, staring rather blindly at the window behind him. "It was bad enough to have the young men go. Now it's the girls too. My Evadne — Edward's Mona — and wait till you see Mab, she's only thirteen —"

5

When the pony-cart returned just before lunch, Virginia was sitting in the drawing room with Tracy Marsh, drinking sherry.

The rest of them gathered round the fire with their own glasses, trying not to stare at him, but obviously mesmerized by so glamorous a figure, fresh out of Warsaw, and on top of that an American, and furthermore a beau of Virginia's.

Jeff contained himself with difficulty, restrained by the awful unwritten law — *you can't print that*. When a man is at his ease among friends with a drink in his hand, you don't pump him for the newspaper. He may talk a million dollars' worth of front-page stuff, but you can't use it.

He told them very little anyway that had not already been in print or rumor. The point was, he had seen it. His mere presence in their midst, untalkative, unexcitable, unpretentious, but authentic, made the nightmare of Warsaw real. It was plain that he had digested his experience, accepted it, made his deductions, and reported accordingly to those who sent him there. He had no desire to shock or frighten his present audience with hair-raising tales. But small anecdotes and word vignettes could not help but emerge if he so much as opened his mouth — the flame-streaked rubble and blood and terror of a bombed city — the raw-boned Stukas in a screaming dive on the target — the stumbling, sobbing lines of refugees shattered and panicked by a hail of machine-gun bullets from above — the old lady dressed in her Sunday best and riding in a wheel-barrow — the child who carried a dead bird in a bent and battered wire cage — the boy who wept beside a dying cart-horse. . . .

He had seen a fallen Government go into exile in the crowded border towns of countries which were so far safe — and their faces wore the same dazed hopelessness as the faces in the roadside camps set up by people who had no money to buy shelter and nowhere to go. A world had ended. A nation had perished. Tracy was there when it happened, and it had marked him, but he was not one to dramatize it.

Virginia, watching and listening with the rest, was wrung with pride and pity. Here was a man to love and to cherish. And some fool of a woman had bungled it and gone off with some one easier. Well, that made two fool women, didn't it. In an hour or so he would be gone again. What could you do in an hour to make up for twenty years? Better to let it go now. Don't look back. Don't entangle him. There was no future. There was only a war.

The talk had moved on to Finland, where the Russians were being made to pay for every inch of ground, but where there was no chloroform for the wounded.

"Aren't we going to help Finland *either?*" Anne cried unexpectedly, and then flushed as they all looked at her with surprise and affection. "Can't we even send them hospital supplies? Performing amputations without anaesthetics is going back to the dark ages!"

And Virginia said, out of her reverie —

"Not as far back as that. It happened in Richmond when my mother was a girl. She was caught trying to carry opiates through the Yankee blockade in her hoop."

"Oh, Gran, they might have thought she was a spy!" cried Mab, entranced.

"That's what they think," Virginia smiled. "But she had red hair, and she told off the whole Union Army, up one side and down the other, and they let her go — *with* the drugs!"

"Those were the days!" Jeff sighed. "I'm afraid it wouldn't work with the Russians!"

"But one would have to *try*," Anne muttered, still smouldering, and "Hear, hear!" said Nigel quietly, so that she sent him a grateful glance and retreated again behind her eternal knitting.

And Nigel thought, A dear creature. Generous and tenderhearted, and brave. And lonely, I should think. Why hasn't some one seen before now, she's well out of her teens. Roger isn't making the most of his time. Younger than she is, probably. Besides, she wants looking after, and he's not able, even if it occurred to him. And then, perceiving the direction of his thoughts, Nigel was astonished and, suddenly reckless, looked at her again. . . .

Luncheon was a bit overhung by the

clock, as Tracy was soon due at Cheltenham and the family had to attend the children's play in the village. When they left the dining-room Virginia found that she had been tactfully maneuvered into seeing Tracy off alone while the others scattered on their lawful occasions.

With his hand on the inner knob of the front door he paused to look down at her.

"Don't come outside with me, it's bitter cold," he said, and took her hand in his free one. "I shan't see you again for a while, I'm afraid. This was just a crazy piece of luck today. Do you ever come up to London?"

"Only once since September, to do the Christmas shopping. I don't know when I'll get away again. How long have we got here in England, Tracy? When will it start?"

"In the spring."

"Where will you be?"

"Hard to say, by then."

"If you are in London — *when* you are in London — can you let me know?" She had not meant to say that, and she instantly regretted the flare of hope in his face.

"I probably can't give you much notice. But you'll hear from me," he promised, gripping her hand and letting it go. "Now and then."

The heavy door closed behind him. She stood a moment, staring at the panels as though she could see through them to where the car moved away down the drive.

As she turned back into the hall Sylvia was coming down the stairs with her floating dancer's tread which made no sound on the carpet.

"*He* is a lamb," said Sylvia. "Mind you have the good sense to keep track of him!"

"It's a bit hard to do," Virginia smiled.

"But worth some effort," said Sylvia. She was wearing a brown fur cap on her honey-colored hair, and carried a fur-lined coat over her arm. "The cart is coming round again, and the bikes are still there. How do you mean to transport this gang to the Parish Hall?"

"I hadn't thought," said Virginia, with unaccustomed vagueness.

"Shall I cope?" Sylvia asked sympathetically.

"Please."

"Very well, you and Phoebe and I in the cart. Jeff and Mab can take the footpath, and the others can use the bikes. That comes out even. O.K.?"

There was nothing to do but nod assent, though Virginia felt a dim reservation somewhere.

"We can switch round coming home, if we like," said Sylvia, and sat down on an oak chest to put on her overshoes, glancing wisely at Virginia as she did so. "He'll be safe enough at Cheltenham," she said, and Virginia laughed.

"At least he doesn't seem to be headed for Finland," she remarked with relief.

"He's been to Finland," said Sylvia, stamping into her boots. "Or St. Moritz. That was a snow-tan. You don't get it sitting round the Ritz bar in Paris." Her direct blue gaze dwelt affectionately on Virginia's confusion. "That's quite a boy you've got there, I only hope you gave him a little encouragement!"

"Well, I — nobody knows when he'll turn up again."

"Keep your fingers crossed," said Sylvia

cheerfully as the rest of the party began to trickle down the stairs.

Jeff felt that to object to Sylvia's innocent arrangements would have been more noticeable than to accede to them without comment, and so found himself setting out alone with Mab along the narrow path which wound through a little wood and across a stream and past the old grey church to the village.

It was probably only an accident that they had never walked there alone together since the time a few days before his marriage to Sylvia when he tried to find words to comfort a broken-hearted child who would not admit even to him that she was suffering. You mustn't hold this against Sylvia, he had said that day. We grew up together, we've always been in love — some day I'll be coming to your wedding, he had said, feeling futile and heavy-handed. Promise to let me look him over first, won't you — promise to wait for me, wherever I may be. . . . But that wasn't at all what he had meant to say, and when she leaned against his shoulder, shaking with suppressed sobs, he had thought, but she's a *child,* she'll get over this — it's worse than I thought, I mind it myself, he discovered. And then the swift inner uncertainty — shall I feel like this when Mab marries? — what is this between us, as though she wasn't a child at all? — if it wasn't for Sylvia, he had thought in astonishment — but it *is* Sylvia, it's always been Sylvia, for me. . . .

Now it was three years later, and Mab was less of a child. And only this morning Oliver had said he must be careful.

She was taller now, walking beside him in one of their easy silences — more self-possessed, more knowing. But still not wise enough to hide it, Oliver said. She had hidden it at the wedding, though, composed and smiling in her pink bridesmaid's dress. How does it feel, he had wondered then, to watch the person you love best in the world being married to some one else? And now he thought unwillingly, Some day I shall know. Some day it will be my turn, to see Mab married. Because she must marry, he thought, walking beside her in the narrow path, their shoulders brushing. She must not be allowed to waste her life, because of me. Somehow I must make her see that she must look beyond me, for love. Perhaps if she did go to Williamsburg — that might be the pattern — there might be some boy there who is meant to make her forget me. . . . But he knew very well that Williamsburg was not the answer. At Williamsburg she would find Julian.

"Are you thinking about the last time we walked here?" Mab asked quietly at last.

"Well, no, I wasn't — not exactly," he answered with his new caution. "When was that?"

"You know when," said Mab. "It was just before your wedding and you were going to America for your honeymoon, and I begged you not to come back here if there was a war, and you said, What kind of heel did I take you for? And you said I was the one who would be in America if there was a war, and I said I wasn't a coward."

"So we agreed to ride it out together, didn't we," said Jeff. "Well, here we go."

"I'm afraid I'm not so brave as I thought I was."

"You mean you'd like to go to Williamsburg now?"

"Oh, *no,* I couldn't leave Gran! But I hate the *waiting!* It's a funny thing to say, but I think we'll all feel better once the bombs begin!"

"Well, yes, I think you've got something there," said Jeff. "As a matter of fact, Oliver was saying somewhat the same thing only this morning."

"People like Oliver must be pretty disgusted, they went to so much trouble to settle it a few years back, and now look!"

"It was only an armistice in 1918," said Jeff. "Funny how we got used to that word, forgot its real meaning, and expected it to last."

"Funny how you get used to almost anything, if it goes on long enough."

"Do you, Mab?" He glanced at her quickly.

"Oh, Jeff, I can't stand all this tip-toeing!" she cried, half laughing, half exasperated. "Everybody but Sylvia goes round holding their breath for fear Sylvia will find out that I love you more than anybody in the world! Sylvia already knows that, she's always known it! It's nothing new, it hasn't made any difference to Sylvia and me, I love her too, and you'd be lost without her, I can see that! She's not afraid I'll put poison in her tea, in fact when you're away we hold each other up!"

"I see," he said with some difficulty. "What brought this on?"

"It's just something in the air, lately, as though — as though there was something *wrong* about my feeling the way I do about you, and about Williamsburg! Well, after all, it's not a book we're living in, is it, or a play! Nobody's jealous or miserable or going crazy or committing suicide to provide a third-act curtain! Suppose I do know that there'll never be anyone to hold a candle to you as long as I live, I'm not going to die of it! That's what I mean about getting used to things, though I suppose I haven't said it very well. When you married Sylvia I thought it would kill me, but I realize now how childish that was. I see you all the time just the same, and Sylvia and I depend on each other. I couldn't do without her now, any more than you could. I've got *used* to it, Jeff."

"Yes, I see," he assented, still groping. "The thing is, Mab — Well, it's looking ahead a bit, but perhaps it's a question of your not being willing to give anybody else a chance to make good later on, if you go on thinking I'm so all-fired perfect —"

"You're not perfect!" she cried, and laughed at him.

"Oh, is that so! What's wrong with me, then?" he demanded, pretending dudgeon, and she laughed again, and pausing in the path threw her arms around him gaily, her face buried in his coat.

"I don't know, I just had to say that, you looked so smug, there must *be* something, but I don't know, don't you see, I'll never know, because I love you so —"

He was silent, standing still in the path with one arm laid lightly around her while she clasped him in that childish embrace, which loosened suddenly as her head came up. Their eyes met, his smiling, puzzled, and compassionate, hers questioning and alert, for she had felt through the heavy coat the muffled drumbeat of his heart.

"Jeff?"

"Yes, dear?" He could find no other words to answer the sudden uncertainty in her tone. Her hands were still on his sleeves, her upturned face was very near — green eyes, like Tibby's — it was as though the portrait stood there, breathing, between his hands — as though time itself had slipped and shifted, and Julian stood with Tibby in his arms again — my darling — *Tibby, my darling.* . . .

"Jeff, is it all right now?"

"You are sure nothing will cure you of this?" he said, unaware that they were Julian's words, not his. "You are quite sure you won't just wake up some morning able to see that I am a very ordinary sort of man, no better than a lot of others, and maybe not so good?"

"I shall never see that, as long as I live." She laid a small warm hand — Tibby's hand — against his cheek. "What is it?" she whispered. "You look very queer."

He drew in a giddy breath, not moving under her hands.

"I feel very queer," he said.

"Why? Why do you look like that, Jeff?"

"Like what, my darling?"

"Almost as though you were sorry for me."

The bright, cold world in which they stood steadied round him again. He found her hands, and loosed them from his sleeves.

"I wouldn't presume," he said gravely, and she was not sure what he meant, but moved on with him obediently in silence, till they came to the church at the top of the village street, and life engulfed them again.

IV.

Whitsun at Farthingale.

1940

1

What with Finland's surrender in March, and Denmark overrun in a single day in April, and Norway going under before your eyes as May came in, it got so you dreaded to turn on the radio each morning. Virginia had a portable in her bedroom, and Mab usually joined her there for early tea. Together each day they learned what Virginia called the Worst, before they faced the world downstairs. After dinner each evening in the drawing-room the nine o'clock News awaited them again, inevitable as doom.

Spring had come in with a rush, after the coldest winter in living memory. Easter was in March, and it seemed as though everybody but Michael had four days' leave, and got about with hoarded petrol and did reckless shopping and noted — with an inward prickle of apprehension — that the crocuses were out, and it was Time.

ARP tightened up, after the winter's sag. Gas-masks were dusted off, though nobody carried them any more. The Lowlands braced themselves again, obstinately refusing Allied offers of what was tactfully called "preventive aid" and clinging desperately to their forlorn and futile neutrality.

When the blow fell, on April ninth, it was the usual shock. Hitler had gone for Norway instead.

"Caught on the wrong foot again," said Virginia crossly. "Everybody's in France, watching the other mousehole!"

Everybody but the Fleet, which at once began to distinguish itself and take punishment. Michael was there, on a destroyer — not one of those that were sunk at once. And Mona's chin was well up.

"Now we're getting somewhere," she said.

But it wasn't enough. Poland had gone down before sheer, crashing weight and numbers, rolling in over a flat defenceless countryside. In Norway Hitler uncorked a new technique — the back door, the dagger from behind, wholesale blackmail and treachery and murder, the Fifth Column. Once more the free world had to watch, angry and impotent, while a brave, bewildered nation went down fighting. Courage was not enough in Norway either, and neutrality was a delusion. If Norway had not been so busy being neutral while Finland was defending itself last winter, Bracken said, she might have stood a better chance now. Neutrals wanted to have it both ways. But even now, if Belgium and Holland could learn quickly from Norway's dreadful lesson . . .

Finland had held out one hundred and three days against the Russians. After twenty-five days the Norwegian Government was evacuated by British ships under heavy fire, and British troops were admitted to be falling back towards their embarkation ports from impossible positions. The country was lost.

"We will never win this war with Chamberlain in Downing Street!" cried Virginia, and there was acrimonious debate in the House along the same lines, and shouts of "Resign!" But the stubborn, unspectacular, pathetic old man would not concede defeat.

"Who else is there?" Mab asked, for it was hard to remember a time when Neville Chamberlain had not been Prime Minister.

"Winston," said Virginia without hesitation.

"But he's got the Admiralty!"

"They should move him up. He could run this war singlehanded better than Chamberlain and his whole blithering Cabinet put together!"

"But I thought they said he was wrong when —"

"Of course he's been wrong sometimes!" Virginia interrupted impatiently. "They all make mistakes! But I'd rather have Winston at Number Ten making *his* kind of mistakes than put up any longer with Chamberlain's howlers!"

"Was it a howler to try to help Norway?"

"No, we had to do *something!"*
(Nobody could discuss Norway any more
without shouting, Bracken said.) "But
somehow it wasn't done *right!* I don't
know, but we've got to do better than
this! There's got to be a change, this
won't do at all!" Virginia rose briskly and
rang for Melchett. "Let's have some tea
— port wine — Ovaltine — what'll it be?
I need something to brace me up, don't
you?"

"I'd like some hot tea," said Mab.
"And some cinnamon toast."

"All right. Whatever you say!"

"I'm cold," said Mab, rubbing her
fingers and haunching her shoulders.
"And it's too late to start a fire."

Melchett came, and the order was given.
As she turned to go, she hesitated.

"Perhaps you ought to know, madam,
that one of the Bank young ladies has had
bad news from Norway."

"Oh, dear. Which one?"

"Miss Merton, madam."

The one called Claudia, Virginia thought.
The one who wept all the time anyway.
Her boy. It would be.

"Is he — does she know —?"

"He's dead, madam."

Melchett went away to get the tea.

In the quiet room, which was so suddenly cold, Mab and Virginia looked at each other in silence. Somebody killed. First blood for the house this war. It had moved much closer, in one tick of the clock. The long, horrifying casualty lists of the other war had not yet begun. By Christmas in 1914 they had lost half a million men. Now it was starting again.

"I suppose it's wrong to be glad it wasn't Michael," said Mab finally. "What shall we do?"

"What *can* we do?" Virginia threw out her hands. "She'll be giving Anne Phillips a bad time, though."

"We might send them up our tea when it comes," Mab suggested practically.

"Brandy, more likely. Perhaps I should take it up myself." Virginia stood a minute, gazing blankly at the empty hearth. "We should have had a fire tonight," she murmured. "It's this war — you go without common comforts — no more this — no more that. Well, there's still some brandy." She moved with decision towards the door. "You go ahead with your tea when it comes. I won't be long."

When Melchett returned with the tray Mab was still sitting motionless, her hands pressed together in her lap.

A week ago Jeff had gone out to France, wearing a correspondent's uniform. Just a routine job, he said — Paris, Nancy, Arras, Luxembourg — it was a sort of joke that everybody went to Luxembourg, where you could watch the guns in France firing while you drank your coffee on the hotel terrace. The tourist's war, said Jeff with sarcasm. But after months on the diplomatic run, writing think-pieces in London, he was thankful for any change. A group of them had all gone together — like a guided tour, said Jeff. British Headquarters were very fussy about who saw their war, and the French had wound themselves up in a web of red tape in Paris which was even worse. Still, it was a step in the right direction, said Jeff. Mab and Sylvia were only thankful that it was a step across the Channel instead of northward, towards Norway. He would be perfectly all right in France, they had assured themselves.

Mab thanked Melchett for the tea and said Good-night as usual, but made no move towards the tray. The mere fact that an unknown boy had got killed in Norway did not mean that Jeff was any less safe in France than he had been while that boy was still alive. But it brought the war in. It made the war a member of the household, even though Claudia Merton's Harold was not one of the family. It set you counting up the ones that belonged to you — Michael somewhere off Narvik, Roger at an East Coast aerodrome, all those at their posts in London, Jeff on his correspondent's beat — and everybody knew he was not the kind to write the war from the Ritz bar in Paris. . . .

Virginia came in, looking puzzled.

"I'll never understand that girl. She's been snivelling for weeks and now she keeps saying, 'I knew this was going to happen, I knew he was going to die!' Perhaps a little more faith might have saved him!" She sat down and began to pour out their tea.

"Sylvia says we can only lose him if we let go and get frightened," Mab agreed, staring down at her cup, and Virginia gave her a compassionate glance.

"Jeff's all right where he is," she said gently. "There's precious little shooting in France so far!"

The next day brought a message from Mona. Michael had been wounded, not badly. He was in London, and if they could both get leave might they come down for the Whitsun week-end? Virginia replied cordially that Mab would give them her room and double up in Virginia's and everyone was more than pleased.

And so on that Friday morning when Virginia woke and turned on the early News, she and Mab sat up in bed staring at each other while the neat, precise voice of the BBC announced in its pear-shaped tones that Amsterdam and Brussels had been bombed at dawn, and the German invasion of the Lowlands had begun.

Churchill was moved up in a hurry then, and by nine o'clock News time that evening he was Prime Minister. Well, now we're for it, everybody said. Winston will

275

show 'em. And then — inevitably — everybody chuckled.

2

It was another oddity of an odd war that when the long-awaited attack finally came, Michael should be safe at Farthingale with his arm in a sling, and Jeff, the non-combatant, should be missing. He had been in Paris on the Wednesday, doing his regular weekly broadcast. He had found Paris still eating well, going to the theater, cheating on its blackout, hoarding its man-power — and criticizing the British for what happened in Norway. Jeff's French was too good. He heard too much. He was riled at Paris. More than he could say out loud.

So far as Bracken knew, Jeff was to have left Paris with a group of correspondents on Thursday for a motor trip to the British sector. He was due to report from there on the Saturday, visiting the fighting squadrons of the RAF and spending a night among the blockhouses of the British Line facing the Belgian frontier. Therefore the first news of the invasion must have caught him at British Headquarters near Arras, where there was conceivably a lot going on.

By Saturday night, when he should have made contact with London, the British Army had hurled themselves forward into Belgium to meet the German advance, and the whereabouts of the Press units had become hazy.

The Sunday papers were full of horrors, and once again a new one — this time Hitler was dropping parachute troops behind the lines among a defenceless civilian population; ruthless fighting men and saboteurs, often wearing civilian disguises or Allied uniforms, and speaking the common tongue, so that they came upon their objectives unsuspected, as it were unseen, and things blew up, and crossroads were held, and false rumor and panic were started like a prairie fire in the rear of the defending army. It was a refinement of the old two-front war — an embroidery on treachery that crisped the nerves.

Suppose, thought Virginia, Germans just suddenly rained down out of the sky into the garden, and walked in with guns. Invasion? But this was Martian.

By Sunday night the whole civil defence system in England had sprung to attention, and the air wardens — who were unarmed — had been ordered out on a dusk to dawn patrol to watch for parachute landings. But surely the Germans had enough on their hands on the Continent just now? Surely they couldn't just hurdle the war there and start on England too?

Now, thought Virginia, lying in bed on Sunday night with Mab apparently asleep beside her, *now* I am going to be afraid. I remember now how it feels. I thought I was awfully sensible and not a bit nervous and could cope with the whole thing quite steadily and be a credit to everybody. Bombing didn't seem very likely down here, and gas didn't seem very likely anywhere — but parachutists in the garden! What would I do? Should I get out a gun? What if Mab just suddenly met a German coming at her, *what would I do?* This is nightmare, thought Virginia.

This is going to tell on me. . . .

Whitsun was forgotten. Michael and Mona, after less than two days at Farthingale, returned to London for Mona's stand-to with the ambulance, though Michael's leave had still two weeks to run. He was furious. The lilacs were out, the weather was perfect, it was going to be a honeymoon. That bloody awful little man Hitler *again.*

"It's like having the war begin all over again," said Virginia, trying to sound casual. And when once more the raids over England didn't come — "It's that same feeling we had last September — as though you've stepped down a bottom stair that wasn't there."

There was one difference, though, Mab thought. When the war first began they knew where Jeff was.

Useless to comfort oneself now with the capital C for correspondent in gold thread on his cap and the green tab with its gilt legend on the shoulder of his uniform to show he was not a combat man. The dive-bombers screaming down over Belgium wouldn't notice that. Sylvia in London would be the first to hear when he did communicate, and one could trust her to pass on any news at once. Now was the time, Mab reminded herself, not to let go and get frightened.

On Monday the Dutch Royal Family found refuge in England, safely transported by the British Navy, and there were sinister German references to a "secret weapon" in use in their swift advance. The same evening on the BBC Mr. Eden appealed for men over and under the military age or otherwise exempt, to form a new force to be called Local Defence Volunteers — for special training to deal with possible landings of German parachute troops in England.

Virginia's midriff went cold when she heard. If the Secretary for War was entertaining the same nightmare as her own, things were really bad. But she felt in a way comforted. She was not alone. She glanced at Mab, sitting silent and self-contained on the other end of the sofa listening to the News, and wondered what Mab thought about parachutists — if Mab had room for any anxiety beyond Jeff's immediate safety.

The telephone rang, and their eyes met, startled and apprehensive, as they both moved towards it. It was so little used these days, this would have to be something important.

It was Bracken, calling from London to say that Jeff had filed a dispatch at Lille that morning, passed through the British censors. He had been as far forward as Brussels and Louvain, which were now behind the new British lines. He had seen the long, agonizing processions of Belgian refugees bombed and machine-gunned on the roads by German planes, had seen the smoking, deserted villages they had left behind them — as Tracy had seen in Poland last September. The American Ambassador was still in Brussels. So far, the main German pressure appeared to be on the French Army around Sedan, and the British in their sector to the north were not as yet heavily engaged. Holland was all through, Bracken said — done in by expert Fifth Column and parachute work.

The Dutch had lasted four days.

When Bracken's three minutes were up

they returned to the drawing-room and sat down rather limply where they had been before, while the BBC Light Music which followed the News burbled gently in the corner.

Mab pressed her hands together and kept her eyes down, striving to conceal even from Virginia the mixed relief and apprehension which possessed her. He was safe, as late as this morning. But there was nothing about his coming away from the war in France. Almost by accident he had got caught in it, and being Jeff he would stay on the story, which was the British sector of the Belgian Front. And the secret hope that she and Sylvia had shared that Jeff might by good fortune write the war from England was lost.

Virginia, also with something to hide, was thinking that when the German Army established itself on the Dutch coastline as they were now free to do, they would be less than two hundred miles by air from London, whereas the German cities were still as far from British bases as they ever were. But surely the French Army was still formidable? Surely the Belgians would hold? Surely Hitler must still fight a whole campaign across the Channel before he could spare planes and troops to invade England too? Unless he risked everything all at once in one colossal knockout blow . . .

Louvain, Liège, Namur, Dinant — all the old, haunted, dreadful names again, till people who could remember 1914 began to feel as though they were living in one of those vivid dreams where everything has a weird familiarity — I have been here before — I have already done this — how — when — who am I. . . .

Jeff was reporting now from Boulogne, where the correspondents had been (they felt) unfairly and too hastily shunted as the British Army continued to fall back to protect its exposed right flank facing the crumbling French divisions around Sedan. Boulogne was being bombed, as the Germans came nearer.

Cambrai, Péronne, St. Quentin. . . . The British front line continued to withdraw as the French continued to reel back upon them, and the Germans kept on coming. General Gamelin was replaced by General Weygand. Churchill's broadcast on the Sunday night left England both stimulated and aghast. The Maginot Line was turned, he said, making no bones about it — the French had nevertheless promised to fight to the end — (how else?) — and finally, said Churchill, would come the battle for what he called Our Island — blood, toil, tears, and sweat. . . . Winston knew how to talk to his countrymen.

Arras, Amiens, Abbéville. . . .

"The men who fought in the old war and are treading the same ground in this one must feel like ghosts," Virginia said to Rosalind on Tuesday afternoon, when she and Mab had bicycled over to the Dower House for a Red Cross working-party and stayed on to have a drink after the other members had scattered homewards in time for the six o'clock News.

"The old war," Rosalind said thoughtfully, turning her glass. "Have you noticed how often we say that? Almost with a fondness, because this one is so much more terrible.''

"And have you noticed,'' said Virginia, "that instead of being frightened or discouraged everybody is suddenly full of beans? Old Mrs. Thingummy this afternoon, with the feather in her hat — instead of beetling off to the back of Wales, she's been getting out her father's cutlass, or whatever, and wants to make kerosene bombs! And darling Winifred organizing the First-Aid Post all over again, and apparently visualizing streams of refugees arriving from our own coast towns! And the men — the old crocks and babes-in-arms drilling with rook-rifles and spears! Aren't people wonderful?''

"Does it seem to you,'' Rosalind began a little too casually, "that the French are keeping very quiet?''

Virginia stared at her.

"Well, there's not much news — I mean, how do we know they aren't reacting the same as we are?''

"I don't know how I know,'' said Rosalind.

"You mean you think they're going to let us down?''

"I can't help wondering."

"*What* an idea!" said Virginia, shocked.

"I know. I shouldn't have mentioned it," Rosalind agreed guiltily.

"Jeff mentioned it, 'way back at Christmas time when he was here," Mab said, having been very silent all afternoon, and they both looked at her in surprise.

"To you, maybe," said Virginia. "What did he say?"

"He said there must be something we didn't know about the French. I didn't think much about it at the time, there were so many other things going on. But if Mr. Churchill had to go over to Paris just to prop them up a few days ago —"

"Was that why he went, do you think?"

"Well, it looks that way," Mab said apologetically.

The evening News after dinner did nothing to hearten them. Virginia turned with a sigh from the map hung up on the wall — Archie's map from the old war, where twenty-six years ago the same French towns had been marked with the same little red pins. It had looked bad then too. In 1918, even, it had looked the worst, just before the tide turned towards what became the November Armistice. The Germans would finally have to stop for breath this time too — neither men nor machines could keep the pace. They would run out of bridges and petrol soon. Unless there was something one didn't know about the French. . . .

Somehow by the twenty-first of May the German Army had swung clean round against the British right, *away* from Paris. And with Abbéville gone, Boulogne was next.

That night at bedtime Mab put out the light in her room, opened the blackout curtains and the window, and slid to her knees with her arms along the sill and her face buried from the full moon which streamed down over the fragrant garden. It was not praying, it was not crying. She stayed there a long time, and then rose, chilled and stiff, and got into bed.

It was quite a while before she could keep her teeth from chattering. Finally she dozed, exhausted, and roused to confused sounds below, the motor of a car, doors closing, voices — she sat up, holding her breath, trying to hear more above the thumping of her heart. Noel was erect on his cushion in the corner, rumbling in his throat, glancing at her for a clue — a sharp, nervous bark escaped him as they listened, and she hushed him with a quick word. . . .

Running footsteps came down the passage, some one tapped at her door and opened it briskly.

"Mab! Wake up! He's here! He's got back safe, come and see!"

It was Sylvia. Generous, loving Sylvia, sharing the first hours of Jeff's return by coming to Farthingale, and where had they got the petrol! She was closing the window and the curtains, and Mab reached for the bedside light and a dressing-gown.

"He was asleep on his feet when he got to London — the correspondents had a very lively time at Boulogne and were taken off by the Navy in one boat as the Guards landed from another, bombs coming down all over the place!" Sylvia was saying. "He and Bracken talked while he changed and had some food, and then

I put him into the back seat of the car to sleep while I drove — you never saw such a *thing* as the trip we've just had getting here, they've got road-blocks and barbed-wire the whole way from London, and they kept waking Jeff up and shoving a light into his face to make sure I wasn't carrying a German spy unawares! It took both his Press pass and my face, besides our identity cards, to get us here. At one road-block they said nobody but an American girl would have thought she *could* get out of London tonight, and what was the hurry, and I said Jeff had to rest fast and get back on the job. And at another they said, 'Give us a song, Miss Sprague!' and I said, 'Hush, you'll wake my husband, he's just back from Boulogne,' and Jeff stuck his head out and said, 'Careless talk!' and everybody was very jolly, and I sang 'em a song since Jeff was awake anyhow, and here we are! Bracken's given Jeff a few days off to pull himself together and do a story on the LDV's down here, and Evadne found some one to take my duty at the Animal Post so I could get away too.''

By now she had bustled Mab, dazed and delighted, to the staircase, and with the dog in a joyful scamper behind they ran down to the drawing-room to find the lights all on and Virginia in a dressing-gown administering a Scotch and soda to Jeff, who looked pretty much at the fag end, in spite of a bath and a shave and fresh clothes in London.

Without a second thought Mab flung herself headlong into his arms and he swung her clean off her feet and set her down again in their standard greeting after overseas absence, and Sylvia said, "I'm starving, let's go and scramble some eggs, oh, I forgot, there's a war on, *are* there any eggs?" And Virginia, who was still shaking because she had been quite sure it had to be German parachutists knocking up the house at that time of night, said there was some nice meat paste which would make sandwiches and that would have to do.

And with the characteristic family disregard for the clock they all adjourned to the kitchen to have a snack.

Boulogne went on the Thursday, and from then on the news became more hair-raising every day. On Sunday the *Observer* so far abandoned the national policy of understatement as to come out with a headline which said: *Britain At Bay*.

Jeff spent a night out with the LDV patrol under the searchlights and the waning moon, got his story, and went back to London with Sylvia. When he had gone and it was too late, Virginia realized she had not asked him what to do about parachutists if they came, and Mab discovered that she had had no chance to talk to him without a lot of other people milling around. The whole visit had been like seeing somebody off on a journey — you think of all the things you meant to say after the train has pulled out. And there was no knowing when he would get another chance to come to Farthingale.

Every day the British Army was pushed back in a diminishing semi-circle around Dunkirk, their backs to the sea. It was plain now that Hitler cared less to take

Paris than to take that Army where it stood, and then try for London. England was his objective, not France. England he hated, France he could deal with. And he still did not comprehend that the easygoing English now meant to have his head if they never had anything else again.

One woke each morning dreading what the day would bring. One kept one's face on straight and ate and smiled and answered when spoken to, and performed the necessary tasks of living, and the additional jobs imposed by the effort to meet whatever might be coming, and regained the privacy of one's room at night with a relief too profound for tears. And above all, one faced perpetually the threat of the Unknown. How would it come? When? Where? and let me not disgrace myself.

So far as possible no one deviated from the normal routine, in order not to give Hitler the satisfaction. Small social engagements were faithfully kept, family anniversaries were soberly observed, shopping, queueing, working-parties, local entertainments, all proceeded as usual.

Virginia had arranged early in the spring for Mab to have tennis lessons from one of the young women at the infant school who had been a games-mistress. It made something definite for Mab to do, Virginia maintained, and for the uprooted games-mistress it meant a little welcome pocket-money. Twice a week Mab walked or bicycled to the village and from there a penny bus ride took her to the gates of Overcreech House where the infants and their attendants were housed, and she returned home the same way in time for lunch, after a workout on the neglected tennis court which had seen such gay parties in Virginia's not too distant youth.

On the twenty-eighth of May Mab arrived back from her tennis lesson breathless, and flung herself at the silent radio in the drawing-room. When it responded the midday News had gone by. She snapped it off and ran for the stairs, where she encountered Virginia on the way down for lunch.

"They're saying in the village that Belgium has quit!" she cried. "Without any warning! They say that leaves our

Army uncovered on the left! They say we're going to bring them back in rowboats!''

"Good Lord, I missed the News!" Virginia looked at her watch. "Who told you this?"

"Some people in the queue at the grocer's, first. Then I asked at the Post Office and they had heard it too. Old Mrs. Pelham says King Leopold ought to be put up against a wall. He *asked* for our Army, didn't he!''

"When it was already too late."

"Jeff was worrying about the French!" said Mab. "And here it's the Belgians instead! What if —" They were descending the stairs hand in hand towards the dining-room where the table was laid for lunch, and fresh flowers filled the vases, and sunlight sparkled on the silver and mahogany. "What if the French should cave in *too?*" said Mab.

"Oh, it's not possible!" said Virginia sanely. "We're so cut off down here, for tuppence I'd run up to Town on the 2:10 and ask Bracken what on earth is going on!''

"Oh, do let's! We could spend the night with Dinah and see *Gone With the Wind!*"

"Not a good idea, I'm afraid," Virginia said hastily, abandoning her impulsive jaunt to Upper Brook Street. A second evacuation was already being talked of. "Oh, well, we shall know soon enough, I expect, if we stay right here."

Belgium had lasted eighteen days.

For a matter of hours, then, England staggered and groped. Their Army was trapped between the Germans and the sea, with both flanks uncovered. They had been let down, right and left. Then slowly the word began to spread, even down in the West. There were trains full of weary, cheerful troops, unshaven, still damp and sandy from the Dunkirk beaches, but safe home again — the miracle of the little boats had happened, the inspired civilian rescue of an army had come off. Dunkirk had passed into history.

What next? Everyone felt a little silly to mention it, but the invasion of England was probably next.

The weather was still heartlessly beautiful the day Mona's letter came — very brief, too unemotional. With several days of his leave still to run, Michael had fallen in with some Navy cronies who had got hold of a Dutch skoot lying in the port of London — and when it headed for the Dunkirk beaches in the fleet of small craft which flowed towards the sea, often without charts or instruments, Michael was aboard. German dive-bombers machine-gunned the decks off La Panne and he was killed, though the skoot survived and stayed afloat to bring back her load to Dover.

All that brightness, all that joy — finished. He hadn't had to go. He wasn't with his own ship when the call came. He might have stood back. But not Michael. Not Mona. They had always gone to meet things.

The war was moving in.

"We are told," said Mr. Churchill in the House on June fourth, *"that Herr Hitler has a plan for invading the British Isles. This has often been thought of before."*

There was laughter in the House, of course, for Winston was at his best that day. But buried in the majestic rumble of his trumpet call to arms was a phrase which few of his hearers failed to notice with a suspicion shared by those who read the speech next day. He said:

"I have myself full confidence that if all do their duty, if nothing is neglected, and if the best arrangements are made, as they are being made, we shall prove ourselves once again able to defend our Island home, to ride out the storm of war, and to outlive the menace of tyranny, if necessary for years, if necessary alone."

There was no emphasis on the word, but England's ears went up. Alone. Winston had been in Paris again last Friday for a meeting of the Supreme War Council. People looked at each other.

And there was more.

"Even though large tracts of Europe and many old and famous States have fallen or may fall into the grasp of the Gestapo and all the odious apparatus of Nazi rule, we shall not flag or fail," the speech rolled on. *"We shall go on to the end, we shall fight in France, we shall fight on the seas and oceans, we shall fight with growing confidence and strength in the air, we shall*

defend our Island, whatever the cost may be, we shall fight on the beaches, we shall fight on the landing-grounds, we shall fight in the fields and in the streets, we shall fight in the hills; we shall never surrender, and even if, which I do not for a moment believe, this Island or a large part of it were subjugated and starving, then our Empire beyond the seas, armed and guarded by the British Fleet, would carry on the struggle. . . ."

All very true. Very well said. But what had Winston learned in Paris last Friday?

It was a thing which Bracken too wanted very much to know, as Hitler pressed home a new attack on the Somme where two British divisions remained in the line with the French, besides a considerable number of RAF squadrons. Hitler was now in a real hurry. The British Army at Dunkirk had got away from him, and might some day be in shape to return and fight again. But the French kept on falling back.

On June tenth Jeff returned to France with a Press unit, bound for the new British Headquarters at Le Mans. It was inconceivable that the French would not make a stand before Paris, as they had done in the other war. Backs to the wall again. And that would be a story.

At six P.M. the same day, about the time Jeff went ashore at Le Havre, Italy declared war and attacked on the Alpine Front.

4

France lasted about three weeks longer than Belgium. The French Government fled to Tours, then to Bordeaux, and the Germans walked into Paris unopposed, and Marshal Pétain asked for an armistice.

"So now we know what Winston meant by alone!" said Virginia, not at all in despair, but with a visible satisfaction that a mystery was solved.

And then the thing that no one had foreseen and that Hitler would never comprehend took place in England. When Belgium went under, England had reeled with angry protest. Now, with France gone too and America standing well back out of Hitler's way, overnight the English steadied, spit on their hands, and went round grinning. Let 'em all come. There's nobody to desert us now. We've nobody to count on but ourselves. Nobody to save, nobody to save us. The Army was home, the family was together again, inside the moated fortress with the drawbridge up. Alone. Just let him *try*.

Virginia had reacted like everybody else, with an unreasoning elation. It made no sense. Things could hardly have been worse, without Hitler actually coming ashore from the Channel. But there it was. They were in the Finals now. The main event, as usual, was between Germany and England. The Island-devil, mentioned by that unfashionable fellow Kipling a generation ago, was now awake, and as he had pointed out, never cool for being curbed.

In the midst of the characteristic upsurge of British morale now that the worst had happened, there arrived at Farthingale a letter from Irene, announcing her decision to evacuate Basil and Mab to America at once. Bracken had had a cable from Fitz and Gwen at Williamsburg, offering to take as many children as they cared to send, whether members of the family or not, to be met in New York and escorted to Williamsburg for the duration. Irene thought it an excellent opportunity, and several of her friends preferred it to the Government scheme for sending children to the Dominions, which was already under discussion in the House.

No bomb could have caused more consternation in the Farthingale household. Even Basil's nurse was against it.

"That's all very well for the Dutch," she said, referring to Princess Juliana's recent arrival in Canada with her little daughters. "Their country was shot out from under them, as you might say. But he's not in England yet, nor ever will be, if you ask me."

What they were asking her, Virginia tried to explain through a certain gratification at Nurse's attitude, was if she would act as escort to the children during the voyage, and stay at Williamsburg with them, at least for a while, if that could be arranged.

"Well, madam, I don't say I won't," said Nurse cautiously. "If it's decided on, that is. But I do think it's a bit much at this time, if you ask me."

"Then I can tell Mrs. Poynter that you are willing to go," said Virginia, who heartily agreed with everything Nurse said, but could not admit it.

"Well, I suppose if it came right down *to* it —" said Nurse, obviously with many reservations. "But Basil is sure to be upset, being sent away from his Mummy like that, and he's always a bit of a handful when he's upset."

Basil, of course, was not consulted about going to Williamsburg. If he had been, he would have voiced a strong preference for staying as near as possible to his Mummy. But Mab was of an age where her views had to be heard, and Virginia was not surprised when she dug in her heels.

"That's all very well for small children like Basil," said Mab. "But I shall be fourteen in August."

"But I thought you *wanted* to see Williamsburg," Virginia suggested feebly.

"I do. But not like that," said Mab.

"There's no disgrace about it, you

know. Lots of children will be leaping at the chance. There was something about it on the BBC and I thought at the time —"

"And *I* thought at the time what mugs they were to think of such a thing!" said Mab, who very seldom interrupted. "They'll all feel pretty silly if Hitler doesn't come after all!"

"Perhaps we ought to try to get your mother on the telephone," Virginia murmured weakly, for she couldn't but agree with Mab.

"It's Basil they're worried about," Mab said without resentment. "He can go, he's too little to understand."

"Well, after all, Mab, the bombing is sure to start now, if not an actual invasion, and if Hitler should go into Ireland, and some people think he will, it won't be any safer here in the West than in London, and —"

"When Jeff left England I was here," said Mab, too quietly. "How would it look if I wasn't here when he came back?"

Jeff had last reported on Press Wireless from Tours, which was an extension of chaos and the French censors had allowed him to say so. At that time he intended to follow the Government, which had already gone to Bordeaux. And there he was expected to find a boat which would bring him to England.

"I'm sure if we could consult Jeff he would recommend a trip to Williamsburg now," Virginia insisted, hoping she was right. "A voyage in convoy is no great risk these days, and we might even get you on an American ship —"

"There won't be any more American ships," said Mab, who read the newspapers.

"Unless they send one specially for evacuation, there's some talk of that."

"Gran, it's for *children!* I'm almost fourteen!"

"But darling, what am I going to tell your mother?"

"Tell her Basil will go, and I won't."

"But don't you think it would save a lot of trouble and argument if —"

"No, no, *no,* I won't leave England while Jeff is away!" cried Mab, and ran out of the room.

Oh, dear, well, I can't tell Irene *that,* thought Virginia. And then — I suppose it's a good thing, she thought. In some ways Williamsburg might be more dangerous for Mab than anywhere in England. Perhaps this way she will escape a different kind of risk. This way she won't see the portraits of Julian and Tibby. Gwen seems to have forgotten about that in her anxiety about invasion.

The next day Nigel arrived on the afternoon train from London, preceding his telegram by an hour or so, so that he had had to share the only taxi as far as the crossroads and walk the rest of the way. Virginia was almost as much surprised as she was pleased to see him.

"I couldn't use the telephone," he explained, "and I have only twenty-four hours clear, but I felt I had to come and make sure you were all right."

"We're just the same as usual," Virginia said.

"That's what I was afraid of," said Nigel. "Now, there are certain things you must attend to at once."

"Such as burying the silver in the

garden?'' she asked flippantly.

"Such as having your passport and identity papers and spare cash in a safe place. And a bag packed with necessities. I know that sounds fantastic and futile, but I'd feel better if you'd pay attention and take a few precautions.''

"Nigel, do you really think they're coming?''

"No,'' said Nigel deliberately. "But if they do, I shall be stuck in London and you will be here, practically alone, and I shall want to know I've done my best for you.'' He took out his wallet and removed from it a number of crisp banknotes. "I don't want to seem theatrical, but first of all I want you to sew some of these inside the lining of a warm coat which you will keep handy, and have some of them always on you, somehow, and hide some in your room — in the lining of the curtains, or some such place.''

"But Nigel, I could go to the bank here —''

"If you like, but don't draw out a lot, not down here. I want you to find a stout bag or knapsack, and pack it with what I have written down here —" He gave her a neat list. "Most of it will be in your store cupboard, I expect. What sort of shape is your passport in?"

"Bracken keeps it up to date. But I won't —"

"Where is it?"

"In my desk."

"Please bring it to me. And your identity card. How do you carry it?"

"In my hand-bag."

"Let me see."

While they were in the midst of this, Mab came hunting for Virginia, and was charmed to find Nigel too. She was carrying a sort of circular, printed on both sides, which looked rather like a cheap advertisement.

"I say, have you seen this?" she said, handing it to Virginia. "Isn't it gruesome?"

The paper was headed by the Royal Arms, Issued by the Ministry of Information, and began in large type: *If the invader comes. What to do — and how to do it*. With their three heads together, silent, with a growing incredulity that the thing had actually entered their lives, they read the seven numbered paragraphs. . . . *You must remain where you are. The order is "Stay Put." . . . When you receive an order make quite sure that it is a true order and not a faked order. . . . Keep watch. . . . Do not give any German anything. Do not tell him anything. . . . Be ready to help the military in any way . . . felling trees, wiring them together or blocking roads with cars. . . . Remember always that the best defence of Great Britain is the courage of her men and women. . . .*

Why, Virginia wondered angrily, aware that her hand holding the flimsy sheet was not quite steady, *why* should it be so frightening! It was designed to inform and reassure. There was really no excuse for the sickening wave of pure terror which had run through her as she read. *Make sure that no invader will be able to get hold of your cars, petrol, maps, or bicycles.* . . . Make sure how?

"Maybe old Mrs. Pelham was right to oil up her grandfather's duelling pistols," she heard herself saying.

"Darling, you must be serious," said poor Nigel.

"And do you think Mrs. Pelham isn't?" she heard herself ask lightly.

"Irene expects to have the children's passage by the end of the week," Nigel went on, deciding to ignore her. "Nurse's too, of course. They'll go by way of Montreal and will have to take a train to New York. The Spragues will meet them there."

"I had an idiotic letter from Gwen, begging me to come home with the children," said Virginia, folding the paper once across and laying it aside, wondering if her face looked as stiff as it felt, hoping her voice sounded right. "I wasn't taking any notice of it till Irene went off her head too. They seem to think in America that England is all through, and we haven't started yet!" she added, as though she had not seen the seven rules sent out by the Ministry, emerging to her own surprise from the first paralyzing shock. "Anybody'd think we were Belgium!"

"Mummy, they're only facing facts, in America," Nigel told her patiently.

"Even Churchill said —"

"I know quite well what he said. And there was nothing about sending our children away." Virginia began to listen to herself with an impersonal admiration. "What's got into you, Nigel, I never thought that any son of mine —"

"I haven't given up, any more than you have," he assured her firmly. "But now Hitler has got to *try,* and it's going to be hell's delight here for a while. If I had a child —" He hesitated.

"Well?" said Virginia relentlessly.

"I can only thank God I don't have to decide," he concluded, with his rare, slanting smile. "Anyway, in the case of Mab and Basil, it's all in the family, and Mab has always wanted to see Williamsburg."

There was a silence. He looked from one to the other inquiringly.

"I'm not going," said Mab. "Just Basil and Nurse."

"Oh, Lord." Nigel put a hand to his head. "It's all settled for you to go. What does your mother say?"

"She thinks I'll come round, but I

won't. Even Nurse is against it. She says it will upset Basil far worse than a few bombs here."

"My dear child, it's not just a question of a few bombs here any longer," Nigel explained, as though he spoke to some one who was a little lacking. "If the Germans contrive to occupy even a part of this country, even for a short time —"

"You don't really think they *will,*" said Mab.

"No, I don't," he agreed promptly. "But neither did the Dutch and look at them now. We have to assume the worst and prepare for it. I should think you'd jump at the chance to go to Williamsburg for a while."

"Grandmother Tibby didn't go looking for a refuge when the war came to Williamsburg," said Mab.

"That was a little war. You could put it in your pocket."

"The colonists were ragged and hungry and short of guns and men, and far worse off than we are now," said Mab. "And the British Army must have looked just as bad to them as the Nazis do to us."

"Now, look here —" Nigel began.

"Anne says I'm right not to go," said Mab, producing the clincher. "Anne says that when it's all over and Hitler never set foot in England after all, the ones that ran away won't know where to look."

"You see?" said Virginia to Nigel, with an expressive gesture. "Young England!"

Nigel, worried as he was, couldn't but grin.

"I must see Anne while I am here," he said, almost to himself.

"She came in when I did. I'll tell her you're here." Mab started for the door.

"Ask her to come in here," Virginia said. "Nigel is telling us what to do and what not to do, better than the Ministry can." And when Mab had gone she added, "I suppose they haven't much extra money, those girls. We shall have to look after them too, you know, if anything really bad begins."

"Yes, please let's not lose sight of Anne," said Nigel, and Virginia glanced up at him with interest, and then took a good look at Anne as she entered the room, holding back a little on Mab's hand, smiling her wide, unself-conscious smile at sight of the visitor.

"Hullo, are you the man about the invasion?" Anne asked cheekily, and sobered under his steady gaze.

"Have you got a passport?" Nigel asked her in his most legal manner.

"No. I've never had one. It's a bit late now, isn't it? Holidays abroad aren't what they used to be."

"Have you any spare cash?"

"I don't know what you mean by spare, I've got about two pounds, nine, and thruppence."

"But haven't you got a bank account?" Nigel insisted, rather like a kindly uncle.

"No. I only work there."

"You mean that two pounds is all you've got in the world?"

"Just about. I sent some money home last week, they're fixing up their shelter."

"Then you really must allow me —" Nigel's hand went again to his breast pocket.

"What for?" Anne asked bluntly.

"Emergencies," Nigel replied as bluntly, and held out to her two five-pound notes.

"Call it a loan," he said.

"Well, thank you very much, but I don't see any need for it," said Anne, making no move to take the money. "We're told to stay where we are and not go on the roads if there is any sort of trouble — and the Bank is responsible for us here. Unless, of course —" She turned a suddenly apprehensive look on Virginia. "— unless your mother wants to close up the house or —"

"Nigel is behaving a bit like a mother hen," Virginia said unfairly. "I have already assured him that I'll look after you like my own, no matter what happens."

"That's awfully kind of you both, but I really have no right to —"

"Don't be so stiff-necked and obtuse," said Nigel in his incisive lawyer's voice. "When this war is over I want to know where you are, and I want to find you alive and well."

Three pairs of eyes stared at him in varying degrees of doubt, suspicion, and incredulity — Anne, Mab, and Virginia could think of no possible explanation of the above statement except that Nigel must be — well, interested. It came as an equal astonishment to each of them, in a different way.

Virginia recovered first.

"That I will guarantee to undertake personally," she said.

"Thank you," said Nigel formally, and as Anne would not take the money, he laid it down in front of Virginia. "I'm sorry to be so abrupt, but I feel rather pressed for time."

And Mab, looking from him to Anne, saw that Anne was blushing from the V of her blouse to the roots of her hair, and wondered if Nigel had just proposed, right there in front of everybody, and what Anne was going to do about it.

"And now," said Virginia, rising with all the bank-notes in her hand and the list of things to be packed in a bag, "Mab and I will go and gather all this together —"

Mab followed her from the room, resisting a backward glance as she closed the door.

There was a long silence when they had gone.

"I am most terribly sorry," said Nigel at last, not a bit like a lawyer. "I can't think why I did it like that, except that I'm a bit rattled like everybody else. Will you forgive me? It's only Mummy, after all, and she was bound to catch on soon."

"But — I don't —" Anne put both hands to her face with a sound half gasp, half laugh.

"Naturally, you don't," said Nigel. "I can't expect you to. But now that I've put my foot in it, I might as well say that there hasn't been a day since I last saw you that I haven't thought of you — wondered about you — and looked forward to seeing you again. This warden job I'm in now leaves a lot of time for thinking, when one might otherwise be reading, working, killing time with friends — especially on the night shift, as I am. When you came in the door just now, so smiling and sweet and safe, I got it right between the eyes — that nothing must happen to you if I can prevent it. I know it was clumsy of me, I do apologize."

"Oh, *no* —" Both her hands started towards him, protectively, and then were withheld. "You mustn't sound as though you had done something rude! It was only —" Again the lovely blush swept upward, and this time he saw it.

"Only —?" he prompted, watching.

"It was as though you had read my mind, I — didn't know where to look."

"Read your mind?" he repeated, and took her hands, and when she tried to draw them away he held them, still resisting, in his. "Anne —?" he said, with a question.

"I had let myself dream," she confessed, looking down at their hands. "I had let myself *pretend*. I've always told myself fairy stories, it's childish of me, I know, but as soon as I came to this house it sct mc off again on another make-believe."

"The house, yes — but where was I?" And when she would not answer — "Anne?"

"We — don't know each other," she gasped, pulling at her hands, and he let them go, and she rose and walked away from him down the room.

"Anne, was I in the dream?" He

waited, standing where he was. "Oh, yes, I know it's all too sudden and too soon. It's not fair to press you now, when everyone is overwrought."

"Yes, that's it," she agreed faintly. "You might — feel quite differently when things are normal again. And I feel sure they will be, don't you?"

"You misunderstand me," he said gently. "My mind is quite made up. But you have a right to some sort of proper courtship when things permit."

"C-courtship —?" said Anne incredulously, and turned to face him across the room.

"Flowers — little dinners — dancing — house-parties — if those things ever come again. Anyway, a chance to know me well enough to decide if you can put up with me."

"B-but you can't mean — how can you possibly —"

"I don't know how it came about, if that's what you're asking. I only know that you're always with me now — your eyes, your voice — I'm just as surprised as you are, I suppose — except that I'm getting used to it and it's just been sprung on you entirely in the wrong way, I admit. Perhaps it's those long lonely hours on night duty. Perhaps it's the long lonely days and nights before that began. I was going quietly crazy with my loneliness, until I saw you. I couldn't seem to lay hold of anything — there didn't seem to be anybody I needed or wanted — I was empty and dreary and old before my time. And now I need you. You comfort me. I'm going to love you very much. Do you mind?"

"Oh, my dear —!" said Anne, and opened her arms.

5

It was not a thing which Virginia had anticipated, but she was quite content that an engagement should exist between Nigel and Anne Phillips, whose first name she had never used till the toasts were being drunk. Anne was gentle and sweet and soft, and plainly would worship Nigel all her life, and that would be good for him, which was all that mattered these days. The wedding would come later, when things had a little resolved themselves. Meanwhile there would be the deep satisfaction to each that the other was aware — and there was the post, which still functioned regularly.

Anne, watching timidly for reservations on the part of Nigel's mother, began gradually to hope that it wasn't just good manners, and that she might be welcome in this magic household where she had so allowed her imagination to run away with her. She still could not quite believe that she would ever belong here as a member of the family — she understood that it was a formidable family, headed by the fabulous Bracken Murray, who was Nigel's uncle — but so far there was nothing to make her feel an outsider. Anne bloomed during dinner that night, with a new brilliance in her mysterious, heavy-lidded eyes and a new tilt to her generous mouth. Being engaged makes a girl *feel* pretty very quickly, and it shows.

During the evening they listened to Churchill's broadcast, and thanked God again for such a leader: *"Therefore, in casting up this dread balance sheet and contemplating our dangers with a disillusioned eye, I see great reason for intense vigilance and exertion, but none whatever for panic or despair,"* the strong, fighting voice declared into the quiet room. *"The whole fury and might of the enemy must very soon be turned on us. Hitler knows that he will have to break this Island or lose the war. If we can stand up to him, all Europe may be free and the life of the world may move forward into the broad, sunny uplands. But if we fail, then the whole world, including the United States, including all we have known and cared for, will sink into the abyss of a new Dark Age made more sinister and perhaps more protracted by the lights of perverted science. Let us therefore brace ourselves to our duties, and so bear ourselves that if the British Empire and its Commonwealth last for a thousand years, men will still say, 'This was their finest hour.'"*

When they realized that he had finished, they looked at each other, their throats too tight for speech. Tears were slipping quietly down Anne's face. She wiped them away with her fingers, and her eyes followed Nigel's tall figure as he moved to shut off the radio.

It was Mab who first found words.

"He sounds like a tired lion," she said.

Not even Virginia knew what it had cost to make the decision from which Mab never wavered after that day. The coveted chance to see Williamsburg had been presented at last, but with too high a price-tag. To see it without Jeff there would have been disappointing enough at best. To use it as a bolt-hole while Jeff was out reporting a war which was being fought to preserve what Williamsburg stood for became impossible.

And yet one lived with fear. It was fear which rolled in across one's consciousness like surf on a beach as one woke to each new day, and set one's insides to churning so that one was never sure that food would stay down — though one ate conscientious meals as they came in order not to be conspicuous in the general self-possession which prevailed. To go off one's feed now would be regarded as dramatization, which was always frowned on in the family, and which as a rule only Basil descended to. Once Jeff was back in England, she promised herself, it would be easier. More than half the fear was for him.

His telegram came the same day the French armistice terms were published. After four days in an overloaded, unseaworthy cargo boat from Bordeaux he had arrived at Falmouth and sent off identical messages to Farthingale and London: *Home again. Love. Jeff.* Then he got into a crowded train and walked in the door at Upper Brook Street an hour ahead of his telegram.

So there was still time for Mab to accompany Basil and Nurse to Williamsburg with Jeff's approval, and the pressure was still on from everybody but Virginia and Nurse. The fear was still there too, in the pit of her stomach, for the French were going to be even less use than anyone had supposed.

Mab fought it out again that night in her room. No fair waiting just to see what Jeff would say. She was old enough to make up her own mind. A long time before war had come to England Jeff had once recounted to her a family legend to the effect that a hundred and fifty years ago Tibby at the age of sixteen had dressed herself in her twin brother's clothes and gone to meet Lafayette's army before Jamestown, in order to be near Julian who was one of Lafayette's aides. There was nothing to prove that Tibby was not frightened too.

When the time came for Basil and Nurse to sail, Hitler had begun to bomb the English ports as foreseen, and getting aboard a liner was likely to be a nervous business. Jeff came down with Irene to escort them to Liverpool, but this time Sylvia stayed on duty at the Animal Post in London, where there were occasional alerts without bombs.

Irene had reluctantly surrendered Mab's passage to another child, giving up on the long distance argument. As usual her attention was centered on Basil but now she had begun to have qualms about losing sight of him, and for his safety on the way.

Mab sat next to Jeff at dinner that night, in a quiet ecstasy at his being there within reach of her hand, although nothing but general conversation was possible in so small a gathering. After coffee in the drawing-room Irene went up to see Basil in bed, assuming that Virginia had nothing better to do than accompany her. When they had disappeared up the staircase Mab found Jeff's speculative eyes upon her and hunched her shoulders in a small, derisive movement.

"I'm in disgrace with Mummy," she said.

"So I gather." He set down his coffee-cup and prepared to give her his undivided attention. "I was kind of surprised myself. It's a good chance for you to see Williamsburg, isn't it?"

"Now, don't *you* start!" said Mab.

"I'm probably wrong," Jeff said, "but I happen to think it's better this way."

"You mean you think he won't come."

"When I left France I thought he would. There is something about defeatism that spreads and penetrates. I shall never understand what happened over there. As

325

a matter of fact, I don't understand what has happened here, either. But now I've got a funny sort of feeling that he is not going to take England."

"Well, of course he isn't!" said Mab, and he sat looking at her in silence for a long moment.

He was still readjusting to Churchill's Island. He had returned to London in time, he thought, to assist at the end of the world. And once there, he found England happily convinced that it was "just going in." When he expressed surprise, Bracken had said only, "The English are tough. You'll see."

Jeff's first retreat from France before Dunkirk had been more or less official in nature, and he had crossed the Channel in a British destroyer. There had been, for all the haste and confusion, morale — dignity and discipline and decency. Since then, returning to Paris only a day before the Germans overran it, he had seen France crumble from the top down. Instead of barricades and mounted guns he had found only deserted boulevards, shops with all the shutters down, hotels which refused admittance — and instead of gunfire, a great silence. He had made his way on foot to the office of the permanent Paris correspondent, arriving there hungry and angry and incredulous. He was not expected, and was freely advised that unless he meant to wait for the Occupation — which the Boss in London would not approve — he had better get going. For a moment he had hesitated. But the Paris story would be covered, and the Government had gone South. He was able to locate and join a carful of fellow journalists who were headed for Tours and bedlam, where Press Wireless still functioned, at eightpence a word.

Stocking the car with what food and drink and petrol they could buy at Tours, they had set out the next day for Bordeaux, to which the Government had preceded them. They travelled by roundabout lanes away from the main highways, which were choked with hysteria and horror. They passed sunny villages whose inhabitants seemed still unaware that the Germans were in Paris. But as they neared Bordeaux the panic there overflowed and swamped them. They stopped for coffee at a small café when Pétain's voice came over the radio in the kitchen, announcing that he had asked the Germans for terms. The waitress who served them was in tears, and the gilt letters which spelled *American War Correspondent* on the shoulders of their uniforms drew hostile glances in the hot, frantic streets.

Through the Embassy they got passage on a small Dutch cargo boat which was on its way back from South Africa. The harbor at Le Verdon was bombed as they steamed out, with roughly eight times the ship's normal complement aboard. And although few could have survived a hit in the circumstances, the exhausted passengers on the crowded decks remained almost indifferent to this final hazard. Food was short, they lived on two skimpy meals a day for an endless, blistering voyage. At Falmouth a group of cool, smiling women from the WVS had met them with tea and sandwiches. Looking into their serene faces, Jeff could only conclude that no one in England had been listening to the news from across the Channel.

Not so, but quite otherwise, said Bracken. Look around you. And Jeff saw the Home Guard drilling with wooden guns, and the sentries and barbed wire in Whitehall, and the old carts and ploughs strewn on the fields against troop-carrying planes, and the guerilla warfare school at Osterley. . . .

And now Mab, as tough as any of them.

"Tell me something," he said. "Why aren't you afraid?"

"But I am!" She glanced over her shoulder towards the stairs. "I'm terrified. Don't give me away."

He made a rueful shrug of laughter, with an affectionate smile.

"You don't believe me, do you," she accused him. "Well, it's true. I'm not like the rest of you. I'm a coward. I'm only praying that by the grace of God it won't show when the time comes."

"Well, believe it or not, by the grace of God it usually doesn't," he said.

"What happens?" She was watching him intently, for now he had been there, he had heard bombs, and seen people die, in France.

"You find you have a sort of extra gadget," he explained. "They call it adrenalin, I think. But they're only guessing. It's really just your own personal gadget, and it works. I promise you it will work."

"So that nobody knows you're afraid?"

"So that you don't disgrace yourself," said Jeff. "So that sometimes you even surprise yourself."

"How do I know I've got one too?"

"I'll bet you," said Jeff, and took out a half-crown and laid it on the mantelpiece. "Let it stay there. If ever you have hysterics — it's yours, I lose."

"Oh, Jeff, if only we could be together now —!" She went to him blindly and buried her face against his coat, while he held her, his cheek against her hair. "The worst part is worrying about you," she said, muffled. "Nothing will happen to us down here in the country, unless the invasion actually comes off. But in London you'll be in the front line, whatever happens! Every time they drop a bomb on London I'll wonder about you

— and you can't be forever ringing up to say you're all right! I promised myself that if you just got back to England I could bear the rest. But it's hard to make do with that. It's hard!"

"I know," he said, holding her.

"If only I could be in London *too* —" she heard herself saying to her own astonishment, for she had always believed she was thankful — and ashamed — that she was not obliged to be in London. Now it seemed to her suddenly that the one thing that mattered was to be beside him, wherever he went — so that if anything happened to him she would be there, so that she need not sit helplessly miles away waiting for second-hand news. The world might be coming to an end, but all the more reason not to lose sight of him now — because if Jeff were going to die she had to die too, beside him where she belonged.

"That would be worse for me," he said quietly, and she looked up at him, in his arms. "I can worry about you less if you're here at Farthingale," he said, appalled to find that his voice was not quite steady. Her eyes — the green eyes of Tibby's portrait — were swimming with tears, which dazzled him — her lips were set against the working of her small throat. He felt her trembling from head to foot, and it ran through his own body from hers, like a current. . . . *Tibby — it felt like this with Tibby.* . . . He was keyed very high with controlled nerves, he had gone short of sleep for weeks, braced for an ordeal which no one could predict. And now he recalled suddenly, in a dizzy wave, a night in Boulogne when a bomb came down in the square outside the hotel and he had come to lying on the floor in the approved air-raid posture, face down, hands locked behind his head, and in the reverberating silence of the wrecked room had distinctly heard himself saying, aloud: *"I will come back to you, never fear — you are mine, Tibby, I want you —"* In the press of more recent sensations he had forgotten that lightheaded interlude at Boulogne. The *Times* man had come shouting down the corridor to rescue him, and they had prudently retired, shaken but unhurt, to the basement shelter where restoratives were available. Now, in Virginia's drawing-room, he heard his own voice again saying, "I will come back to you, my darling, never fear —" and checked himself on the brink of the abyss, a ringing in his ears.

"Jeff, I want to say a sort of charm, do you mind?"

He shook his head, unable to speak, and voluntarily she drew away from him till only their hands still held, warm and strong, between them.

" 'There shall no evil befall thee,' " said Mab, looking into his eyes. " 'For He shall give His angels charge over thee, to keep thee in all thy ways. They shall bear thee up in their hands, lest thou dash thy foot against a stone.' " Then she bent, and laid her lips against his hands that held hers. Neither of them was aware that Tibby had spoken again across the generations, the same words Julian had heard in the Sprague parlor in Williamsburg the night before the army marched to Yorktown.

"Mab —" Jeff drew her to the sofa and made her sit down beside him, her hands

333

in his. "Mab, I feel very humble. I don't deserve all this."

"It isn't something we can choose or refuse," she said simply. "I was born loving you, that's all. We can't do anything about that now."

"No," he agreed gently. "There isn't a thing we can do about it. Remember that part of it, won't you, Mab."

V.

Autumn in London.

1940

1

Life in London itself at first remained fantastically normal, and many evacuation areas heard sirens and bombs before London had so much as an alert. But even at Dover, which was being shelled now as well as bombed, the British were staying put. Well, if they think they can *scare* us, people said, sweeping up glass and digging each other out of débris.

Meanwhile, methodical as a white mouse in a laboratory, Hitler pursued his terrible pattern. After the war of nerves and prophecies of doom came the bombing of shipping and the Channel ports, the attacks on the forward aerodromes, the surprise spot-bombing to confuse and scatter the defending forces — all gathering momentum as July ran into August. The RAF had its own pattern, prompt and deadly, rising to meet each new onslaught, taking toll, taking losses.

Unmoved except to derision by horrendous German threats to "Make England blind and deaf," they set about arming their fortress with a kind of grim gaiety that got things done. The beaches bristled with barbed wire and blockhouses, concrete road-blocks went up, every field and golf course that provided landing-room for a horsefly was ploughed into ridges or strewn with derelict vehicles and machinery. It was everybody's war. And "You can always take one with you" became a kind of password.

Jeff had been fascinated and amused. What he had experienced within himself, he now saw happening to a whole country. When it came, you stood up to it. More than once in France it had seemed to him as though his heart hit the roof of his mouth, during the long downward scream of the bombs, but when the bang was over and the walls had bulged and settled back again and the floor had ceased to heave, his heart was still there on the job, still in the groove. He wasn't an invalid, he wasn't even a handicap case, he didn't have to depend on the bottle of pink stuff in order to stay on his feet — he could take it just as well as people who didn't have dicky hearts. And this was in itself a miracle.

"That's not to say I never turn a hair or bat an eye," he told Sylvia after his second return from France. "I'm not bragging, understand that. I'm all green around the gills, no doubt, but I don't have to lie down flat the way I used to if I so much as tried to catch a train."

"Oh, stuff," said Sylvia, pleased. "You've been catching trains ever since I married you."

"That's what I mean," he said earnestly. "If you hadn't married me, I'd probably have my knees under a nice safe desk in the New York office."

"And you'd probably live longer," said Sylvia.

"Not necessarily. I wasn't a very good

risk a few years ago."

"And now you're just as good a risk as anybody in London."

"Just about. No more. No less. But it's not my heart I'll die of."

She came and sat down on his lap, rubbing her cheek along his.

"It's been good, hasn't it," she said. "Even with all this hanging over us, hasn't it been *good!*"

"Honey, there's no need to sound as though it was over!" he objected, cradling her.

"I never said it was. But even if there wasn't any more — oh, Jeff, nobody's better off!"

"So you wouldn't trade me for some guy with a red band on his cap and three rows of ribbons?"

"Nope."

"Thank you," said Jeff politely.

Even if there wasn't any more. She could not have told why she said that, so casually, without apprehension — except that the future no longer stretched ahead to a comfortable three score and ten, the future was *now,* before whatever was coming arrived. The future was what you could make out of whatever you had left, for it was no longer possible to assume that everything would be the same a year, a month, a week from now. There was only today, and what you already had. Tomorrow might not be so good. Tomorrow, in fact, might not bear thinking of. But today, thought Sylvia, nobody was luckier, nobody was better off. And because tomorrow couldn't change that, couldn't spoil what had already been, because that much was already perfect, inviolate, and safe, tomorrow could come, and do its worst. You were still ahead.

And this, though she did not know it, was the turning point of Sylvia's war. Like Jeff, in her own way she had crossed the bridge and left panic behind. Like Jeff, she knew without ringing any bells or blowing any trumpets that by the grace of God she could take it.

On August fifteenth, when Hitler had promised to enter London for his triumph, he hadn't even dropped a bomb on it, and people were laughing about a German broadcast which described the English population as fear-crazed. "It's a British panic — they've got it backwards," said one of the American correspondents at the Savoy. On the twentieth, Churchill's ringing tribute to the boys of the RAF somewhat explained why Hitler was delayed — the English still owned the air over their island. On the twenty-fourth German bombers actually got to London and the sirens went, and there were bombs at last, and casualties. But the Germans had losses too. Three to one in planes, fifteen to one in personnel. He'll have to do better than that, people said, digging out.

And so Mab's birthday had come round again, in a world at war. Jeff sent regrets that he could not take his eye off Hitler long enough to come down to Farthingale and drink her health. He also sent a hamper of goodies from Fortnum's, and a parcel of books from Hatchard's for blackout reading. Hitler took no particular notice of the day.

At the end of the month, however, he made another speech — he would raze

British cities, he said, in retaliation for recent visits from the RAF to the Reich, which had apparently begun to get under his skin. Let him get on with it, then, people said. Three months since Dunkirk, a year since the declaration of war, and no invasion yet, they said. If he can't do it now he can never do it. What's he waiting for?

There was a general feeling that the mid-September tides and moon would be his last chance this year, and that now he must make his try. Along with what Bracken called the Come-on-damn-you attitude, a growing tightness in the midriff had begun again, as the London raids got heavier. He was due to spring something new again. He always had something up his sleeve. Now for the secret weapon. Gliders full of troops, some thought. Cross-Channel destruction on an undreamed-of scale was mentioned seriously. Or gas.

As September came in, the pattern changed. He had given up trying to destroy the ports, to knock out the aerodromes, to kill off the RAF. He had gone to work on London's nerves. Day and night now the sirens went. At first people watched the dogfights from the streets, cheered the Spitfires, and scattered from machine-gun bullets when the German planes flew low. Harrod's Store got a hole in its roof which upset its sprinkler system, and it shoppers got the giggles.

Even with the nervous ones, the strange adaptability of the human fabric began to operate. It was almost impossible to be frightened to death half a dozen times a day. You finally had to eat and sleep and work, without bolting into a shelter every time there was a warning, even without rushing up to the roof to see the fun. Theaters and restaurants resumed their routine, functioned steadily right through the alerts. People began to ask one another casually if the raid was still on, because they had forgotten to listen for the All-Clear — though you could always tell by looking at the nearest policeman, he wore his gas-mask round in front at the ready, if there was a raid on. . . .

But Hitler was getting down to it now.

His time was running out. He was always a dirty fighter, anything could happen now. . . .

The household in Upper Brook Street was having tea, that first Saturday afternoon in September. Bracken had happened to come home early, it was Sylvia's day off, and Dinah was just arriving from her office at the WVS when the sirens went. Only Jeff was absent.

"They're at it again down the River," Dinah said, in the queer moment of dead silence which always seemed to follow the first howl of the alert. "I thought I heard crumps even before I started for home. Apparently they're coming up this way now." She poured her tea with a steady hand, and carried it to the window, still wearing her hat. "It's getting pretty noisy towards the south."

"Churchill paid a visit to Dover the other day," Bracken said. "Maybe they're going to raze it in retaliation."

"They're nearer than Dover," said Dinah, and the telephone rang, which, when a raid had started, meant something pretty drastic.

"Blast," muttered Bracken as he reached for it. "I'd just got settled in." The conversation was very brief. "Man can't even get a cup of tea any more," he complained. "Take it easy, now — I'm off."

"What's happened?" Sylvia set down her cup with a clink. "Where are you off to?"

"The East End. Something's up. If you get hold of Jeff ask him to get in touch with the office." He collected his gas-mask, for they were being done again, and his tin hat, and kissed his womenfolk, and was gone.

"I think," said Dinah when the door had closed behind him, "that this is going to be a nasty one."

"Just in time to spoil dinner," Sylvia remarked, for one had to say something. She wondered if any amount of familiarity with the sound of the siren would ever eliminate that first sick crunch in the stomach. It was humiliating, degrading, and silly, and she was perfectly sure that it didn't happen to anyone else. Not that one could ask.

"That bomb in Regent Street hasn't gone off yet," said Dinah. "You have to go round it."

They ate a rather silent dinner in the dining-room. Bracken did not return and Sylvia began to wrestle again with the familiar necessity to worry about where Jeff was. The maid who served them reported as she brought the coffee that the sky over the City was as pink as dawn, and it wouldn't be much of a blackout tonight. When they had finished coffee they went out on the front steps to look.

Fires. And rolling black smoke. And a smell of burning. There were tremendous great fires down at the docks, which would act as targets all night long for more German planes. In contrast to what was happening down the River the West End streets were ominously quiet, almost deserted. But even while they stood there a fire company dashed by towards the pink sky.

Their warden passed along his beat, and touched the brim of his helmet with a forefinger.

"Better make yourselves cosy in the

345

shelter tonight," he said. "They're really letting go this time!"

But there was nothing directly overhead and they returned to the drawing-room and sat down together, with books and cigarettes, trying to get through the evening. Slowly they became conscious of a vibration in the air, like a giant mosquito with hiccups. A.A. guns barked angrily, and the crump of bombs in the distance came nearer as they listened. Midge, who had gone to bed in his swing, woke up, went down briskly for a drink of water, and began to sing. They exchanged amused looks, and Dinah said, "Bother, I suppose we may as well go downstairs."

Carrying their books and knitting and Midge in his cage, they resettled themselves in the comfortable shelter room, not for the first time, to wait out the night. Sylvia's hands were cold, and she felt a little queasy. Jeff had gone down to Dover again that morning, because once you had been to Dover you couldn't stay away. There was also a conviction among the correspondents that Dover was the place to be when It happened. Sylvia, who would have preferred to have him nearer at hand when the Germans came ashore, told herself once more in exasperation at her own reflexes that she must get used to it. Look at Dinah, she told herself. And Bracken's out in it too.

Towards midnight, in what seemed to be a lull, they went upstairs again and opened the street door. Instinctively they drew back, as from a furnace. There was no blackout. Reflected from the low billowing smoke ceiling which was the sky, the red glow of fire illumined London like infernal day. The smell of burning was everywhere, and ashes settled in their hair. The lull, if there had been one, was suddenly over. Ack-ack fire, the crump, *crump,* CRUMP of a stick of bombs approaching, the mumble and whine of planes, the patter of falling metal, struck them like a blow.

Dinah closed the door and stood a moment with her back against it in the darkened hall — futilely shutting out the sight and sound of London on fire.

"Well!" she said, more in indignation

than dismay. "What a night!"

They made their way back to the basement room, and in its comforting light they looked at each other silently and sat down. Where did the flames stop? How much longer could they sit there in safety? How would they know? What about the rest of them — Bracken — Jeff — Evadne — Mona — Nigel. . . .

"I'm glad it's your night at home," Dinah said at last.

"I don't know — being on duty helps to hold you up, somehow —"

"I was thinking of me," said Dinah with a little smile. "It helps to hold *me* up to have you here."

Sylvia could find nothing to say. It was the first time Dinah had left any such opening. Sylvia decided it was probably just tact, to make her feel better.

She watched Dinah light a cigarette, noticing that her fingers were quite steady. Sylvia wanted one herself, but knew her own hands would betray her. She had never learned, because one didn't discuss it, that everybody had his own secret soft spot of fear — and hers was fire. She had always promised herself that she could stand up to anything but fire, and her knowledge of incendiary bomb drill was exceeded only by her hatred of it. She knew that you couldn't beat an incendiary bomb to death, nor kick it into the gutter, nor stand there and watch it. Her lightning swift manipulation of tongs, shovel, and sand was the admiration of everyone. Tonight all London was on fire. It was only a question of time, Sylvia thought, till the flames reached the street outside.

Dinah put a record on the portable gramophone and sat down again, her face set in its usual serene composure. Almost immediately the house jarred and shuddered from a new impact.

"That's enough," said Dinah, rising again. "They really must come down here."

Gregson, the butler, veteran of the old war, worked at a First-Aid Post around the corner. His elderly wife and the parlormaid insisted they felt most comfortable in the kitchen during a raid, where with their feet on the fender and knitting in their hands and a pot of tea alongside, they kept each other company in the best of humors till the All-Clear came. Tonight Dinah went up and exercised her authority. Mrs. Gregson and Foster the parlormaid descended to the shelter, bringing their knitting and a fresh pot of tea, and soon four pairs of needles were clicking companionably while the gramophone played Gilbert and Sullivan with impromptu twentieth century off-stage effects.

At intervals during the night they groped up to the street door and looked out, marvelling that the fire seemed to come no nearer though it burned higher and brighter as dawn broke, and the air was full of ash and fumes. Their warden caught them there and admonished them, and said the Fire Service was a marvel, and he thought they had tried for Waterloo Bridge, but nothing had landed in this sector so far.

"Can't tell it from daybreak," he said, ruefully staring Citywards. "What's left, I wonder. What's left down there. Well, this is the way we thought it would be. He's a bit late starting, but," he concluded with the cheerful cockneyism, "we can't complain!"

Fleet Street, where Bracken was — and the Temple, where Nigel lived — what was left, down there. . . .

The All-Clear went before five, and the sun rose on a smoky, stolid city which nevertheless still stood, except for dreadful pockets of disaster. Near the River there were areas of smouldering ruin, and groups of dazed, homeless people who carried in their hands all they had left. There were the dead and injured. And there were exhausted, blackened, singed, and undefeated fire-fighters, wardens, rescue squads, and the white-faced, self-controlled ambulance girls, their dark blue sweaters and slacks grey with ash and plaster, their hands scraped and gritty, from crawling about trying to reach something which still moved.

The sun was well up when Bracken returned home. Having found a willing taxi man he had checked up on Evadne and Mona on his way. Both had hailed his arrival jauntily, with drawn, determined smiles. Mona had had the worst of it this time, while Evadne's sector nearby was without incidents. Stephen, she was thankful to say, was out on tour with a concert party, and had had a lively time in Liverpool a few nights previously, although he maintained he had been much worse scared on first nights.

Bracken was black as a fireman himself, and his grey suit was pocked with little brown holes where cinders had fallen, and smudged dark with mud from around a firehose, and on top of that streaked with white plaster dust. Tired as he was, there was a kind of exhilaration about him.

"He can't do it," he said, drinking cup after cup of tea in the dining-room before he went up to bathe and change. "He threw down everything he had tonight, for hours on end, and these people are not stampeded. It's the same everywhere you go — in the shelters, in the rest centers, in the Services — these people will not give in."

"But if it goes on and on like *this* —" said Sylvia.

"They'll sit out worse," said Bracken with conviction. "I've always said so —

and now I'm surer than ever. I saw an old lady out sweeping up glass in the street this morning — I thought she'd come unhinged for sure — and she explained that horses came that way every day and the glass would be bad for their feet! Some of the glass had come out of her own windows. I saw women carrying jugs of water and mugs for tea out to the firemen around the target fires, and standing by *joking* while they drank it. I helped pull a girl-child out of a cave-in and she wouldn't budge even for First Aid till we dug out her mother — dead. I talked to some bombed-out people in a queue waiting for a bus to take them somewhere — they had no idea where. Nobody was having hysterics. Nobody had any idea of asking for mercy. 'This won't do him any good,' they said. I tell you Hitler is licked!" said Bracken, thumping the table. "It may take a while, but London can do it!"

He went away to take a bath. He said Jeff was travelling by car, and would have the sense to stay the other side of the River till things cooled off. He said not to worry, Jeff would turn up.

Which Jeff did, about eight o'clock, when the sirens had just let off again. He was much cleaner than Bracken, but showed the effects of a sleepless night which he had spent with Denis Arnold and another American correspondent between a ditch and a hilltop beyond Gravesend, trying to count the planes as they streamed towards London — picking out the sound of interceptors, and the chatter of machine-guns and ack-ack, and the thunder of bombs as they landed — watching the flames and the fireworks as they mounted the sky over London, and the occasional fiery comet of a falling plane or barrage balloon.

Within sight of the unexpected holocaust, they had got very cold and frightened, Jeff said, waiting for daylight on the roads. Common sense told them that the petroleum tanks on the docks had caught — imagination insisted that they would find the whole of London a burnt-out shell.

In the clear, sunny dawn of that Sunday morning they had driven back through the

East End, past the fires which still burned, and the homeless and the rescue workers. Gradually they perceived that London was still there. Incredulously they beheld the calm, untouched dome of St. Paul's. And the bridges, all intact. And the Tower. And Fleet Street. And Trafalgar Square. And with a solemn elation they had become convinced that London would always be there.

"But you *know* a fire always looks worse than it is," said Bracken, the old-timer, to Jeff, who had been weaned, they said, on printer's ink.

"Sure I know," said Jeff. "That's so we can look forward to hell."

2

That Saturday had begun early at Farthingale, with a lone German plane crashing in a field near the house. In the remarkably short time before the Home Guard arrived on the scene the pilot had extricated himself and was found lying a few feet clear of the wreckage, cursing in

German and bleeding freely.

They pulled him further from a possible explosion and were at once relieved of any obligation to probe the remnants for other survivors by the whole thing bursting into flames. His sidearms were confiscated, First Aid was applied, and he was half-carried to the terrace at Farthingale, while the local policeman took over from Captain Westley of the Home Guard and telephoned for the local ambulance.

While they awaited it the pilot sat, surrounded by his captors, with his back against the balustrade and his knees drawn up, sullen, silent, and obviously suffering.

"We oughtn't to stare at him," Virginia murmured to Mab as they went out through the French doors to the terrace. "Perhaps you should bring him inside and let him lie down?" she suggested to the policeman, who said better not move him again, thanks, which was doubtless more wise than callous.

The man raised his head to look at them, seeming still incredulous that this thing had happened to him. Then he looked carefully around him, as though memorizing his surroundings — and back to the woman and the girl. He appeared puzzled and somehow disgusted. It did not occur to any of them that what most occupied his thoughts was the total absence of excitement or confusion. These people had not been all panic-stricken by his arrival, and now that he was at their mercy they were not angry or threatening. He understood that an ambulance was coming for him. Where was the terror? Where was the revenge? Did they not know that their cities were in ruins? Another thing they did not know was that his navigator, who could still walk though his right shoulder was smashed, had gained the shelter of the hedgerow before anyone reached the scene of the crash.

The ambulance came. He was helped on to a stretcher and driven away. That girl, he was thinking with nothing but indignation — on her face there was only pity. No fear.

The German plane burnt itself out, and the cows in the field soon forgot about it and began to graze again. People drove round to look at it, and some of them came into the house for a cup of tea and a gossip. And sometimes one of them would say, "Is this the beginning?"

It was a question which had crossed Mab's mind too, as she was returning home from Overcreech House later that morning. Virginia believed firmly in doing everything just as usual until the Germans actually landed, and so Mab had continued to work on her backhand with instruction from the ex-games-mistress at the infant school. She had come back by bus as far as the village and then, accompanied of course by Noel the spaniel and carrying her racquet and wearing her tennis shoes, she had taken the footpath through the wood by the stream where she and Jeff had walked together last Christmas.

She often came here with the dog, to sit on a fallen log and think about Jeff, who always seemed very near if she stayed quiet and listened for him. And this was the most dangerous of all the Williamsburg games she played — that there existed in the little wood a certain place where she and Jeff were always together as they had been on the Christmas walk, when she had heedlessly thrown her arms around him and heard his heart beating underneath his coat. Standing where they had stood that day, she would shut her eyes and wait — and somehow it would come again, that secret inner upheaval which had happened when he said with such compassion — "Like what, my darling?"

Unconsciously today she had paused again in the path, waiting for Jeff — and then Noel was barking and scuffling somewhere on the left and she turned, always dreading that he would really manage to catch a rabbit and she would have to rescue it from his jaws. As she ran towards the sound it changed abruptly to a snarling growl, and there was a thrashing in the thicket — and she saw a blur of grey-green cloth on the ground and a snarling, kicking flurry of black dog beside it. A powerful hand had Noel by the collar and was trying to choke him into silence.

For a single incredulous second Mab felt ice-water in her veins, felt rooted, turned to stone. The German lay full length on the ground with the dog struggling in his grasp, but struggling less effectively, gagging and gasping, growing limp —

"Drop him!" cried Mab, and ran in swinging the tennis racquet. "Let my dog alone — *let him go!"*

The racquet bounced harmlessly once, on the strings, and she swung again with the edge of it forward — hard — and again with the edge downwards, *hard.* Noel wriggled free and scrambled away, choking, sneezing, growling, turning at once to face the enemy, groggy but game, coming in again with his teeth showing. But the man lay still on the ground, with a bleeding red welt across his forehead where the edge of the racquet had hit. He was not unconscious. He stirred at once, and raised a hand to his head, and muttered. Mab dropped the racquet, scooped up Noel in her arms, and ran.

In a very few minutes she emerged from the wood into open ground at the edge of the field where the burnt-out plane lay, and saw people running towards her — people who had heard a dog barking in the wood. She dropped to her knees on the ground then, still holding Noel and trying to get her breath, a stitch in her side, a pain in her chest, feeling sick, wanting to scream, wanting to cry. . . .

The first man reached her, panting.

"What happened? What did you see?"

"He's by the stream — he tried to kill my dog — I hit him — look out, he's not dead —"

The man ran on. Others came up and passed her without pausing for questions, racing into the wood. She sat still on the ground while the pain in her chest receded, making sure that Noel was not damaged. He was too heavy for her to carry except in desperate necessity, and she wondered how she had got him as far as she did.

They were still sitting there, congratulating themselves, when the search party returned, leading the man in the German uniform, who still held one hand dazedly to his head while the other arm dangled uselessly at his side.

"My God, girl, you might have been killed!" cried Captain Westley, who had appeared again from somewhere and was carrying her tennis racquet in his hand. "Mean to say you sloshed him with *this?*"

"He was lying down," she explained faintly.

More people were arriving, there were questions, exclamations, even some laughter — "He might have shot her at sight — wrong arm, very awkward for him — lying on his gun when she went for him — in bad shape to start with, lucky for her — doesn't mean she didn't do a job on him — dog all right, my dear? — good for him — could have been worse —"

"Come along up," said Captain Westley hastily, raising her to her feet as though she might be made of glass. "Get you out of this now, or your grandmother will have me court-martialled."

Walking on knees that still shook at every step, supported by his efficient grip on her upper arm, with Noel trotting confidently ahead, Mab reached the terrace at Farthingale where Virginia met them, heard the story with incredulity which became amusement, and sent for drinks all round.

He who would be known henceforth as Mab's German was carted off to the hospital, where he informed them all in perfect English that but for the damned dog he would have been able to evade capture until the arrival of the Fuehrer, who was due in England any day now. And when a nurse bent over him during the dressing of his wound he spat up into her face.

There were no alerts at dusk that night, and the household at Farthingale went to bed as usual, except that Mab had an eggnog with a drop of brandy in it to ward off nightmares about Germans in the wood. So now I know what happens when she encounters a German, Virginia thought, closing the door of her own room at last on the excitements of the day. She deals with it, far better than I could have done. She doesn't weigh ninety pounds, but she was able to save her dog.

Not for the first time since noon Virginia put both hands to her eyes and allowed a long shudder to run through her. Suppose I had had to tell Jeff that

Mab had been shot to death in our own wood, she thought. Jeff — not Irene. Unreasonably she had thought first of Jeff in reckoning up the aftermath of Mab's adventure. All very well to say, with hindsight, that the German would not have wanted to call attention to himself by firing a gun. He carried a gun in a shoulder holster, and there was no telling what he might have done if his right arm had not been disabled, making a difficult draw. Mab had not thought of that, when she swung the tennis racquet at his head. Must I keep her always with me now, Virginia thought wearily, for the impulse was never to let Mab out of her sight again. So much for taking no notice of Hitler and going on just as usual. It wasn't enough to watch for parachutes, neither of these Germans had used one. From now on, Germans could be anywhere. Virginia herself always supervised the locking up each night. Glass doors into the garden were not much use, she thought as she got into bed.

She had no sooner begun to drop off than she was roused again by the ringing of her bedside telephone.

"Westley here," a calm voice said. "The word has gone out. Have everybody get dressed and be prepared."

"You d-don't mean inv —"

The line clicked and he was gone.

Outwardly composed, inwardly what she would have called twittering, Virginia went round knocking on doors, saying the same thing to each startled question from within, moving on before more questions could detain her: "Get dressed and come downstairs. There's some kind of alert on."

Only one reply made any real impression on her mind.

"Oh, dear," said Melchett, without any fuss. "I'd better make some tea."

Virginia had left Mab till the last. She opened the door quietly and went in. Mab was reading in bed, with the blackout curtains still drawn. Noel, who had somehow stolen a lot of the limelight and after being regarded all his life as rather timid and too highly strung had now proved himself a mass of leonine courage, lay on the coverlet guarding her feet —

which was not as a rule allowed. When Virginia appeared he rolled his eyes at her warily without moving, his chin comfortably pillowed on Mab's ankles. Somewhat to his surprise, no one ordered him down.

"We're supposed to get dressed," Virginia said, as though it was eight A.M. of an ordinary morning. "I've just had a phone call from Captain Westley. Some kind of general alarm has gone out."

Mab felt again that trickle of ice through her veins — more Germans — able-bodied ones, capable of shooting a small black dog that barked. And Noel would bark now, every time he saw a German uniform. She reached for him and pulled him along the coverlet into her arms, as Virginia said, "Darling, you must jump into some clothes at once."

"*Listen!*" said Mab, sitting rigid with Noel in her arms.

The churchbells — silent since mid-June all over England in order that their ringing might be the signal that invasion had begun — the churchbells in the village were ringing.

"They've come!" gasped Mab, and swung out of bed, grabbing for her slippers.

Virginia went to the wardrobe and chose warm clothes, though the night was mild — a tweed skirt, a woolen jumper — and tossed them at Mab.

"Get into those quickly and come along to my room."

Outside Mab's door, she ran. By the time Mab joined her, clothed and composed and very white, with Noel on a leash he seldom wore, Virginia was ready too. She had even put on lipstick.

Together they descended to the drawing-room where the others were assembling. With the lights on, inside the blackout, almost in silence they waited.

Melchett brought in a tea-tray, exactly as though it was the usual time of day for tea, and as she set it down a car drew up outside and there was a certain amount of tramping about, and the knocker on the front door banged three times.

Nobody in the room said anything. Virginia followed Melchett into the hall.

"Ask who it is before you open the

door," she whispered, and waited just inside the curtain which masked the shaded light in the hall from the steps when the door was open.

"Westley of the Home Guard!" rang through the oak panels, and Melchett snatched open the door and he came round the curtain — an elderly, competent man who was somehow able to impart smartness even to that rough uniform with the Mons ribbon on its tunic, blinking a little even in the dim hall, a rifle in his hands — and Virginia could have kissed him for not being a German. Instead, she said, "Good evening, Captain Westley. What now?"

"Apparently they're here," he announced gently. "Somewhere. Anyway, the password for invasion has been phoned in, and everyone is standing to. You'll be all right, of course, except for parachutists. I want to leave a man here on your telephone, and two outside, so some one will have to stand by on this door. I should make ready if I were you."

"Ready for what? We're not supposed to move."

"No question of moving. But don't anybody go back to bed. Stay all together, I would. You know the rules — bicycles — maps — petrol?"

She shook her head.

"Kept locked up and hidden. There's a bit of food available, of course —

"Can't do much about what's in the larder now. Besides — you're a household of women. No heroics, mind — use commonsense."

He stepped round the curtain to the door, and she heard his lowered voice outside. Following him to the steps, she made out a small force of men in the Home Guard uniform, a car, a couple of motor-cycles, and what appeared to be a Bren gun. A lad with a rifle passed her and was shown the telephone by Melchett, took possession of it and at once began a cryptic conversation with some one he called Fred.

"It sounds awfully silly," said Virginia, standing on the top step beside Westley in the dark. "But would anybody like some refreshment while you're here?"

"Later, if we don't have too much

company," he said. "Thanks very much."

He got into the car and it moved away, followed by the motor-cycles and the gun.

That sounded as though he might be back. Virginia returned to the drawing-room, unreasonably comforted. There were men about the house.

Mab was sitting on the sofa drinking tea, with Noel lying at her feet. She found it hard to swallow, and the sweet biscuits hastily provided by Melchett were beyond her, but she managed to sip the tea. Everyone looked at Virginia in well-behaved silence as she came in.

"The Guard is here," she said, going to the tray to fill her own cup. "One of them will be on the telephone and two outside. Captain Westley again, God bless him."

"Have they landed?" Mab asked, for somebody had to.

"He doesn't know. The code signal for invasion has been sent out. Now we just have to wait."

They waited all night. Sometimes the telephone in the hall rang, and the lad posted there talked into it. But nothing else happened.

Some of the girls went to sleep on the chairs and sofas where they sat. Some of them smoked endlessly, some tried to knit or read. Putting on the gramophone would drown outside sounds, and everyone wanted to listen — for what? At dawn the birds began.

Mab had brought her knitting to Virginia's side, and found she could not guide the needles for trembling, which shamed her, and she pretended to doze, leaning against Virginia's shoulder. With her eyes closed she visualized Jeff's half-crown on the mantelpiece. He had already won it once today, when she managed not to go to pieces in the wood. Whatever he had bet on had worked and she had even surprised herself, as he had prophesied.

But now was the second time round. If she did anything wrong now he could still lose it. And this was worse, this time you had time to think, and imagine things. If there was a parachute drop nearby and the men outside the house were killed, the man on the telephone might still have time to give the alarm, she thought. To whom? And if before Captain Westley could get back to the house the Germans actually entered it, what would they do to its occupants? In Holland they had smashed things, set booby-traps, used civilians as shields, shot people who resisted. If Noel barked, and he would — If Virginia talked back to them, and she would. . . .

If ever you have hysterics, I lose, Jeff had said when he laid down the half-crown. Tense and silent, her eyes closed, she waited — while her right hand crept towards her left wrist, which was encircled by the bracelet of Jeff's birthday watch, and fastened hard around it, pressing it down against the bone. She tried to remember the touch of his hands the day he put it on for her — and then recalled the evening since then when she had obeyed the recurrent impulse to lay her lips against his quiet fingers. He was not surprised when she did that, she recalled now. He accepted the gesture as not unexpected — almost as though she had done it before. . . .

She contemplated again her own words that evening. Well, anyone could quote the Psalms at need — but she had called it, half apologetically, a charm, perhaps because although they attended the village church nearly every Sunday and had the Vicar to dinner every so often, they were not a noticeably religious family, and suddenly to say something from the Bible, out loud, in the drawing-room, sounded to her own ears a little queer — *almost as though some one else had spoken for her.* . . .

Sitting very still against Virginia's shoulder, clasping her left wrist with her right hand, Mab pursued this new and perilous line of thought. I was born loving you, she had said to him, without thinking twice about it then or since, and he had not been surprised at that either — *as though Jeff knew.* Well, Jeff always knew things. But why did he look like that — as though he was sorry for her. Not just because there was nothing they could do about it, he wasn't meant to do anything about it, that was what she had tried to tell him. Not just because she could never marry anyone else, for love of him. Jeff's compassion was greater than that — as though — her mind groped forward into the mystery — as though Jeff knew something he kept from her — as though he spared her some knowledge she had not yet attained — as though there was something *beyond*. . . .

At breakfast time, when they had opened the curtains and washed their faces and tried to behave like a normal Sunday morning, the car returned, bringing Captain Westley. He came into the hall, brisk and smiling and apparently as fresh as a daisy, and leaned his rifle against the table by the telephone as Virginia went to meet him.

"I think it's a dud," he said. "Would you run to a cup of tea now?"

Virginia, who had already supplied the men on duty with food and tea, drew him into the dining-room where tired, welcoming faces awaited him. And somehow the meal became quite a merry one.

By the time they knew that the invasion had not happened after all, they knew that London had had the worst raid of the war, and that another was already beginning.

3

So Hitler's secret weapon was fairly simple after all. It consisted of dumping everything he could lay hands on — screaming bombs, oil bombs, delayed action, incendiary, and land-mines — over London. He kept it up for fifty-seven days and nights. And on November third, when for the first time there was no alert, London was still there.

So was the family, at its respective posts — thin, worn, sleepless, but holding up. Stephen's mobile canteen had finally arrived from America, and he had left the concert parties to drive it himself nearly every night, where the fires were hottest. The girls would not give in and go to the country even for a breather. Everyone had adjusted with enormous effort to not ringing up everybody every day to make sure they were all right.

Of them all, Sylvia was showing the least strain, and could least have explained it. It was not that she had been left off all contact with human misery and grief, for the search for pets among the ruins was usually accompanied by heart-breaking scenes, working side by side with the wardens and rescue squads, in the effort to save some beloved animal whose owner desperately needed the solace of its continued existence. "Could you please come round to Number 81, miss, they won't let me pass the barrier, and me pore cats is in there somewhere —" And there would be a discussion with the warden or constable on duty and some kind of compromise, and perhaps a long, perilous crawl through jackstraw timbers and a powder of plaster dust, dragging the canvas bag into which one must thrust a clawing, terrified, probably bleeding pussy and drag it out again — tears of gratitude, First Aid at the post, a cup of milk for its supper — and on to the sombre duty of explaining to a quivering child that the limp dog it carried had gone to heaven. . . .

But during the past two months Sylvia had come to terms with her war, in a mysterious inner serenity which was unaccountable even to herself. I thought I was a coward, she would think, in the midst of inferno. Well, I am, of course, down inside. But I didn't know it wouldn't matter. I didn't know you could go on anyhow. It's as though some one else took charge and you just obeyed orders. Very convenient, Sylvia thought. And she went on living every day as though it was the only one she had and if it was the last — they had all been good. Midge the canary saw it through with her, going down to the shelter with Dinah if Sylvia was not there to escort him, singing foolishly as the gunfire grew louder — imitation thunder, usually of an inferior quality — brash and gay and healthy and unaware. Each time she thought of evacuating him to Farthingale she thought how insulted he would be if allowed to decide for himself — and so he remained in the Upper Brook Street house, living his life as he saw it, yiking with joy each time she returned to him, maintaining in his fragile olive-yellow body an essential part of her own secret morale.

"One more for Midge," she would tell herself firmly, even when it was cats. One more of the speechless ones, and nobody understood better than Sylvia what they meant to the dazed, lost, homeless humans who belonged to them. The house fell down, the possessions of a lifetime were dust, but if the warm, confiding body of the pet was restored to empty hands life could begin again, life could go on.

It was not just the helpless, bewildered creatures themselves that Sylvia saved — it was the morale of some one who had lost everything else. Jeff's hair would have turned white if he had seen some of the risks she took. But Sylvia knew where she was now. Sylvia knew you couldn't dodge it. When it was yours, you got it. Until then, everything was velvet. Afterwards — well, you were in good company.

November brought a lull to London, while Coventry caught it instead, and Birmingham, and Bristol. No one expected London's lull to last, but they made the most of it, and invasion was generally considered to be off till spring.

The family took it in turns now to go for a few days to Farthingale, where they slept for hours without moving, had hot baths and changed before dinner, and sat about doing nothing with infinite pleasure. When Jeff and Sylvia came down it was the first time they had all met since Mab's encounter with the German, and although the story had of course been told in letters it had to be rehearsed again with gestures, and by now it had somehow become very funny.

"The first time I hit him the racquet bounced!" Mab recounted with something like a giggle. "Then I got the edge of it going. It wasn't fair, he only had one good arm."

"He was enormous," said Virginia, indicating seven feet of vertical air. "If he'd been standing up she couldn't have *reached* his head!"

"Noel made as much noise as six dogs," Mab said, anxious to share the glory, reaching down to pull the spaniel into her lap and cuddle him. "He wasn't scared, he was being fierce. They don't have all the fun in London, do they, doggie!"

Jeff rose and ostentatiously removed his half-crown from the mantelpiece.

"That tennis racquet is going to cost

you two-and-six," he remarked, dropping the coin into his pocket. "I was betting on a sure thing, anyway."

"The way I was shaking, you really owe me sixpence of it," Mab argued shamelessly.

"If I had sixpence for every time I shook!" cried Sylvia, and laughed.

She longed, that week at Farthingale with Jeff, to tell Mab what she had learned the hard way about living through the war. Once as they strolled along the frost-bitten borders hand in hand she almost succumbed to the temptation to speak out of turn. If anything happens to me, she almost said, look after Jeff, won't you. But that wouldn't do, that would set Mab thinking. Mab would beg her to be careful, and she might with the best intentions upset Jeff. And anyway — if anything happened to her — they would know when the time came what to do, Sylvia told herself. One always seemed to know when it came right down to it, what to do.

The day they left Farthingale for London, with a half promise to return for

Christmas if the lull lasted that long, Sylvia paused a moment looking back at the house in the late November drizzle. It would stand, she was thinking. And London would stand. People came and went. England would go on. The family would go on. Mab would grow up and marry and have children. There was a whole lifetime for Mab to live, when this was over, the kind of life no one had time for now. . . .

Sylvia was feeling again, there in the drive at Farthingale, the same detachment in which she weathered the raids. It was as though one existed oneself within a frame of preconceived events over which one had no more control than an actor confined within the pattern of a playscript. You couldn't ad lib this one. The producer couldn't be argued with. This one had to be played the way it was written. . . .

Jeff was waiting for her, his eyes questioning and kind. She felt a sort of compassion for him, for fear he had not learned what she had, as the war went on. She tucked her hand under his arm, with an upward look under her lashes.

"Next to Williamsburg," she said, "I love this place. If I hadn't ever seen it, I wouldn't have lived."

He recognized again the disturbing echo of finality in her words. She often sounded like an old, old lady looking back without regret on memories time itself could not steal from her. But Sylvia had only begun to collect memories. It was the war again, he thought, changing one's whole perspective, so that only the past was safe, and nothing in the future was sure. Once people like Sylvia could look ahead with some confidence. Once they could say, Next year we'll go home to America, Next month let's go to Paris, Next week let's ask the So-and-So's to dinner. He ached with concern for Sylvia, for whom tomorrow could only mean more fortitude, and to whom a night without bombs was a treat.

4

The Bayswater flat where Stephen and Evadne lived had so far not been damaged, which made things very handy all round, as his canteen lived in a mews near the garage which housed Mona's ambulance, and Sylvia's Animal Post was nearer there than it was to Upper Brook Street. Jeff often contrived to wind up there after his shelter visits and fire engines and pub crawls and broadcasts, just as they were all coming off duty, and Mona sometimes slept on the sofa when she was not on call.

"Isn't it a cosy war," Evadne remarked one night, when they sat drinking tea in her little sitting-room during a midnight calm.

And Mona said, with her mouth full of cheese cut from a whole Cheddar which Gwen had sent from Williamsburg, "Isn't it funny — and isn't it dreadful — how little it takes to comfort us these days? An electric fire which still functions to warm our shins — a quiet night — a parcel from America — equals Luxury! I suppose it all leads back to our stomachs, just as the man said —'' She reached for the tea-pot. "Just to be able to have all the tea we want, because we happen to have some rich relatives in America —''

"But I give lots of it away, to people who have only the ration!'' Evadne reminded her anxiously.

"Darling, I *know* you do! It's only when I've gorged like this that I'm strong enough to feel guilty and gluttonous,'' said Mona kindly. "And I do think cutting down our tea was harder on most people than anything the war has done. It was such a harmless indulgence — that nice 'ot cupper tea when things went wrong.''

"I've done up another pound in little twists of paper, just enough for a pot in each,'' Evadne said. "You must take some with you when you go — to give away, I mean.''

"Thanks, I'd like to.''

They were trying hard not to make a fuss of Mona or seem to watch or cosset her. But they all felt she was taking Michael's death just a bit too well. Somewhere behind that glacial cheerfulness, that unshaken competence and devotion to her hazardous job, was a walled-up grief which was due to crack right across like a mirror and leave nothing but shards. True, it was no greater burden than hundreds of other women carried, nowadays. But it was the way Mona bore it — the bright, defiant, untouchable façade of her sorrow — that was frightening. It seemed impossible that she could keep it up. One wondered with pity and dread how and when she would break.

She had made no outward change in her routine since Dunkirk. She never missed an hour of duty, she even took on other people's shifts in order that they might have time off — "Nonsense, I've nothing better to do," she would say lightly, dismissing their faltering gratitude. Which was true, as they knew very well. She had got thin, and her mouth was drawn and tight at the corners under the bright lipstick. Her hair still shone with brushing, her carriage was still tall, with a new, braced look to the shoulders, as though she faced a high wind, and her chin stuck out at an almost aggressive angle. She would not give Hitler the satisfaction, by acknowledging grief.

"If it doesn't hot up here again before Christmas," Evadne suggested casually, "how about coming down with us to Farthingale for a couple of days?"

But Mona could see through that.

"Thanks very much, but there's sure to be some one who can really make use of some leave," she said evenly. "As a matter of fact, I've already let it be known at the Post that I am available right through the holidays."

"It's time you had a rest," Evadne insisted.

"Nonsense, I'm perfectly fit. Look at Nigel."

The Temple had been hit during October, with heavy damage and casualties. Nigel's rooms had been pretty well demolished and he himself had been buried for several hours without serious injury. But the family knew he was still pretty shaky and subject to prostrating headaches, and there was a conspiracy to get him transferred to the Regional Commissioner's office near Farthingale, where his lifelong knowledge of the countryside and its inhabitants would be of great value; and which if it came off would make it possible for him to marry Anne and settle in for a while.

They were all holding their breath for Nigel. It seemed too much to hope for that anything could work out like that for anyone these days. And Nigel himself, concussion and all, felt guilty and incredulous at the mere prospect of even such legitimate happiness, so accustomed were they all to waiting and losing and doing without. As though he hadn't earned it, Mona would have said. All his most cherished belongings smashed and that nasty crack on the head besides. And Anne? Anne said her prayers each night with childlike faith that all might come right for Nigel, who deserved much more than she asked for him — a new job and herself to look after him, day by day.

"I'd sort of like to go to Nigel's wedding," Sylvia said, with a glance at Jeff, who had had a shaking up recently by a bomb near the office, which had taken out all the glass and the telephone and the electricity, and fired a broken gas-main at the corner. She had promised Bracken, with some misgivings, to try to persuade Jeff to spend Christmas in the country.

"Yes, let's all go to Nigel's wedding," said Evadne helpfully, and then remembered Mona, who never by the flick of an eyelid betrayed anything but simple pleasure at other people's weddings, "I still can't imagine how it happened so fast," Evadne hurried on, because of Mona. "Nigel is not the impulsive type. Mummy says Anne will be good to him, which is all that matters, of course."

"And how different from being good *for* him!" Mona pointed out.

"Well, that too, no doubt," Sylvia said. "And she has a sort of Cinderella state of mind that's very touching. Christmas falls on a Wednesday, I looked it up. I suppose I daren't suggest a whole week away?" And she looked under her eyelashes at Jeff, who pretended not to see.

"If you could get Hitler to take the week off too —" Stephen remarked. "But no, he's much too conscientious for that!"

"Jeff —" Sylvia persisted, looking pretty and beguiling.

"We'll see," said Jeff, unimpressed.

Hitler usually chose the week-ends for the worst of it, and Sylvia knew it was going to be a bad night soon after it began on the eighth of December. As the telephone began to ring, the familiar orange glow in the sky made things uneasily visible as she worked. Then, when it seemed to slack off for a bit, she stood in the doorway of the Animal Post looking out at the sky above St. Paul's — too red — too low and hot. All the poor churches. It was one of the mysteries, that the churches had to go.

She knew a strange reluctance for the night still ahead of her — a lassitude, a desire to go back inside and sit down — a shrinking from the sheer noise. The thought of all the things that needed to be done inside — the wheezing canary who had caught cold because all the glass in his house had been blown out, so he slept each night in the Animal Post with a ball of cotton soaked in eucalyptus in the bottom of his cage; the dog whose feet were so badly cut by broken glass that they had been enclosed in hard little bandage-boxes after the splinters were removed — his master had been taken away to hospital and he couldn't understand that he had not been heartlessly abandoned, and had to be coaxed to eat; another dog with a nervous breakdown, who howled every time a screamer came down; and the mother cat anxiously guarding a family of puny new kittens who had to have a drop of whiskey in the milk — all good excuses to potter and delay and stay off the street. . . .

A woman hurried up, incoherent, in tears, pulling at her sleeve — Sylvia stepped out of the doorway and followed.

Aeons later, though it was the same night, the smell of singed fur on an injured cat went clean against her, so that she turned aside and was apologetically sick in the gutter.

"There, now," said the cat's owner sympathetically, out of her own anxiety. "It does turn you up sometimes, and no mistake!"

"I'm terribly sorry," said Sylvia, trying

to laugh it off. "You come along back to the Post and we'll see what we can do about these burns —"

She noticed as she cleaned and bandaged the cat, which remained ominously silent, that her hands were not quite steady any more. What's the matter with me tonight, she thought impatiently — I must be getting too tired — better knock off for a week soon, she thought, because one's judgment went, one started to make mistakes, one did foolish things and bungled them. . . . We've had nights like this before, she reminded herself severely — buck up, can't you, it must be almost over.

The woman went away with her cat, full of gratitude, and Sylvia forced herself to go out into the street again, dodging into a doorway as a bomb came down near enough to swish, emerging showered with grit and ash as the walls behind her lurched and steadied and somehow remained upright. She was furious now to find herself shaking and cold, with a dry catch in her throat. She hated the smell the bomb had left, she hated the taste of the smell, and the stinging it brought to her eyes. She caught dizzily at a pillar box and clung to it as to a friend. Then she straightened and with her handkerchief wiped the grime and plaster dust blindly from her face. Tears came with it — her cheeks were wet with endless tears. Stop it, now she addressed herself firmly. It's just a bad night. You've seen bad nights before. . . .

Another bomb swished down, and the blast rocked her where she stood — why can't you duck, she muttered — go on like this and you'll get yourself killed. . . .

It seemed to her that tonight's crumps had been too near Evadne's Post on the other side of the square, and she walked towards it, knowing that Stephen's canteen would be somewhere about. As she turned the corner she saw an ambulance at the curb — not Mona's — wardens and rescue men working in a new crater, prying at heavy timbers which were tilted like a giant jackstraw game. Over everything was the Smell, much stronger here. Her hasty glance found the entrance to Evadne's Post undamaged in the light of a flaring gas-main further down the street — dark figures moved efficiently against the shooting flame. It was suddenly quiet overhead, and the orange glow of fire in the sky had begun to merge with a red dawn.

She came to Stephen's canteen, pulled in behind the ambulance, and saw his familiar figure bending to offer a cup of tea to an exhausted warden who sat with his feet in the gutter — she was able to recognize old Smedley, wiping at a trickle of blood down his blackened face, his uniform covered with dirt and plaster, as though he had himself been dug out of something. Sylvia approached them, herself well disguised with grime.

"Hullo," she said, and Stephen glanced up at her and reached for another cup of tea.

"We're in a mess here," he said. "Tilton is missing, and his aunt is being brave."

"Where was he last?"

"They're digging for him," said Stephen briefly. "Evadne's over there, waiting. She had just come in as Tilton and Smedley went out."

Sylvia took the tea and sat down on the curb with it beside Smedley, inquiring how he did, and receiving a somewhat punch-drunk account of the incident. Except for the rescue work the street was now perfectly quiet — traffic had been diverted with No Entry signs and the Germans had gone home to breakfast. Suddenly the sun showed itself through the smoke haze, and another day had begun.

Perhaps it was the tea, perhaps it was Stephen's always bracing presence, or the usual profound post-raid stillness and exaltation — strength flowed back into her with an almost physical impact. There, you see, she reproached herself. It was just a bad night. I told you it would end like this. Anybody'd think you'd never seen a raid before. Tired. Everybody's tired. That's to be expected. Well, anyway — nobody caught me wobbling. Nobody has to know.

"Jeff's here," said Stephen. "He'll be looking for you."

"Where? Maybe he went back to the Post —" She glanced round eagerly. Jeff too. You see? I told you so.

"Try down by the ropes." Stephen pointed to where a policeman was supervising the erection of a barrier around the new crater which had a jagged wall rising behind it. "He went thataway."

The bomb had been down long enough for the dust to settle a bit, though the smell was still very noticeable. The front of the house still stood, the steps, the door ajar on its hinges, the glassless windows, with curtains blowing in and out. Then there was a big piece gone, and beyond it a nearly complete room, open on the front side, with pictures askew on the walls and a bowl of flowers intact on the center-table. Fine plaster dust and house rubble lay over everything and blew along the floor and coated the furniture. It was exactly like a stage-set, Sylvia thought, with the fourth wall neatly removed to face the audience — the kind of set that always drew a round of applause as a tribute to its details and realism.

Jeff had paused there, listening to the policeman beside the ropes. She slid her hand under his arm and felt it gripped against his side as she joined the group. The face she raised to his welcoming smile was serene, if dirty, the tear-marks already overlaid with a more recent deposit from the smoky air. Nobody could tell, not even Jeff, by looking at her, that for once, during the past night, she had wavered. His arrival brought the final reassurance to her recovered morale, and there was another day for Sylvia.

"— one of the miracles," the policeman was saying. "She wasn't hurt. If only they wouldn't try to go back for their bits and pieces, we had quite a time with her about that. That wall can come down any minute now."

The sun looked out again, slanting into the room. The ambulance still waited, its stretchers out. The rescue squad and the wardens were still digging, surrounded by the eerie quiet that always covered the scene of an incident.

"There's three more in the shelter under there, besides the missing warden," said the policeman, pointing next door, where everything was in a heap. "A bad job with

that wall, but if nothing more is dropped
it may hold for a while anyway.''

"Mm-hm." Jeff looked at the wall and
looked away, at the men working below it,
and then at Sylvia standing beside him.
"Are you about ready to knock off?" he
said.

"Back to the Post a minute, to make
sure about Myrtle, and then we can go."
She smiled up at him confidently as the
All-Clear began. "That was quite a
night," said Sylvia. "Let's find Evadne
while we're here, and ask about Tilton."

"Stevie will know where she's got to,"
Jeff agreed, and they filtered through the
little group that always gathered where
ropes were stretched around forbidden
territory.

"There 'e is!" cried a woman's voice.
"There's my Dickie-bird! Listen to 'im,
pore little soul, all unconscious!"

Sylvia paused. Somewhere a canary was
singing. Jeff had not noticed, and she
turned back, trying to trace the sound.

"Under the table, 'e was. I told 'im 'e'd
be safe there, and 'e was!" A stout
middle-aged woman stood with her hands

on the rope barricade, leaning across it towards the room which lacked a fourth wall. Her face was streaked with dirt and tears, one hand was bandaged, her clothes were torn and ruined with grit and chimney soot. "Somebody please fetch my Dickie out of there —"

One of the ambulance girls took hold of her arm.

"They can't get to him just yet," she said soothingly. "They've got to try for the shelter people first, you know. You just wait a bit — he'll be all right."

"Not if that wall comes down, 'e won't. 'Ere, I'll go in meself, it's only a step —"

The girl held her arm firmly.

"No, much better not. Leave it to the men, they know how, they'll get to him, you'll see —"

The canary went on singing. Midge would not have called it a voice. It was high and shrill and common — a cockney canary. But all unconscious, as she said. Something very strange had happened in the night, and nobody had come round with his breakfast, but the sun was shining — a little more sun than usual, somehow

— and so he sang.

Sylvia surveyed the open room thoughtfully. She could see the cage now, on the floor under the table where the bowl of flowers stood. A bright table-cover, laid on cornerwise and now dimmed by the dust, half hid the bird.

She looked up at the wall of the house which had been blown away. It had an angle at the back, which seemed to her practiced eye able to hold it up. The wall wasn't sheer, it had two legs, as it were. There was no fire, the only thing that ever made her hesitate. One more for Midge. . . .

She ducked under the rope and ran lightly across the broken bricks and rubble towards the song. Some one shouted once — the policeman? — and then there was silence intensified.

Jeff, standing beside the canteen with Stephen, looked back just in time to see her enter the shell, and felt Stephen's hand close hard on his arm.

"Stand still!" said Stephen between his teeth. "Don't anybody move, or make a noise."

They waited, afraid to breathe. She was so light, so quick, she moved so easily. She wouldn't set things rolling and drifting, the way she moved. . . .

She had reached the room, which was now in full sunlight. She stooped, picked up the cage, spoke to the bird, and started back with it — light, swift, skimming. . . .

Several squares away a red bus was feeling its way along the roped-off, dishevelled streets — observing its detours, jolting a bit here and there on the ruptured, uneven pavement. It was within its rights, it moved cautiously, everyone had done the right thing. But from it, like a ripple on the surface of a pond, a tremor spread — imperceptible except to the ragged wall, which wavered, leaned, mumbled, and collapsed with an awful slowness, blotting out the sunlit room.

At the same moment Jeff lunged forward towards the rain of concrete. As he passed the rope and reached the fringe a piece of the cornice struck him and he went down.

While the air was still full of débris and

dust, and fragments still rattled down, the rescue men who had been beyond the fall swarmed in. Jeff they got hold of almost at once, and carried him out to where the ambulance stood. Laid on a stretcher, he immediately tried to sit up, with a grunt of pain. His left arm and shoulder were useless.

"Take it easy," Stephen's voice said beside him. "Evadne's here. Hang on to Evadne. I'm going in."

Sitting on the curb with his feet in the road, Jeff swayed blindly against some one who proved to be Evadne. An ambulance girl knelt at his other side, cutting away his coat-sleeve. Some one held a damp cloth against his face, wiping off the grit and blood.

"She only needed ten seconds more," he said.

A cup of tea appeared before him in a hand. He stared at it blankly.

"Drink it," said Evadne's voice.

He took the cup obediently in his right hand, which was raw and dirty and scarred, and felt the hot sweet liquid on his tongue.

"She won't be alive," he said, when he had swallowed once.

"Drink it, Jeff," said Evadne, and the cup crashed on the pavement, splashing them both with hot tea, and he hid his eyes with his hand, making no sound.

Evadne sat beside him, wordless, motionless, holding him against her, and they heard the picks and shovels at work behind them, and low voices, and some one sobbing quietly, while they waited.

VI.

Christmas at Farthingale.
1940

1

There was no longer any question about who would be going to Farthingale for Christmas. Bracken hired a car, Stephen and Evadne put Jeff into it, and rode with him through the wintry Cotswold countryside.

His arm and shoulder were in a bulky cast, but he could still get about on his feet, if he cared to. Until the day they left London he simply sat wherever they put him, quiet, self-contained, docile — no trouble to anyone. They cut up his food for him, and he ate it methodically, with his good right hand. If they spoke to him, he gathered himself together and replied sensibly. If they didn't he was silent, looking straight ahead of him.

Shock was all very well, said Evadne. But it should wear off. Numbness can't last, however merciful.

He had volunteered only one sentence since it happened. When they first brought him home from the hospital in the cast and sat him down in the drawing-room in Upper Brook Street at tea time, Midge on the table in the corner began to sing.

They watched Jeff discreetly, for this was one of the hurdles. At first he seemed not to notice. No one else appeared to notice either. It was normal for Midge to sing at tea time. There was less to sing about lately without Sylvia there, but she always came eventually, he had learned. He was a canary, not a dog with second sight and an always anxious heart. There were voices and lights in the room, and the accustomed clink of china, and he joined in with his song. Sylvia would come.

They made conversation, while Jeff sat silent, drinking tea and not meeting their eyes. Then —

"Take it away," he said, and Dinah

reached obediently for his cup.

"The bird," he said, without emphasis. "Take it away."

Dinah rose, making no comment, and carried Midge's cage into her bedroom and shut the door on him. Nobody referred to him again. But it was one of the signs that they had something on their hands. Midge remained there in London when they took Jeff to Farthingale.

Word of Sylvia's death had gone ahead of him by telephone, Bracken to Virginia, the strong if apparently casual bond between brother and sister eliminating any necessity for breaking things gently or circumventing facts. Each of them had their own problem. Jeff in London was dazed and rebellious, besides his painful injury. Mab at Farthingale would be torn asunder by her grief for Sylvia, her pity for Jeff, and the tragic circumstances of that December morning which could not be kept from her.

Mab would have to know that Sylvia had died bringing out a charwoman's canary — the flattened wires of the cage and the dead bird were beside her body when they got to it. Mab would have to know that Jeff's physical injury would be slow to heal, and that his mental state made him unable to bear the sight of Midge. Mab could not be spared anything, for her own sake, because it was just possible that if she understood, if she herself could be made to face things, she might be able to help them reach Jeff in his dark little private world of horror.

She's too young for this, Virginia thought, standing with both hands to her face when Bracken had rung off. She isn't old enough or wise enough. It will only knock her over too. We have no right to ask this of her now. . . .

And before Virginia had at all got herself together Mab came running down the staircase and stopped short at sight of the quiet figure by the telephone. Her startled eyes met Virginia's and all the color left her face.

"What is it?" she whispered, holding on to the banister. "Who called?"

Virginia collected her from the bottom step with an encircling arm and walked her silently into the drawing-room and closed the door behind them.

"Gran — *it's Jeff!*" Tense fingers gripping — white face upturned — naked terror, for Jeff.

"No — no. Jeff's coming here. He'll be all right. But we've lost Sylvia."

"N-not — *dead!*"

"Very quickly — before they got to her. She didn't have to endure."

Mab drew back without a sound. She did not hide her face, but it became a rigid mask of self-control, undistorted, but frozen, with widened eyes which saw nothing. Virginia reached for her, entertaining a passing fear that she might faint. Without seeming to elude her hands, but somehow untouchable, Mab found the end of the sofa like a blind person and sat down. Virginia moved quietly to sit beside her, waiting. Finally she took one of the clenched hands in Mab's lap and uncurled it, cherishing it in hers.

"A brick wall came down," she said, believing anything was better than the silence. "The raid was over. She went after a canary in a cage, in a bombed house. They heard it singing, and Sylvia slipped under the rope before they saw her. Jeff tried to run in as the wall fell, and it damaged his shoulder and arm. He's in a cast. But that's nothing that won't mend. The shock may last longer. They want to get him down here as soon as possible — get him to stay in bed and rest. Will you mind coming in with me again, so he can have your room?"

No answer. No response. Mab's hand lay lax in hers.

"Mab. We have to help Jeff now. We have to think how we can help him."

Mab spoke without moving.

"I should have gone to Williamsburg," she said.

"You — what —?" Virginia bent closer to hear.

"I shouldn't be here. I should have gone away. He won't want to see me now."

"But of course he will! You may be the only one he wants to see. He can't bear the sight of poor Midge."

"Nor of me."

"I don't see why you say that, Mab. We're all counting on you to be able to do something with him. I know it's a lot to ask of you, but —"

"He won't want to see me. I'll have to go away."

"Mab, this won't do, this isn't like you. Tell me what you're thinking, I don't understand."

Mab said slowly, with great effort, not meeting Virginia's eyes, "Will you please write to Mummy and ask if I can go back home at once?"

"To London? No, I will not!"

"You could say you need my room here."

"Not till I know what's in your mind. I never —"

"Jeff will know."

"Jeff? He can't think at all. He's in a fog. We look to you to help bring him back to normal, so he can face things and go on. Mab, tell me what's behind all this. You'd never let Jeff down. He'll need you now. Why are you funking it?"

Mab looked at her then — wide green eyes in a paper-white face.

"I tell you he won't bear the sight of me either," she said.

"But *why,* I can't see —"

"Because he'll never believe I didn't wish Sylvia dead."

"Mab, you can't —"

"I didn't, of course. I swear I didn't. I loved her. She was the most beautiful, shining person I ever saw."

"But *of course,* darling, nobody could possibly —"

"You all know that I've loved Jeff all my life. It's no secret from anybody — he knows it — Sylvia knew. Sooner or later it will occur to all of you that I must have wished for Sylvia to — wished that Sylvia wasn't —" The unnatural calm broke suddenly into quivering appeal. "Oh, Gran, not you! Promise *you* won't ever wonder if I wanted him to be without her!"

Virginia caught and held the thin, tense body against her breast, and Noel, who had sat awed and unhappy all this while, looking on, put his forepaws up in Mab's lap and nuzzled an anxious, comforting nose against her arm, and for the only time in his life was ignored.

"Mab, my dear, foolish darling,

nobody on earth could possibly imagine such a thing!''

"I loved her — I'll miss her as much as he does — they belong *together,* there's no place for me — I never thought of *me,* Gran, I never wanted Sylvia to die, and I have no right to go on living now, with Sylvia dead —''

Tears at last, and great sundering sobs. Virginia held her, rocking, crooning, saying foolish comforting nonsense, until she was quiet and spent, her face buried against Virginia's shoulder.

"There," Virginia said then, when she could be heard. "There, you see? That's what comes of peering and prying into God's will. We come up with all the wrong answers. How on earth could your loving Jeff bring any harm to Sylvia? Nobody in this family, least of all Jeff, is likely to confuse the Battle of Britain with some kind of witchcraft. My dear — what happened to Sylvia was all a part of this dreadful pattern of grief and destruction we're caught up in. We mustn't try to read into it any private significance or superstition. There is a kind of massive

coincidence at work these days, Mab —
nothing rhymes, and there's no reason
anywhere. It's easy to decide that we are
the victims of a particular cosmic malice
— until we realize that nine out of ten
people must feel exactly the same. You
can't have destruction on this scale
without smashing all the laws of averages
and probability — I'm talking nonsense,
Mab, I'm 'way beyond my depth — all I'm
trying to say is, don't for God's sake try
to run His universe. You must learn to
take it as it comes," said Virginia, groping
after Oliver's philosophy, which was, after
all, just that there was always something
to be said for being alive, even if you had
to wait a bit.

2

They wouldn't let him see her, when the
blanket-covered stretcher was finally
brought out. He remembered firm hands
that held him back, perhaps Evadne's, a
man's voice, roughly kind, that said,
"Don't look, sir, I wouldn't — not now,

sir —" He was not sure, as time went on, that it was for the best that he had not looked, because when he got out of the hospital they had put her away forever, which left him wondering.

And yet, thanks to them, he could only remember her as she had always been — whole and alive and beautiful. And surely she would have preferred it that way. ("Don't look now, I've got me curl-papers in," she would clown it, with her head done up becomingly in a towel after a shampoo.)

And at that point he would pass his good hand again across his eyes, to wipe away the stretcher going past him with the blanket pulled so smooth and tidy across its light burden.

Some one had cried and cried — the woman who owned the bird, Evadne told him — not for the bird, not any more, but for Sylvia, and for him, and for her own unwitting part in what had happened. Had they left the bird there in its crushed cage, or had they brought it out too, for decent burial? He would have liked to ask Evadne. It was one of the things he still wondered about. But even in the car on the way to Farthingale he still could not trust his voice to speak of it.

What had become of Midge, he wondered, since that day when Dinah took him into her room and left him there? Some one would have to take care of Midge, he was accustomed to love and conversation and tidbits. Some one would have to pamper Midge, Sylvia would think of that, wherever she was, it must be done for her. But he had not brought himself to speak of that to Dinah before he left London. Dinah was out all day at her office, and Midge would be lonely. If Sylvia had foreseen that Midge would need a guardian other than himself she would certainly have chosen Mab. But he knew, as the car bore him westward into Gloucestershire, that he could not without breaking down ask Mab to take charge of Midge.

For a bird, Sylvia had died. Not for a child, not for one of the dauntless old ladies who stuck it out in London so as not to give Hitler the satisfaction. For a shrill yellow canary, no less valuable in the eyes of that sobbing widow woman who had lost everything else than the banded, pedigreed, alto Roller who had accompanied Sylvia everywhere for the past ten years. It was not poor Midge's fault that Sylvia was dead, and he must not be allowed to pine. Just so long as one never had to see or hear him again, in the rooms one had shared with Sylvia. Take him, one must say to Mab, and love him, but keep him out of my sight. Always.

That would be easier to accomplish than Mab might realize, at first, because they wouldn't be seeing much of each other from now on. Impossible, now that that strange fourth dimensional attraction between them might get the upper hand, with Mab growing up so fast and Sylvia gone. Mab must be left quite free to fall in love with some one else when the time came. Sylvia's death was a barrier between them quite as final as Sylvia's living presence. There would be no stepping round Sylvia to Mab now, any more than if she were still alive. Sylvia would always be alive, somewhere, his wife, his first and only love. Mab would understand that, he thought, without any futile words from him. Less difficult for them both if they saw less of each other now that the barrier between them had merely become invisible.

Mab was watching from the window as the car came into the carriage sweep and stopped in front of the steps. With her cheek against the cold glass she could see Stephen step down and turn to help Jeff, slow and clumsy in his heavy cast, and then Evadne. Reluctantly she followed Virginia into the hall. It would have looked very odd if she had not been there to meet him. Because of his injury her usual reckless greeting was ruled out in any case. Perhaps he would have to go straight to bed after the journey. Imagine hoping that she wouldn't have to talk to Jeff, or see him alone. She thought she would be able to tell at once by his face, if he was dreading the meeting as much as she did. . . . .

They were coming into the hall. There was the brief, scented smother of Evadne's embrace, Stephen's brotherly kiss, and then Jeff — tall and bulky in the cast — drawn and gaunt, but trying to smile —

nothing in his face but pain and fatigue and something like compassion, the way he had looked at her that day in the wood. . . .

"Oh, Jeff —" she said, and laid her face against the sleeve of his good arm.

"Hullo, Mab." His hand found hers and held it warm and close and let it go. "Don't cry, now, or you'll get me started," he advised in his slow, easy voice.

Virginia took over.

"Jeff, you're to go to bed at once and have your dinner on a tray. You've got Mab's room, and she and I are together in mine, we like it, and there's a radio on your bedside table and some new books, and we'll take turns running up to sit with you if you get bored. Come along, now, Stevie will help you get settled in."

They bustled him away.

Mab stood still in the hall and watched him go up the stairs, Stephen and Virginia on either side of him, lest he overbalance in the heavy cast. When they had all disappeared round the landing, she became aware of Evadne standing beside her.

"He's been awfully good," Evadne was saying. "Too good. It's not natural." She linked her arm in Mab's and turned her towards the drawing-room. "He's got to let go, some time. We thought Midge might do it, but that didn't work."

"What's become of Midge?"

"Dinah's got him. But it's not much fun for him, alone all day and most evenings, he's almost stopped singing, it's as if he was beginning to suspect that Sylvia isn't coming back. Mab — we thought if you would ask Jeff to let you have Midge — to keep, I mean —"

"No — I can't do that."

"Why not? Don't you want the poor little beggar either?"

"I'd love to have him," Mab said simply. "But —"

"Well, then. We thought it might sort of break the ice, if you offered. Jeff won't let us touch her things. Everything is just as she left it. He can't be allowed to go on like this, he'll go gently mad, you know."

"I'm not the one to — intrude on him now."

"Mab, what a word! He knows you adored Sylvia —"

"I'd rather not."

Evadne fell silent, puzzled. There were things at work here too deep for her comprehension. But time was passing. Everyone was pressed and hurried these days, respite was brief, decisions must be made. She lit a cigarette and reluctantly allowed the conversation to drift away into the weather and the question of Christmas presents. Mummy will have to deal with this, she thought. I'll have to leave it all to Mummy.

There was still Evadne's December birthday to be celebrated, belatedly, before Christmas was actually upon them, but it was not a very festive occasion, with only eight at table, the best they could do. Nigel, still feeling much below par, was being accommodated in one of the servants' rooms on the top floor which until recently had been full of local Red Cross supplies, and Anne had all her meals with the family now instead of going to the canteen. They found themselves faced with a delicate problem — for how could there be a wedding in the house, so soon after Jeff's tragedy? And yet time was so precious. Even if Nigel went into the Regional Commissioner's office and remained in the neighborhood — time could run so short.

Oliver had recently been transferred from his London post to a mysterious job connected with the Home Guard program in the West. It kept him travelling about a good deal, and had enabled him to arrive from Cardiff tonight with Phoebe, just in time for dinner. As Jeff was dining in bed as prescribed (with everything cut up and cleverly arranged for a man with only one useful hand) Oliver and Phoebe went up behind his tray, carrying cocktails, so that he could drink Evadne's health and not feel too out of things. It was the first time they had met since Sylvia's death, and he found to his relief that there was no necessity to talk about it, once the first bad moments were passed.

"There is one thing I wish you would do for me," he said when he could. "That's to convey to Nigel however you can that he's not to alter his plans on my account. I would take it very hard if he and Anne were too tactful to get on with their lives just because mine has been knocked up."

"I'll see to it," said Oliver, with his small, wise smile, and Jeff felt that it was already as good as done.

Since Bracken was not there, Virginia found herself glancing for reassurance at Oliver during dinner — Oliver, who always knew what was what. Now that he and Phoebe had seen Jeff, they knew what they were all up against there. But there was also Mab. And Nigel. I must talk to Oliver, Virginia was thinking as the birthday cake came chanting in. There's so little time. Blast the war. Things never got out of hand like this when we could all come and go as we liked.

Everybody admitted to being confoundedly tired, and the drawing-room emptied rather early that evening. When lights were out downstairs, Virginia left Mab reading in the other bed and with a flimsy excuse went along to Phoebe and Oliver's room, where she found them still pottering about in dressing-gowns and was warmly received and offered a cigarette.

Oliver was not surprised at what she came to say. She had not expected him to be. During her recital his eyes went to Phoebe more than once.

"It's too soon," he said, when Virginia had as it were left the whole thing in his lap. "We can't do anything yet. Give it a little time."

"But Mab wants to go away — back to Irene — even to Williamsburg. It's pathetic."

Oliver nodded.

"She won't see much of him for a while. He'll be staying in his room."

"But that's not natural, they're always together when he's here!"

"And you used to worry about that too, didn't you," he reminded her. "We all did, I fancy. I even spoke out of turn to him about it last Christmas. I risked making things worse, of course. One always does, by calling attention and pointing out. Perhaps without the blasted war it wouldn't have come on so fast — If things could have wagged along in the usual way —" He broke off with a sigh.

"Maybe we can't blame the war this time. The pattern was already there."

"Going all the way back to Tibby's portrait at Williamsburg," said Virginia. "But they're wrong to feel guilty. It might just as well have been Jeff that got killed instead of Sylvia. He was out in the blitz nearly every night, taking just as much risk as she did."

"Cast your mind back," said Oliver, and she groped a minute — back to 1916, when his first wife Maia had been killed in a Zeppelin raid.

"But that was different," she objected uncertainly, for nobody could honestly miss Maia very much, and she had made his life a misery for years.

"It's always diffcrent," he agreed. "But the feeling of guilt was there, just the same. Phoebe and I were in love, and Maia knew it. Her death seemed an awful retribution — for somebody. It took quite a while to work out what we thought must be the right answer."

"And what was it?" Virginia asked.

"Well, what it boils down to — and it sounds easier than it is — seems to be that we aren't running the show. Are we?''

"N-no —'' said Virginia, following slowly.

"We don't dispose. There's somebody upstairs who does that. When Maia died, no amount of self-sacrifice by Phoebe and myself could alter the fact. It seemed just possible that it was all a part of the pattern which had brought us together in the beginning. At least, I would as lief assume a pattern somewhere as just a blind, higgledly-piggledy aimlessness everywhere. Nothing but good has come of my happiness with Phoebe. No possible good could have come of the two wretched, frustrated people we should have been separately. And I cannot believe that it matters any more to Maia, either way.''

"Then you think there is a sort of design,'' said Virginia thoughtfully.

"There must be. Sometimes we can't see it, whichever way we look. Sometimes it seems to stick out a mile.''

"Can you get Jeff to accept that?''

"It's too soon,'' he said.

During the usual Christmas shuffle, when three of the Bank girls went home on leave, and Claudia departed permanently to join the ATS, it seemed to be a good time for Nigel and Anne to establish themselves together in the room she had hitherto shared with Claudia. They were married very quietly in the village church at the week-end, which they spent in a small hotel in a nearby Cotswold village, and returned to Farthingale on Christmas Eve.

Dinah had rung up from London that morning.

"If you're going to do anything about this bird," she said, "you'll have to hurry. He won't eat now. He's pining. He knows."

Virginia said perhaps if Mab would take care of him, talk to him, get him to come on her finger — and had they tried ice cream? Midge always fell for ice cream.

"Tracy Marsh is here," said Dinah. "He's coming down to spend Christmas with Rosalind and Charles. He and

Charles are driving down in a Consulate car, and I can send Midge with them."

"Wh-when did he turn up?" Virginia asked weakly.

"Tracy? He just walked in yesterday at the office, and Bracken brought him home to dinner. He's been in Paris. He says."

"Well!" said Virginia, and "What?" said Dinah, and "Nothing," said Virginia. "I was surprised, that's all. I hadn't heard a word from him, and had no idea —"

"Oh, well, you know how Tracy is," Dinah said easily. "Now you see him and now you don't. Anyway, he and Charles will drop Midge off there on the way to Cleeve."

"Is he all right?" Virginia asked stupidly. "Tracy, I mean."

"There's nothing wrong with Tracy, it's Midge we're worried about," Dinah reminded her.

"We'll do the best we can. Jeff's still in his room, he needn't know."

And so, with Nigel and Anne causing a certain amount of upheaval in their way, and with a certain amount of doubt about how Mab would feel about having Midge to look after, to say nothing of finishing the tree and the presents, which Evadne could take over, and Christmas dinner, for which they were short-handed in the kitchen now, Tracy Marsh was going to walk in again. Charles would be coming with him — the house was full of people — what was there to be so nervous about? It would be Hello and Good-bye again. How long would he be at Cleeve, though? Did she *want* to see him alone?

Virginia found herself staring at her own face in the mirror. Her hair was definitely whiter this year, and that was not unbecoming. She would do her face over after lunch. Would it be cheating to change into the little black dress she kept for special occasions? You hussy, she said to the woman in the glass. He's got trouble enough. And so have you, she added firmly. This way you can bear it. It would be much worse if he belonged to you.

She turned away from the mirror and went to find Mab, who accepted the responsibility of Midge without enthusiasm, but so long as Jeff didn't

427

have to know —

Somehow Virginia was wearing the little black dress when Tracy's car came up the drive that afternoon. Somehow Anne and Nigel were in their room unpacking. Somehow Phoebe and Oliver had gone for a walk. And somehow Tracy stepped out of the car alone, carrying the covered cage in his hand.

"Charles was anxious to get home," he said casually. "We stopped there first. He said we must all have a drink together soon."

Mab set the cage on the table in the hall and peeked under the cover. Midge sat bunched on the perch, and showed no interest in his surroundings, which was most unusual for him. She took him away to the room she and Virginia shared, with Noel trotting jealously at her heels, and Virginia was left to lead the way into the drawing-room. Tea was not due for half an hour. He declined a drink with thanks, and sat looking at her across the hearthrug.

"Well, Tracy — what do you think now?"

"Well, now we're thinking about the

next thing," he smiled.

"Which is —"

He shook his head.

"There's so little time," he said. "Let me just enjoy this."

"Yes, I know, but where are we with this war? What about Greece?"

"Done for."

"And then?"

He leaned forward in the big chair, linking his hands loosely in front of him, smiling, composed, but rueful.

"Virginia," he said, dismissing the war. "How about coming to America now — as my wife?"

"*Tracy!*"

"Now, don't pretend to be surprised," he said, amused.

"Why are you going to America?"

"Sent for," he said briefly.

"Something new?"

"Mm-hm."

"Gas?"

"Even if I could tell you, my dear, I wouldn't."

"Tracy, it wasn't Paris, was it? Tracy, have you been in Germany?"

"What does that matter?"

"The secret weapon," she guessed acutely. "When?"

"I think I'll change my mind about that drink," he said.

She rang for Melchett.

"Would you take Mab to America for me, before it happens?"

"Sweetheart — there was no secret weapon in my proposal to you. I'm going to Washington by and by, for quite a spell, apparently. I would like to have you with me. It's as simple as that."

"When do you go?"

"Not for a bit. The point is — will you come?"

"Tracy, you know I can't. Not for a variety of reasons. We've got our hands full here, in the family."

"Yes, I understand that," he said quickly, with sympathy. "Bracken told me a little."

Melchett answered the bell, and returned at once with a tray, and Tracy sat a while with a full glass in his hand, attentive, intelligent, alert — listening to the family dilemma.

"Oh, do forgive me, I've been running on," Virginia said penitently at last. "It's so good to talk to some one — adult," she explained in confusion. "I miss Bracken, I think. I'm tired of trying always to be the oracle myself."

"I'm sure you must be," he said, gravely. "Now let us be practical a moment. Jeff, after all, has his own mother here, as well as Bracken and Dinah and his job, which he will be able to get back to before long. Nigel has a wife now, they tell me. And Mab, after all, has parents, hasn't she?"

Virginia tried to explain further about Mab, and how especially since Basil's birth she had seemed to belong at Farthingale more than with Irene and Ian.

"I see," said Tracy gravely. "Would you consider bringing her with you, to Washington?"

"Tracy, you're being very difficult, aren't you?"

"Am I? Would you rather I said no more about it?"

But then she was silent, looking down at her hands in her lap.

"I want very much to be of some use to you," he said, holding on to himself with an effort. "We have left it very late, Virginia, but there is still a little time, if we make use of it."

"We've been so long apart —" she began rather breathlessly.

"That we are strangers?" He contemplated it. "It's hard for me to realize that. You have been so constantly with me, all this time. But you have had a great many other things to think about," he added, naïvely discounting his own career and achievement. "I shall be several days at Cleeve, I hope. With any luck we may see something of each other —"

"Tracy, I'm wrong to let you entertain any such ideas — my life is here, my roots are very deep, I must do first what comes to hand *here* —"

"And mine is just one more demand," he said gently.

"Oh, no, it's *good* to be needed!" she cried involuntarily. "Don't think you aren't tempting me, Tracy, because you are! Just the thought of some one like you *back* of me, bigger than I am —" She broke off, keeping her eyes on her hands. "You see, I've thought of you too," she confessed.

"Then please go on thinking of me. Think hard. Think fast. There is so little time."

"When — when must I decide?"

"You can decide any time. But it will probably be several weeks before I sail."

"*Weeks!*" she cried in despair. "Oh, no, I can't think of it — it's impossible —"

"You could always follow me. We probably couldn't travel together anyway, they always fly me," he said simply, but his hands were knotted now, and there was a tense little muscle working in his jaw. "You may think I'm a bit cool about this thing," he said with difficulty. "How else can I be, with an open door behind you and the clocks striking tea time? But never doubt, my darling, that I want you in my arms. You gave yourself away just now when you said that about somebody bigger than you are. You have gone it alone long enough."

"I'm anything but alone," she began to protest, and Melchett came in with the tea-tray, and cups for nine.

Tracy stood up, towering, and his smile was casual and kind.

"I promised to turn up at Cleeve for tea," he said. "And I've sat gossiping here all this time." He took both her hands in his, before Melchett had left the room. "Charles has plans for tomorrow — you'll hear from him. Until then —" He raised her hands to his lips, and she felt his kiss in her palms. "Think," he said. "Think about it, please."

When he had driven away, and no one showed up for tea, Virginia went slowly up the stairs — even in one's own room, privacy was a casualty of the war. In order that Jeff might have a room, she must share hers with Mab. Outside the door she arranged her face, lifted her chin, and went in.

Mab sat beside the cage, offering a variety of tempting food, while Midge took no notice of her. His olive and gold feathers were rumpled and lustreless, his eyes had gone into his head.

"He's sick," said Mab, turning a tragic face towards the door. "He knows now that she won't come back. What can I do — if he dies, what can I tell Jeff?"

"He may pick up after a day or two here," Virginia said. "He needs attention. We must talk to him — make a fuss of him — play him some music."

But Midge took no notice.

The next morning — Christmas morning — he was sitting in the bottom of the cage, apparently without strength to hold to a perch. Mab hung over him, weeping for sheer despair, coaxing, crooning, trying to tempt him with food. As Jeff had not left his room, even to see the tree, he still did not know that Midge was in the house. Late in the afternoon, Mab came to a decision. She went and knocked on his door.

"Come in," he said, and when she opened the door he was sitting by the window in an armchair, an open book on his lap.

"Perhaps I'm doing the wrong thing," she said, with the knob still in her hand. "Will you forgive me, if I am?"

"Naturally," he said with a faint smile, and closed the book.

"Jeff, I know how you feel, but — I have to tell you. I've got Midge here. And I think he's dying. I know it will be hard for you, but I thought if he could just hear *your* voice — I've tried everything else —"

He made no answer, turning his head away towards the window.

"Jeff, it's not *fair* to him — he's dying of loneliness —" The words broke in spite of her.

"Yes," he said, and sighed. "You're right, Mab. Bring him in here."

She brought the cage, with Midge sitting motionless in the bottom.

"Hi, there," said Jeff to Midge, in their standard greeting, to which the standard reply from Midge was *"Yike!"* with a rising crest. But the sunken eyes, the uncared-for plumage, told their story. "Are we going to let it lick us?" Jeff asked him gently.

Midge took no notice.

"I guess we are," said Jeff. "He's all done, Mab."

"Oh, Jeff, *try!*" Tears were running down her face. She opened the cage door and took Midge in her hand, trying to warm him. "He's lighter than air," she said. "He's starved himself — even his feathers are cold —"

"He doesn't care," said Jeff. "We're no good to him. We're the wrong people. Your Noel would be the same if he lost you. Don't cry, Mab —" He laid his good arm around her shoulders in the old, instinctive gesture. "Oh, for God's sake don't cry —!"

They sat together, in tears, while Sylvia's bird died.

It was a dreadful Christmas.

4

And so, by dying Midge did in a way break the ice. Useless to insist that he was better off now, or to imagine that he had flown straight to Sylvia, wherever she was. There is something about a dead bird that breaks the heart entirely, and even after the soft, limp, weightless thing which had been so much joy and beauty was enclosed in an old silver jewel-box of Virginia's and laid away in a hole dug by Stephen in the rose garden, the little tragedy lingered.

Then to the family's secret terror, Jeff got flu, and Virginia sent for Phoebe at once and they took it turnabout to watch him day and night. Jeff was not allowed to have colds, much less flu, for his rheumatic fever history made respiratory ailments a cruel hazard. The decision about going to America was taken out of her hands by Jeff's illness, although she had almost begun to contemplate it as a possibility before Tracy returned to Town at the new year. She was tired, and lonely, and she apologized to him because for once she did not know her own mind clearly. But it was better, she told herself now, that she had not raised his hopes by going off half-cocked while he was there. Obviously, her place was still at Farthingale, and theirs was a dream, a holiday madness which had no chance of survival in the middle of a war.

Confined within the cast, Jeff was in danger of going on into pneumonia, which was likely to mean a recurrence of the old heart trouble. He knew that, as well as any of them. And lying very still in Mab's bedroom, hot and aching and defeated, he counted his heartbeats and waited for the old stutter and lunge he had almost forgotten since his marriage to Sylvia — and discovered slowly to his surprise, it might almost be said to his fury, that he was not yet ready to die.

Why can't I just let go gracefully, he thought, while his heart pumped steadily on. Midge knew how. Midge didn't fool around, he went after her, the only way he knew. It would become me to do the same. . . . But in spite of himself, as it were against his will, he responded to expert care and treatment, he fought off the germ, he licked the fever, he held his heart steady, and began to mend.

"You're going to be all right," Virginia told him one day, beaming with relief. "You're going to come out of this as good as new."

"Like the damn' fool I am," he muttered sourly, and drew a long, cautious breath in a sigh. "Well, that just shows you, doesn't it."

But by the time Jeff was out of danger,

Tracy had gone back to Washington, via Lisbon. *I wish I could say, with a reckless gesture, that if ever you wanted me I would come from the ends of the earth,* he had written her, the night he left London. *But I must put it the other way round. If ever you will come to me, I want you.* She kept the letter. She read it over and over, and sometimes it blurred a little as she read. What would it be like, she wondered, and what sort of woman would she be, to lay all this down and run to him, where there were lights, and luxuries, and where she would have some one of her own, bigger than she was, as Rosalind still had Charles. . . .

Because he was infectious, Mab had not been admitted to Jeff's room during his illness, but more than once in the small hours Virginia had found her huddled in a dressing-gown on the top stair opposite his door, her back against the banister, her eyes fixed on the line of light which showed above his threshold.

"You'll get chilled and catch it yourself," Virginia had scolded, but gently. "I can't have the two of you on

440

my hands. Run back to bed like a good girl.''

"What's his temperature now?" Mab would ask wanly, and Virginia would tell her, sometimes knocking off a degree for luck, and out of sheer pity would give her some small errand to accomplish, make her drink a glass of port wine as a dose, and shoo her off to bed.

But as he began to improve, the logical thing was for Mab to read to him, to share his tea-trays, and bring him the small gossip of the neighborhood. Virginia noted with dismay that this did not seem to transpire. Mab was always somewhere else now. And Jeff did not ask for her.

Finally, being Virginia, she took the initiative again.

"Jeff, I think it's time you did something about Mab," she announced, pouring out a cup of tea for him and another for herself, at his bedside.

He took the cup from her, awkwardly still, and glanced up at her under his brows.

"So long as it doesn't need two hands," he said. "What should I do?"

"I don't know." He saw that for Virginia she was very serious indeed. "Haven't you noticed that she isn't visible?"

"I'm contagious."

"Not any more."

"You mean I must send out invitations?"

"Jeff, she's convinced that you'd rather not see her."

He set down his cup with a little smack, not looking at her.

"I don't know what you have in mind yourself," Virginia went on after a pause. "But I know that Mab has got it into her head that you will hold her to blame for Sylvia's death."

That brought his eyes around to her.

"How on earth does she figure that?" he asked incredulously.

"I don't quite know how. But it's very real to her. I hope I'm not meddling," said Virginia warily. "But it oughtn't to go on like this, she's very unhappy. She seems to feel that the love she has always had for you might act as a wish to — eliminate Sylvia. It's very complicated," she finished faintly.

"Look, Virginia, I don't think I feel up to this if you don't mind, not today, couldn't you possibly —" He met her eyes with reluctance now. "You want me to tell her that I don't believe in voodoo?" he suggested.

She looked back at him without smiling.

"Perhaps that's it," she said.

"This isn't going to come out the easy way, if that's what you're driving at," he said after a minute.

"No," she agreed meekly. "Things never do, do they." And then she thought of her own love match, in the dawn of history, when the world was young and sweet and simple, and the Germans stayed at home. "Not any more," she qualified wistfully.

"Will she come to see me now?" he asked.

"If I say you inquired."

"Very well, consider that I have inquired," he sighed, and she rose.

"If I can find her," she murmured, and went away.

After a while he opened his eyes, and

Mab was standing beside him.

"Hullo," he said, sounding to himself quite normal. "Pull up a chair."

She did so in a silence. It was the first time either of them could remember when there had not been something to say. He reached for a cigarette and she supplied the light.

"Thank you," said Jeff. "Well, have I missed anything, being laid up like this?"

"Bristol's caught it again," she said, with a glance at the radio beside him. "And Cardiff cathedral. You'd think God would protect His churches."

"That's a hard one," he nodded, and she moved an ashtray within his reach.

Again there was a silence.

"Any local news?" he prompted, conscientiously entertaining a backward caller. "I mean — what have you been doing yourself?"

Sitting on the stairs outside your door, she might have said. Watching and praying. Waiting. Wondering. All for you. Nothing that wasn't for you. But the words wouldn't come. One said things like that so easily and naturally while Sylvia

444

alive, but now one thought first —
it wouldn't sound right now.
.erything sounded different, without
Sylvia. So that was one was afraid to
speak. Afraid of sounding as though
Sylvia wasn't there. And groping with Jeff
was a new and horrifying experience. But
now one never knew what a thoughtless
remark might lead to, or what blunder one
might innocently commit. Confidence, and
comfort, and companionship — all gone
with Sylvia. Nothing left but pitfalls.

"Oh, nothing much," she said like an
awkward schoolgirl, which she had never
been. "Going for walks with Noel."

"No more Germans in the woods?"

She shook her head with a dutiful smile.

"The invasion is supposed to be off till
spring," she remarked. "Will they try
again then, do you think?"

"Probably."

Another constrained silence settled
between them, frightening in its
implication that they no longer had
common ground for easy companionship
without words. Jeff's listless attitude, his
averted gaze which rested indifferently on

the window, his simulated interest in h
daily doings, were frightening too.
remembered a remark of Virginia's th
Jeff must get back on the horse soon. The
war had thrown him, hurt him badly, but
if he went on like this, withdrawn, almost
insensible, he might lose forever his ability
to face up to things. Besides, he was
needed. Bracken was overworked and
short-handed at the office.

The main raids were still passing
London by, and the continued lull there,
Virginia said, would give Jeff a chance to
ease back into it, now that the cast had
given way to a sling. But he gave them no
clue to his intentions, keeping to his
room, looking at them remotely,
uncommunicative and ingrowing, and
more and more unlike himself. No one
supposed that he was afraid to go back to
London. It seemed merely that it had not
occurred to him. He must have an
incentive, Virginia said, mulling it over
aloud. If we told him that Bracken wasn't
able to go — or if we told him that Dinah
must come away for a rest and he should
go back to keep Bracken company — but

as so[...] [...]n [...] got [...] there he'd find out
[...] [...] [...]ly had some special
[...] [...] [...]f together. . . .

"Jeff [...] [...]o go to London," said
Mab.

It took him completely by surprise, but
he came into focus slowly, turning his
head till his eyes rested on her, as though
he had to think back with an effort to
what he had heard her say.

"Visitors are not encouraged just now,"
he said.

"Not as a visitor. Not just for a
week-end. I haven't been there since the
war began. I think it's time I went. Sybil
Fenton's got my room at the flat, because
of being bombed out, but if Mummy was
willing. I could stay at Dinah's, couldn't
I?"

"Dinah's got room for you, I suppose,
as far as that goes," he admitted. "You'd
better make sure they've got all their glass,
though, it can be beastly cold without it.
And you can't count on hitting a dull
patch in the raids, you know, just because
of Cardiff and Bristol."

Well at least now there was something

to talk about, she thought cautiously. At least now she had his attention.

"He's slacked off for a while over London," she said — unconsciously everyone spoke of the Germans as "he" — Hitler, without whom there would be no Germans over London. "And anyway — I think everyone should know what it's like to be in a raid."

"You won't enjoy it," he prophesied. "But in a way, I see your point. Living through an air raid has become a sort of graduation exercise to qualify as a citizen of this cock-eyed world."

"Oh, Jeff, you *are* intelligent!" she said gratefully. "Everybody else would say I'm too young, or that it's a foolish risk, or that I'll be sorry — or they'd think I'm showing off! I'm not, and I know I shall be terrified. I don't *want* to go, any more than one wants to go to the dentist, but it's something I just feel as though I can't not do!"

"Yes, and what does Virginia say?" he inquired, for everything came to that at Farthingale sooner or later.

"She doesn't like it, of course, because

of Sylvia." The name lay there a moment on the quiet air, while they both forced themselves to hear it without visible emotion. "But she wants to go to London herself, and she has to agree that I'm old enough to decide some things for myself now, and she says if I'm really determined to go she'll go with me. As soon as you can be trusted here alone, that is, and if the lull goes on in London."

"Correction," said Jeff. "As soon as I can go along. Which ought to be pretty soon now."

She looked at him doubtfully, wondering if she had done the wrong thing after all, to turn his mind Londonwards again. But you must always get right back on the horse that has thrown you, and Jeff was still a war correspondent with a job to do. Sylvia had always been the first to point that out with pride. Sylvia would never have tried to keep him here, in this walking trance of grief, just to keep him safe.

"If you — when you're sure you feel up to it," Mab said, with a lingering uncertainty, and his brows came down.

"If you think you're going to go racketing around London in an air raid without me there to look after you —" he began, almost like old times, and she reached a quick hand to his.

"Oh, Jeff, I promise to go to the shelter — and that's the worst of it," she added, frowning. "Do you think I could have claus — claustrophia, and not know it?"

"You'll know it in a shelter, fast enough," he said. "Why?"

"Because I dread being *under* something," she confessed. "When we tried the refuge-room here, after it was built, I — couldn't stay in it long. I felt the whole house on top of me, *pressing* — I felt it in my chest," she finished lamely. "Like smothering."

"But you go in lifts. And in the Underground."

"I can. But I hate it."

"Dinah's refuge-room is quite a normal sort of place — you hardly know you're in the basement," he said. "Maybe with a little practice you can get used to it."

But not without me, he was thinking. She's not going through any raids without me. She's had no training, and she'll have no duties to fall back on. And if she really can't stand shelters — lots of people can't — some one must stay upstairs with her. That will be me. Of course she oughtn't to go at all, but Virginia must know what she's about, even to consider it.

He was at the moment too tired to take issue with Virginia, even on what was best for Mab, who had had a mind of her own last summer too, and the invasion had not come to prove her wrong. The least he could do was to see her through it himself, and he had to go back to London some time, it wasn't fair to Bracken to go on like this. Whatever Mab was trying to prove to herself, Jeff faced an important test case of his own in the first raid he encountered now. Without Sylvia in the world, he was no longer sure of his heart. His talisman was gone, his good angel, his guarantee. And so his heart could go back on him again — any time.

The tension between them was eased at last, with no mention of voodoo and with the pitfalls seemingly avoided. In his own unhappy preoccupation he had failed for once to read her mind with his usual ease, and did not suspect that she had first conceived the trip to London as a debt to Sylvia she had to pay. It seemed to her that the least she could do for Sylvia now was to hear German bombers herself, and not stay safe in the country all through the war, like a child. And now, as it was working out, she saw it also as a way of bringing Jeff back to himself. He would go to London now, as habit reasserted itself, to try to watch over her. And once there, more habit would claim him — the newspaper routine, the daily round with Bracken, Dinah's serene and comforting presence — that way his salvation lay, especially if he could come to it unaware, believing only that he went because she might be frightened in a raid. Might? She would be terrified. But with Jeff beside her, it might not show. It must not show. Sylvia had seen much worse than anything that happened in London now. Perhaps when she had heard a few bombs herself, she could bear to think of Sylvia again. And Jeff, back on the job with Bracken, would gradually be able to bear it too. . . .

"Of course it's a worry about Noel," she said, to cover her own thoughts from Jeff's uncanny perception. "If I go to London, he will have to stay here, because of his walks. Gran says his walks might be very inconvenient, if there was a raid on. It will be the first time we've been separated."

"You shouldn't be away from him too long," he pointed out, seizing a useful argument against unnecessary risk. "One raid is pretty much like another. See one and you've seen 'em all."

VII.

Spring in London.

1941

1

Everyone was relieved that Jeff wanted to go with them to London. It meant, at least, that he had not resigned from life entirely. No one suspected that it represented to him a challenge that had to be met. He had to find out if he could weather a raid, with Sylvia gone. And secondly, by undertaking to see Mab through it, he had placed himself in a position where he simply could not afford to collapse.

Early in March, they arrived in Upper Brook Street to find Bracken's glass intact, and Dinah worn and serene and smiling, and very glad to see them. The crocuses were out in the Parks, and much of the winter bomb damage had been swept up and tidied away in the recent respite. There was even a little theater life, in the daytime, and people seemed to have given up carrying their gas-masks again, in spite of more invasion talk now that spring had come.

There were a few alerts, but no noisy nights in that part of London — nothing that sent them to the shelter, during the first few days of their stay. And then, on the nineteenth, without any notice, the blitz was on again.

It began before they had finished dinner, so that the china chattered on the table and the chandelier shuddered above their heads.

"Oh, well," said Bracken, bored. "Let's have coffee downstairs, then."

They all rose from the table at their leisure, and Dinah collected her knitting-bag from the drawing-room and Virginia chose a new book. Mab's palms were wet as she picked up a copy of *Punch,* and she found Jeff close beside her when they descended the stairs, followed by Gregson who carried the coffee-tray. And Jeff, to his horror, felt his heart beginning to lurch in his side. Out of practice, he told himself firmly. Got to get used to it all over again. With a difference.

They sat down in the light, comfortable basement room. Dinah poured the coffee, Bracken handed round the cups.

"How it takes one back," Virginia said, and her eyes went round the substantial furniture and the astonishingly normal look of things down there. "The same beastly sensation of having one's stomach hit the floor, the same old pretence that one doesn't give a damn. Except that we used to sit on a hard bench in the scullery, with the Zeppelins overhead. Nothing so posh as this."

"If we had had to spend as much time on that bench we'd have done something about it!" said Dinah, and the noise from outside began to penetrate their sanctuary. The lights flickered, but stayed on. Dinah rose and brought a candle and matches to the table beside her, and resumed her knitting. Bracken was filling his pipe.

Mab sat with *Punch* open on her lap, staring down at the page. Her hands were cold, there was lead in her middle, her ears sang with her own heartbeat.

It seemed to her that the house above them jarred and settled several inches stealthily. She glanced round at the walls, refused to look up at the ceiling. Jeff moved his chair so that it nearly touched hers, and sat there quietly, smoking, not watching her — within reach of her hand. She realized that she was sweating all over now — like a horse, she thought.

Dinah and Virginia chatted on, without apparent effort — reminiscing, mostly, about the other war. Bracken joined in, and made them laugh. The noise outside increased. Steady, damn you, said Jeff to his heart. I can't, I can't, thought Mab, sitting still.

"Bracken, I think the servants really should come down," Dinah said at last. "Go and be firm with them, they'll listen to you."

He rose and went upstairs to the kitchen. It was a point of honor with the Gregsons not to budge from there unless it got really bad. Mab's eyes followed him with longing to the door which led to the stairs. She did not know her teeth were clenched.

"It's noisier up there," Jeff murmured without moving. "And you've still got three stories above you. Do you want to try it?"

She looked at him dumbly, and managed to move her head from side to side in negation.

"Mab, are you all right?" Virginia asked sympathetically. "Does being in the shelter bother you worse than the raid?"

Again she signified No. But they had looked at her now, and in the effort for self-control she began to tremble visibly. Jeff rose and laid a casual hand on her shoulder.

"Let's see how it is upstairs," he said gently. "We can come back if it doesn't help."

Punch fell to the floor as she stood up to follow him, and they left it there. Walking woodenly with the effort not to break into a run, she reached the door of the shelter. At the top of the stairs they met Bracken returning with the servants.

"Change of air," said Jeff, covering her

with his good arm, and they nodded comprehendingly, and went on down into the shelter.

He closed the door at the top of the stairs behind them, put out the light in the hall, and led her to the front door. It opened inward on a blast of cold air and reverberating sound — a smell of cordite and burning — a flare of fiery sky. She stood with his arm around her, braced against his shoulder, gazing out — and was not trembling any more.

"Well, that's it," he said after a moment, and closed the door, and guided her back to the drawing-room where the lights had been dimmed to one or two. "We're just as well off here, for a little while anyway. I'm sorry you ran into this one, it's the worst in some time." He went to a side table and poured two liqueur brandies and came back with them to the hearthrug where a dying fire still cast some warmth towards the sofa which faced it. "Come and drink this," he said, and put a glass into her hand. "All of it. Right down."

She obeyed him, and he set the empty

glasses aside, and sat down on the sofa with his good arm towards her.

"Come here," he said, and she went to him gratefully, and felt the warmth and strength of him, and hid her face against his coat. Crrrump — *crrump* — CRUMP! — a stick of bombs seemed to hurdle the house, leaving behind an uncanny quiet. "Missed," said Jeff, his arm tight and steady around her. "That will be the nearest, probably, for tonight."

"I'm all right now," she said. "I think it really was the shelter, even more than fright. I couldn't get any air. I never meant to disgrace myself."

"You were doing fine," he assured her. "It's always a good idea to look outside now and then."

"Jeff, is this really a bad raid?"

"It's a humdinger. Nothing like it in weeks. He must have known you were here."

She sat up, spreading her hands palms up, and rubbed them together.

"See?" she said with some satisfaction. "I do feel better up here. I've stopped sweating and shaking."

"Sure you have. That was claustrophobia."

"But you haven't got it. You ought to go back down."

"Hell's bells, Mab, I'm used to being *outside* when it's like this!"

And so was Sylvia, she thought. This is what Sylvia went through every night. There was a long, whistling whine, with a bump on the end of it.

"Oops," said Jeff. "Back again. They come in waves."

The house seemed to curtsey and rise again. He pulled her to him, shielding her against his body.

"Go ahead and be scared!" he said, against her ear, making himself heard above the guns on the ground. "You got a right!"

She clung to him, battered and bruised by the noise.

"Some of it is our own guns, you know," he said. "You get so you can tell the difference."

"This is worse than Jamestown," she said. "At least it was daylight then."

"What about Jamestown?" he asked, to

keep her talking. It was a queer thing, he had noticed before now, what people found to talk about in a raid. The effort to function at all — the need for normal speech — the determination not to show fear — often laid bare the deeper layers of consciousness and reserves. He had heard strong men resorting to almost total recall in the process of keeping a conversation alive during a raid. "What about Jamestown?" he repeated, willing to fall in with whatever game was going.

"When Wayne made a mistake, beyond Green Spring — Lafayette was furious, he hadn't wanted a battle there — we had the whole British Army after us, he swore at Wayne up one side and down the other —"

He bent his head to hear, above the London guns. And while he listened, time seemed to shimmer and slip and fall away, and he began to remember. . . .

"— but Lafayette got us out of it, that night, up the Neck —" she was saying, and her lips were smiling, her eyes were wide and dark and fixed on the dying fire. "— he was a darling man, you couldn't ever fool him — you could look at him barefaced and lie and he knew it, but he wouldn't give you away — he spoke wonderful English, but he couldn't spell it — he always put two n's in enemy —"

She was silent in the close circle of his arm, as though drowsy — but when he roused himself to look at her, her eyes were open on the fire, and the present caught him again, like a slow awakening from a dream, and he sat very still, contemplating the extraordinary thing that had happened in the noise of the guns and the pound of bombs falling much too near. Was it the brandy, which she had never tasted neat before? — he had poured rather a stiff dose, for her first. Was it the raid, establishing some sort of fourth dimension, like his own hallucination that night at Boulogne — he had nearly lost his moorings again just now. . . .

"It was so hot, and we felt so sorry for the horses," Mab went on, seeming not to care whether he heard or not. "We were thirsty all the time, remember? — and the water always tasted bad, when we did get it — Julian, I want a drink of cold water —"

It ran down his spine in a tingling shock, which he instantly suppressed, without moving. She had used the wrong name — she had spoken as Dinah and Virginia spoke in the shelter, of the old war which lay within their mutual memory. We sat on a hard bench in the scullery, said Virginia of 1917 — we were thirsty all the time, said Mab of 1781. . . . Once more, he held the portrait of Tibby in his arms, alive and warm and breathing, and time had no meaning. She had come back to him. They were together again. As it was in the beginning. . . .

She stirred against him, and sighed.

"I suppose it's the brandy that makes me so thirsty," said Mab. "Is there any water on the tray?"

"Soda water," he said, glancing round at the siphon.

"Never mind," she said. "Don't go away. Like this nothing matters."

"No, nothing matters now," he said, and laid his cheek against her hair.

"We've got past it, haven't we."

Crump — *crump* — CRUMP —

She ducked closer to him as the stick went over again, and his arm tightened as he leaned above her.

"It's wrong for you to stay up here," she murmured in the ensuing pause. "They'll think it very odd downstairs."

"They know why we're here."

"It wouldn't matter so much if I got killed, just because I couldn't stand a shelter. But Bracken couldn't get along without you."

"Nor I without you," he said.

"Oh, Jeff —" She raised a face streaming with tears. "Oh, Jeff, I would have died *instead!* I should have been the one! You didn't need me!"

"We don't know," he said, and took out his handkerchief and wiped her cheeks. "We never know — we aren't running this show — you said it yourself one day — you said we can't choose or refuse —"

CRRUMP — *crump* — crump —

Again they leaned together instinctively while the house rocked around them.

Again the din receded and left them limp and incredulous, clinging. But now Mab could not stop crying, and he gave up trying to dry her face, and sat quietly while she wept away the weeks of unnatural composure and fortitude, not from fear now, for she was past fear and hardly heard the noise — tears of exhaustion and despair and a hopeless yearning for what she only dimly understood — tears of relief that somehow, anyhow, she was here beside him with constraint and uncertainty knocked out of them by the raid.

Then the lights went out.

"That always helps," said Jeff calmly. "I didn't bring up a torch."

"What does it mean?" she asked, without real apprehension, sitting up away from him in the fireglow.

"They've busted a main power line somewhere. It often happens. There are some candles on the mantelpiece if we want them."

In the faint light from the coals he saw her put her hands to her face, wiping it with her palms in a childish gesture, resolute and pathetic.

"Well, now you owe me that half-crown," she said, and he laughed.

"Not after a crack like that!"

"I'm sorry, Jeff."

"For what?"

"I couldn't stick the shelter. I cried and made a general fool of myself up here. I'd better go back to the country where I belong."

"Where you can really get in amongst the Germans," he amended.

"I say, are you all right up here?" said Bracken's voice at the door, and the beam of his torch found the sofa.

"We're fine," said Jeff cheerfully. "Come and join us. Have a drink. Make yourself comfortable."

"Damned if I don't," said Bracken, and turned the torch on the table which held the tray. "They've buggered off again now. That's all for tonight, no doubt. Brandy?" he suggested with his back to them, busy at the bottles.

"Just a spot." Jeff rose. "Our glasses are somewhere over here."

Perhaps it was the brandy — his heart

had given no more trouble.

2

The March nineteenth raid took the heaviest toll of lives for many weeks. It caught Irene and Ian dining out with friends. They were not far away from their own flat — but far enough so that if they had stayed where they were they would not have been killed in the direct hit which demolished the house where they lived. And while Mab had always preferred to be with Virginia, and had come almost to regard Farthingale as her home, to lose both parents in a night, and every trace of their possessions and mutual life as a family, was a knockout blow.

They got her back to Farthingale and put her to bed. Jeff went with them, though it was Virginia she turned to now. She seemed not so much grief-stricken as unbelieving and lost. She did not want to be alone. Her eyes followed people as they moved about her room, as though dreading that they might go away and leave her. She wanted a light at night, she wanted a radio playing on the bedside table, she wanted Noel under her hand. She clung to tangibles against the void.

Jeff sought out Oliver, as usual.

"Do you think," he asked directly with no beating about the bush, "it is time now for her to go to Williamsburg?"

"Can you face the consequences?" Oliver put it to him as directly.

"Yes," said Jeff without blinking. "That's what consequences are for."

"You learn," said Oliver.

"Slowly. And with difficulty."

They smiled at each other, with understanding and affection.

"Shall you go with her?" Oliver asked.

"Oh, no. Not yet. You see — I may have got myself sorted out a bit by now — so that I can see my way. But she's had another haymaker. She won't be able to see straight for some time to come. Even without that, I'm not sure I could have handled it alone." He paused. "She will have to go back to them," he said. "Back to Tibby and Julian."

Oliver nodded, without surprise.

"In ordinary times I would have said you were playing with fire," he said. "Psychologically. But these are not ordinary times. She has had a terrible shock — more than once. If she is not allowed to escape in one way, she may find another — less suitable. Always provided you are ready to follow through on it."

"I'm afraid I have never had much choice," said Jeff.

"Sometimes it seems as though we don't. Are you going to fly her over?"

"That's a problem," said Jeff. "On account of the dog. I shall let her decide, of course, but I doubt if she'll leave him behind and I doubt if he can go on a plane."

"Be sure that she understands what a voyage in convoy means."

"I have a hunch that if this comes off at all, Virginia will go with her," Jeff said.

"Do her good," Oliver agreed.

So the next thing was to approach Virginia, which Jeff did as soon as possible, with Oliver to back him up.

"We'll have to go by sea," she said matter-of-factly. "They wouldn't take a dog by way of Lisbon."

"You mean you'll *do it?*" His voice cracked delightedly.

"There's no one else to do it," she said, "She can't possibly set out alone. Are you going to break it to her or am I?"

"It's mine," said Jeff and went up to Mab's room and knocked.

She was always glad to see him, of course. But there was a layer of air between her and the world which nothing penetrated any more. She existed behind it, alone, forlorn, enduring. He sat down beside the bed and took her hand in both his.

"Mab, there's something I want you to do. For me."

"Of course," she said without interest.

"I want you to go to Williamsburg now — with Virginia."

"Without you?"

"Perhaps I can fly over, later."

She lay looking up at him, her hand in his. And while he watched, her eyes filled with tears which spilled over and ran down her cheeks. Instinctively he reached for her, gathered her into his arms.

"How did you know?" she gasped, holding to him convulsively. "Oh, Jeff, how do you *always* know?"

"Know what, my darling?"

"I want to go!" she sobbed. "I've *got* to go! But it looks like running away!"

"No such thing," said Jeff. "You've had your war, and you've stood up to it."

"It's not that," she sobbed. "It's not the war."

"What then, Mab? Tell me."

But she had no words to say that she both feared and craved his daily presence, until the strain of a daily renunciation was too much, on top of everything else, to contemplate. And that the only alternative, never to see him at all, was a prospect which filled her with despair. Overwrought and physically exhausted by months of tension and inner conflict, she wept hopelessly in his arms for what she believed was the last time.

"Now you listen to me," Jeff said, shaken by her sobbing. "You and Virginia are going to Williamsburg. You'll have a nasty ten days at sea, but Noel can't fly and I know better than to ask you to leave him behind. I shan't know a moment's peace night or day till I get word that you have arrived safely, but the risk is not too bad now. You will live in my house in Williamsburg, you will sleep in my room, in the very bed I was born in. You will have Basil and Nanny and Virginia for company, besides your Cousin Gwen and Fitz, who live a few streets away in the house Evadne stayed in while she was there. You'll have all Williamsburg, from top to bottom, at your disposal, with Jamestown thrown in. And pretty soon you'll find that you have come home, and things will look a lot different to you."

She had stopped crying, spent and resigned. Home it might be, in the end, but now it was exile. And it was best. Even he could see that it was best for them to be apart. He laid his lips against her temple, and settled her back on the pillows.

"Old Doctor Day himself has prescribed," he said. "It's going to be kind of dull around here without you, and I may prescribe a trip for myself by and by. Meanwhile you'll be in time for a Virginia April — and that is something to see. Will you write to me?"

"Yes, Jeff."

"Don't think you're being sent into exile," he cautioned, reading her thoughts with his usual ease. "You have been there before."

She tried to smile, looking up at him from the pillow — very small and thin and white.

" 'Thy people shall be my people,' " said Mab.

" '— and the Lord do so unto me, and more also, if aught but death part thee and me,' " said Jeff, and forced himself to rise and take his gaze from hers. "I'll tell Virginia to start packing. And you'd better break it to Noel that he's going to be seasick."

VIII.

Spring in Williamsburg.
1941

1

"Do you know where you are now?" Fitz asked quietly, keeping his eyes on the road as he drove.

Richmond lay behind them, as the day drew in. The trees either side the road stood tall and aloof, cutting off the setting sun, too close together to allow more than a suspicion of the River on the right. Little dusty lanes led off at angles, with obscure, tipsy signs. Almost uninhabited crossroads occurred at long intervals.

"Jamestown will be somewhere on the right," Mab said, looking straight ahead of her. Her hands were clasped tight in her lap, her eyes were enormous.

"Another ten miles. We just passed

Westover. Farthingale plantation used to lie over there. It burned down during the War Between the States.''

''Is there anything left to show?''

''Used to be a few bricks when I was a kid. We don't own the land any more.''

Soon the car emerged into a clearing, with a lane to the right, and Mab looked back.

''Jamestown,'' she said softly.

''That's it. First fine day we'll have a picnic there. Kind of spoiled now, with the museum and the turnstiles and the picture postcards. But we still go there, and eat our sandwiches beside the River.''

The long, blacked-out voyage was over. There had been a dazzling night in New York, which was ablaze with light — the kind of dinner you couldn't get in England any more — and a bed which stood still in a large hotel room whose uncurtained windows looked out across a spangled park.

And now, with Gwen and Virginia in the back seat, and Noel sitting erect and watchful between herself and Fitz in front, they came to Williamsburg. A cable had

476

gone back to Jeff — and although she felt unreasonably that every mile took her further away from him, a mounting excitement had her by the throat, as though the curtain was about to go up on a new play.

She saw the College, with its sweep of lawn — the Duke of Gloucester Street, under arching mulberry trees — the brick church, standing as it had always stood in its simple yard — the Palace Green, with a glimpse of gates and cupolas at the end of it — the Court House, just where she looked for it — the car turned off to the right, then left again. . . .

"Here we are," said Fitz, as they came to a stop in front of a long white house with green shutters and a portico. "This is Jeff's house, Mab. Ours is just across the way."

"I feel very strange," Virginia announced, stepping out of the car rather slowly, and pausing to look around her. It was the house where her mother had been born, and had fallen in love with Cabot Murray the Yankee, when to love a Yankee was out of the question in the

South. It was the house to which she had come many times as a girl, turning young men's heads at the Christmas parties with her New York clothes and her travelled, transatlantic ideas of what she wanted her future to be. Well, it had all come true — Archie, and Farthingale, and the children — a great love affair, in its quiet way, a story-book life, before the first war — then tragedy and loss, and a sort of serenity, before the next war began — and now she was back, as it were, where she started from, but with a telegram in her handbag which had been awaiting her at the hotel in New York, and which said simply: *May I come and see you? Tracy.* And somehow she had not had the heart to leave it behind in a waste-basket, even though she had not yet had the courage to answer it, yes or no. She had brought it with her, and that was a bad sign, she thought, as she stood beside the car, gazing at the house, which would be so full of memories. "I feel rather like a ghost, after all these years," she said slowly. "The house hasn't changed, Fitz."

"We're putting everything back the way

it was," Fitz said. "In between was the bad time. You missed that part."

Mab had got down even more slowly, entangled in Noel's lead, and she too stood still, absorbing her surroundings.

"I had forgotten —" she began, and left it there.

No one questioned her. Fitz gathered up some of the luggage, and the front door was opened by Hagar, who had been born since Virginia left Williamsburg for the last time, but who was always in charge of the Day house when it was inhabited nowadays.

"This is Delilah's daughter Hagar," Gwen said, and Virginia said, "Oh, of course," and held out both hands to the smiling colored woman, who clasped them warmly and said, "Welcome home, Miss Virginia, you bin a long time gittin' heah!"

"I have indeed," Virginia agreed. "And this is my granddaughter Mab."

Mab offered her hand, and Hagar took it in both her black ones, her eyes fixed solemnly on Mab's face.

"Ain't it a miracle!" she murmured.

"Mas' Fitz, you done tole me ahead o' time, but would you believe it? It's de Ole Mistess come home again, as suah as you'ah a foot high. You done *tole* me, but I nebbah believed —"

There was a scurry on the stairs and Basil was among them, grown, and happy, and less (as Virginia perceived at once) objectionable, now that Nurse had had full charge of him for a while. Things went into a welter of dog and small boy and Mab and Nurse and smiling colored faces as the luggage was carried in — and Mab found herself finally in the drawing-room with lights coming on and a late tea-table beside the wood fire, and the sound of ice in a cocktail-shaker — "It's a Daiquiri, Virginia, do you mind?" from Fitz, and Virginia who had drunk nothing but Martinis for years accepted a Daiquiri with enthusiasm, and Mab and Gwen had tea with a smitch of rum in it from a slender silver jug.

And suddenly, holding her cup and laughing at Noel who sat with his paws up beside Gwen asking for buttered toast, Mab glanced higher, above the mantelpiece, and met her own eyes in the portrait of Tibby — with the same sensation as when one encounters an unexpected mirror. She sobered involuntarily, gazing back, and it seemed to her that the painted lips deepened in a smile. Fitz followed the direction of her gaze.

"Yes, there she is, waiting for you," he said, as though Mab had spoken. "Are you surprised?"

"N-no," said Mab gravely. "Jeff said she would be here. But even then, I had no idea —" She put down her cup and went to stand beneath the portrait, looking up. "We are alike, aren't we," she said, pleased.

"It was rather a long drive," Virginia said, and rose, with a glance at Gwen. "And Mab is supposed to rest before dinner. You'll stay and have it here with us, won't you — there's still so much to talk about."

Fitz said he would just run the luggage home and come back in half an hour. Gwen led the way for Virginia and Mab up the wide uncarpeted stairs.

"First door on the left for Mab," she said. "That's Jeff's room, which was also Tibby's. It looks out the front. She liked to keep track of things in the street, they say."

"I'll bet she did," said Virginia, and they followed Mab, who paused on the threshold of the big front bedroom, enchanted.

A fire had been lighted on the hearth. The furniture was old mahogany, burnished by generations of loving black hands. The wall-paper was sprigged with flowers, and the ruffled curtains were as crisp as a ballerina's skirts. A deep armchair stood by the broad window, from where they could see Fitz in the dusk outside turning on the lights of the car and driving away. Gwen touched a wall-switch near the door and shaded lamps came on all round the room.

"No blackout!" sighed Virginia with rapture. "I shall never get used to that again!"

Light caught the bright brass bales on the chiffoniers, warmed the rosy rug, spilled across the counterpane of the great canopied bed, turned the window-panes blue, and illuminated the little reminiscent smile on Mab's face as she advanced into the middle of the room — where she stopped short, staring at the portrait which faced the bed from the opposite wall.

"It's Jeff!" she cried, as though he had walked into the room.

Virginia and Gwen exchanged glances.

"That's Julian," said Virginia. "Didn't Jeff tell you?"

"He told me I looked like Tibby, a long time ago," said Mab. "He never said that he was Julian!"

"Well, there you are," said Virginia gently. "We'll leave you now to get settled in, but you'd better tuck up on the bed for a few minutes first of all. Come along, Gwen, I want to put on a new face before dinner."

Alone in the room which was hers and Jeff's and Tibby's — and Julian's — Mab sat down slowly in the armchair by the window, and when Noel came and lay down across her feet as he always did in a strange room, she leaned her head against the back of the chair and closed her eyes. Home again, she thought — *you have been there before,* Jeff said. It was for this that he had sent her on that nightmare voyage in a blacked-out ship, with the lifeboat drills and the depth charges going off and the swing of a zigzagging run, and the competent, smiling crew, and the determinedly cheerful passengers — all behaving as though the *Athenia* and the *City of Benares* had never been heard of. For this homecoming, this undreamed-of peace which was like a fragrance in the air she breathed.

And sitting there under the eyes of the portrait she drifted into a doze, her head against the wing of the chair, the dog's warm body against her feet. Grief and tension and the daily necessity to be strong beyond her strength drained away. Already she had begun to heal.

They found her there when they looked in on their way down to dinner, as Fitz drove up again outside. She woke without effort when they spoke to her, smiled at them, skipped into the bathroom to wash, and arrived downstairs with an appetite.

"Butter," she said, as she had said last night in the New York hotel. "I never thought butter could be so important. Can I have lots?"

"Oh, Gawd bless de chile," said Hagar, almost in tears, as she served them. "Dere's all de butter in de state ob Virginny effn she wants it!"

"I am a pig," said Mab without compunction. "But they won't have any more in England if I have less here, will they?"

"It's not only the rationing and shortages that make meals difficult over there," Virginia explained to Gwen. "When your stomach is in a knot because of the latest News Bulletin you don't even relish the food you've got."

"I know it's wrong to feel so happy here," said Mab, gazing dreamily at her full plate. "But I don't think Jeff would mind." She looked round at them doubtfully. "It's not *possible* it's the same world," she marvelled. "Hitler's still there. But look at us here. There may be a raid over London this very minute."

"They won't be any safer if you

worry," Virginia reminded her.

"I know. And I don't worry, really, any more. There's something about this place," Mab said gravely, "that makes it *unnecessary* to worry."

They sat a long time over the meal, and Mab listened fascinated to reminiscences that went all the way back to the war in Cuba in '99 — where Fitz as a correspondent had so far forgotten himself as to get a rifle and shoot back at the Spaniards, which was against the rules. How Mab would love to be here tonight, Evadne had said, hearing the same stories in the autumn of '38. And now Mab heard them, breathless and aglow, and begged for more.

Then Noel had his evening walk, in the soft southern dark with lights shining behind the windows and the undimmed street-lamps overhead, to Mab's renewed delight, and the Spragues drove away. Once more Mab climbed the broad stairs, accompanied by Virginia and Noel — to find that Hagar had provided a sumptuous cushion for Noel in the corner nearest the bed, dropped the Venetian blind across the window, unpacked Mab's bags, laid out her night things, and turned down the covers.

Virginia kissed her good-night, and they laughed together at Noel as he took possession with a comfortable sigh.

"I'm just across the hall, in what used to be Cousin Sue's room — it's all so cosy, isn't it, to think my own mother shared it when they were girls — so long ago, and yet —" Virginia sighed without sorrow, almost with contentment. "— perhaps they're not very far away, after all. Be sure to let me know if you feel strange, or can't sleep." She closed the door gently behind her.

Mab got ready for bed, the little smile on her lips again. She had seldom felt less strange in her life. Tomorrow they were going to lunch with Fitz and Gwen at the Sprague house, and all Williamsburg lay ahead of her — the Palace — the Capitol — the Raleigh Tavern — all put back the way it was. And down at the end of Waller Street, where they said there was only a railway bridge and petrol pumps — what? Now she would see for herself. . . .

She got into bed — a bed so deep, so soft — so wide, so fragrant of something that was not lavender — the pillows received her tired body like heavenly arms. There would be no depth charges tonight — no German planes overhead — just stillness and safety and peace, for miles, hundreds of miles around.

The bedside table held books and a small radio, all her own. She looked at them blissfully, but without curiosity. Later. Tomorrow. There would be lots of tomorrows. One could afford to wait.

With all the lights out except the one within reach of her hand, she stretched herself in the big bed, feeling small and snug. Noel had already begun to snore softly, which meant that he was all worn out. Let him. There was no one else to hear.

She raised her eyes to the portrait which faced her from the opposite wall, as Tibby had done every night during all the years she had lain there alone after Julian was dead and gone. She had married at sixteen — he was older, he was the schoolmaster. . . . Now it was Mab looking up at the portrait, another link in the chain, waiting for it all to begin again. She smiled at Julian, secret, sure, secure — waiting.

"Good-night, Jeff," she said aloud, and put out the light.